INTRODUCTION TO THE GISMO:

THIS IS A GISMO
IT IS A DUPLICATING DEVICE—
IT WILL DUPLICATE ANYTHING—
EVEN ANOTHER GISMO.
TO OPERATE, SIMPLY ATTACH A SAMPLE
OF WHATEVER YOU WISH TO COPY
TO THE LEFT HAND ARM
OF THE GISMO, AS SHOWN.
THEN PRESS THE SWITCH,
AND A COPY WILL APPEAR
ATTACHED TO THE RIGHT HAND ARM
OF THE GISMO.
WARNING:
DO NOT ALLOW THE OBJECT BEING COPIED
TO COME IN CONTACT WITH
ANYTHING ELSE.

A
FOR
ANYTHING

Damon Knight

A BERKLEY MEDALLION BOOK
published by
BERKLEY PUBLISHING CORPORATION

For Justin Leiber,
a good Joe

"ἐν τούτῳ νίχα"

"In this, conquer"

Words accompanying the vision of the
cross seen by Constantine, on the eve
of his victory over Maxentius in 312

BERKLEY MEDALLION EDITION, SEPTEMBER, 1965

BERKLEY MEDALLION BOOKS are published by
Berkley Publishing Corporation
15 East 26th Street, New York, N. Y. 10010

Printed in the United States of America

ONE

This happened, not in 312 A.D., but in August, 1971.

A retired bank vice-president named Harry Breitfeller, who lived in a comfortable duplex in Santa Monica with his wife and other relatives, stepped out on the cement porch a little after nine one morning to pick up the mail. There were half a dozen envelopes, mostly bills, in the mailbox, and a whacking big cardboard carton on the porch under it.

Breitfeller picked up the carton, thinking it must be something his wife had ordered, but saw that his own name was on the label.

There was no return address. According to the postmark, the box had been mailed late the previous afternoon in Clearwater, which is about thirty-four miles northeast of Los Angeles.

Breitfeller could not think of anyone he knew in Clearwater. Remembering stories he had heard about bombs in the mail, he shook the box gingerly. It seemed too light to have a bomb in it, and it rattled.

He took the box inside and set it down, pulled up a chair, and put his half-smoked cigar carefully in an ashtray.

His wife, Madge, came in from the kitchen drying her hands. "What's that?" she asked.

"Don't know." Breitfeller had his pocket knife open, and was slitting the brown paper tape that sealed the carton.

"Well, who's it *from*?"

"Don't know," said Breitfeller again. He turned the two halves of the box top carefully back. Underneath was a little crumpled newspaper, and under that, something made of wood. Cottage lamps, was his first thought, but they were unstained and there were no shades, and no light sockets.

He pulled the two objects out of the carton and set them upright on the table. His wife looked over his shoulder, and so did her sister Ruth who had just followed her in from the kitchen. The objects were two identical wooden crosses. They were about a foot and a half high. Each one stood on a thick wooden base, and had some kind of wiring attached to the upright and crossarm. On the base of each one was a typewritten paper, stapled down, which read:

5

THIS IS A GISMO
IT IS A DUPLICATING DEVICE—
IT WILL DUPLICATE ANYTHING—
EVEN ANOTHER GISMO.
TO OPERATE, SIMPLY ATTACH A SAMPLE
OF WHATEVER YOU WISH TO COPY
TO THE LEFT HAND ARM
OF THE GISMO, AS SHOWN.

(There was a careful pen sketch in the margin.)

THEN PRESS THE SWITCH,
AND A COPY WILL APPEAR
ATTACHED TO THE RIGHT HAND ARM
OF THE GISMO.
WARNING:
DO NOT ALLOW THE OBJECT BEING COPIED
TO COME IN CONTACT WITH
ANYTHING ELSE.

Breitfeller read this through twice in silence, ignoring the heavy breathing of the two women leaning on his shoulders. He was a pink-faced man, rather popeyed and without very much chin, but stronger than he looked.

He inspected the two crosses unhurriedly, up-ending them to see if there was anything on the bottom, then examining each part of the wiring.

"It's a trick," said Ruth over his shoulder. "A silly trick."

"Maybe," said Breitfeller, putting his cigar back in his mouth. He saw that the wires stapled to the crossarms of the two Gismos were really loops, and that the curious little metal-and-glass blocks which hung from them were suspended by these loops.

There was just the one circuit, that looped over to one of the little metal-glass blocks on the left side and then looped over to the other on the right side. The rest of it, attached to the upright, was nothing but a pair of dry cells and an ordinary mercury light switch.

Breitfeller thought he could build one of these himself, in half an hour, except for the little glass-metal blocks. He had never seen one of those before.

He leaned over the table and peered closer. The glass was a curious-looking cloudy stuff, possibly not glass but a plastic, and it was coated with copper on both sides. On the bottom side of each block there was a small copper hook. It looked to Breitfeller as if the glass or whatever it was would be plenty to insulate that hook from the feeble current that would go through the loop of wire: so the Gismo couldn't actually do anything, much less what it was advertised to do.

6

But when he looked at those little metal-glass-metal sandwiches, he wasn't so sure.

His older son, Pete, came in saying, "Dad, I'm going to take the car over to Glendale this morning, okay? Whatcha got?"

"Gismos," said Breitfeller wryly, around his cigar. He was frowning at the nearest cross. You closed the switch *here*; the current went up *here*, through these little contacts, and around *here*, past the left-hand glass-metal block but not through it, and then over *here*, doing the same to the right-hand glass-metal block, and then back to the dry cells. It seemed to him that nothing could possibly happen if you tried it. His fingers began to itch.

"Hey," said Pete, reaching, "let me see that."

Breitfeller forestalled him. "Keep your hands off," he said indistinctly.

"Dad, I know all about that electronics jazz."

"Not about *this* electronics jazz, you don't." Brietfeller got up with a cross in each hand.

"Harry, what are you going to do?" his wife asked, looking alarmed.

"*I* think you ought to call the police," said Ruth, behind her.

Breitfeller said, "I'm going out behind the garage. By myself." He departed, past his brother-in-law Mack, who was just up and looked half asleep, but had curiosity enough to say "What's that?" as Breitfeller went by.

He went out through the kitchen and the back porch, banging the screen door behind him, and walked across the yard to the alley. There was about three feet of space between the side of his garage and the fence, and nothing across the alley but the back of a brewery warehouse, so Breitfeller figured that if anything should go wrong, there would not be too much damage.

He set both the Gismos down carefully on the stack of scrap lumber and stared at them. "TO OPERATE, SIMPLY ATTACH A SAMPLE OF WHATEVER YOU WISH TO COPY . . ." There was a little coil of bare copper wire wound handily around the copper hook under the left-hand crossarm; that was one detail that half convinced him. The other thing was the metal-glass blocks; another, now that he thought of it, was the grain of the wood, which looked identical in the two crosses, and the fourth thing, the one that really made his heart beat faster, was just the fact that there were two Gismos and not one.

Because if it was a gag, why would there be two? But if it was real, then with two Gismos you could make a third one, a fourth, a fifth . . .

Well, you never got anything without taking a little risk.

Breitfeller, with a sardonic gleam in his eye, fumbled for

7

his money clip and withdrew a one-dollar bill. He uncoiled the copper wire, wound it around the folded bill, and carefully attached it to the little hook on the left-hand side of the Gismo. He slowly put out his middle finger to the switch. Slowly he pressed it down.

He blinked. Swinging from the right-hand arm of the Gismo, as if it had been there all the time, was a second, folded, green one-dollar bill.

"Lord God Almighty," said Breitfeller, fervently.

TWO

The sun, just past the meridian, made a glaringly bright rim of light around each of the closed dark shades. Except for this brilliance, and two or three random bits of metalwork picked out by the sunlight, the room was in hot half-darkness. The air was close and stale. On the laboratory bench was a clutter of electronic test equipment, carelessly piled. A book had been knocked to the floor, where it lay disheveled among wads of paper, dust, bits of insulation and wire. In the far corner, half a stack of massive loose-leaf binders, precariously piled atop a filing cabinet, had fallen. From under these protruded the legs and body of a man.

The piled books stirred, rose and parted with a gravestone clatter. A head emerged, crowned with dust. A hand came up to hold it. There was a groan.

Mr. Gilbert Wall, of Western Electronics, sat up painfully and looked around him. His hair was rumpled, his tanned face covered with grime. There was a large bruise, beginning to turn yellow and blue, around his right eye, which was swollen half shut. Wall touched this bruise, gingerly, and groaned again. "Maniac," he muttered to himself.

He sat up straighter, looking momentarily apprehensive. "Ewing?" he called. There was no answer.

Blinking, Wall turned and noticed the brightness against the drawn shades. He started, and looked at his wristwatch. "Quarter after one!" he ejaculated. He looked around wildly, then scrambled to his feet and wincingly went to the bench. His hands did not find what they sought. He glared around once more, half distractedly. "My God!" he said.

On the wall beside the door there was a telephone. Wall saw it and went there. He took the receiver down, heard a dial tone, and dialed "O."

"Operator," he said shakily, "get me Los Angeles." He gave the number. "I want to speak to Nathan MacDonald—

Nathan—N as in nut—that's right, and hurry. This is an emergency call."

"My trunks are all busy to Los Angeles," said the voice. *"Will you wait, or shall I call you back?"*

Wall swallowed. "Operator, this is Roy M. Jackson of the Federal Bureau of Investigation speaking. This is a matter of the national interest. Now put that call through, if you please."

There was a pause. *"May I have your identification number, sir?"*

Damn. "Operator, I've just been assigned. I do not have an identification number yet. You'll just have to take my word for it. This call must go through."

"Sir, I can't break in on a trunk call unless you have an identification number."

"Give me the head operator."

After a few moments there was another voice. *"Sir, this is Miss Timmins. May I help you?"*

Wall repeated his story, in a voice of passionate sincerity.

"Sir, one moment, I'll have the operator connect you with the office of the Clearwater chief of police."

"I don't want the police, I want Los Angeles!" said Wall, glaring.

"That's the best I can do for you, sir. If Chief Underwood will vouch for you, or if you would come to the telephone office and show your identification—"

"Put the Chief on," said Wall. He was thinking: Underwood; now why did that name ring a bell?

By the time he got the man on the line, he had remembered. "Underwood, this is Gilbert Wall speaking." (If the operator was listening in, let her.) "Perhaps you remember me. We met at the Masonic convention two years ago—Norm Hodge introduced us, do you recall?"

"Why, yes, sure I do, Mr. Wall," said Underwood's voice. (The old memory never failed; Wall could see the man's face clearly in his mind's eye, jowly and obsequious, a typical disappointed small-town public servant.) *"How are you anyway?"*

"I'm just fine, and yourself?"

"Well, not too bad, I can't complain. What can I do for you?"

Wall's hand went to the knot in his necktie. "Underwood—what do they call you, uh—" (what was the man's name)—"Ed?"

"Ed, that's right."

"And you'll call me Gil, won't you? Ed, here's my little problem. I'm in Clearwater for the day on some confidential work, I can't tell you over the telephone, but between us two, a Mr. Hoover is very, very interested in this."

"Oh, is that right? Well, you know, anything I can do—"

9

"Just one thing if you would, Ed. I've got to make an urgent call to L.A. and it happens the trunks are busy. You see I'm working against time, Ed, you understand, and every minute counts. So if you would call the head operator, Miss Timmins her name is, and more or less vouch for me— Incidentally, before we hang up, I wonder if we could have dinner together before I leave. I can explain this thing to you then in a little more detail, of course."

"Why, sure, Gil," said Underwood, *"that would be great. Now let me see, you want me to tell the head operator—"*

"Just that you know me and so on, and ask her to do us the courtesy of putting my call through. Tell her I'm at—" He read off the number of the phone from the dial card. "And, ah, I'll call for you at home say 'bout eight o'clock, family too, of course, will that be all right?"

"Fine."

"Fine, Ed, I'll be seeing you and thanks a million." Sweating, Wall hung up and rummaged in his pockets for a cigarette.

A few minutes later the telephone rang. Wall snatched the receiver down and said, "Gilbert Wall speaking."

"Mr. Wall, are you the party who called a few minutes ago with reference to a call to Los Angeles?"

"Yes, that's correct, operator."

"Sir, that was not the name you gave me then, was it?"

"No," said Wall coldly, "that was my cover name I gave you. I was obliged to give my *under* cover name to Chief Underwood, to get him to identify me."

There was a slight hesitation. *"Well, I'll have the operator put that call through for you,"* said the voice uncertainly. *"Just hold the wire, please."*

Wall waited, smoking nervously. He smoothed back his sleek hair with his palm, fingered the gold cufflinks to make sure they were still there, noticed a loose shirt button with annoyance. His billfold was in his breast pocket; fountain pen, keys, notebook, all right.

"Hello?" An unfamiliar male voice.

"I have a call for Mr. Nathan MacDonald. Is he there?"

The right number then; but where was Miss Jacobs, the switchboard operator?

"He's tied up, can I take a message?"

"Hello," said Wall, interrupting the voice of the operator, "this is Gilbert Wall—let me talk to MacDonald."

"Oh, Mr. Wall. This is Ernie, the office boy. I'll uh, I'll put you right through."

Another pause. *"Hello, Gil."*

Wall exhaled with relief. "Hello, Nate. Boy have I had a time with this call, but never mind that now. Listen, that Ewing is a maniac. I mean it. First of all, Nate, our tip was

10

correct, that gadget of his, that Gismo *really works*. There is no doubt about it." The silence struck him as odd. "Hello, Nate? Are you listening?"

"I heard you." Wall could see the heavy-jawed face, all straight lines—mouth, flat nose, narrow eyes, gray hair combed straight across, tops of the horn-rimmed glasses as straight as a ruler. MacDonald sounded like that, dry, unemotional even in crises, and yet there was something in his tone that bothered Wall.

"Well, it's just as bad as we thought. Or worse. He absolutely would not listen to reason, Nate, and what's worse, the s.o.b. got away from me." Wall touched his temple gingerly, and winced. "It may have been my fault, I more or less lost my head and made some threats, trying to throw a scare into him, and— He took me by surprise, I never thought he had it in him, and he knocked some books over on me, and that's why I haven't called until now. Nate, I was out cold all night, until just a few minutes ago. I'm still not myself. Now, my idea is, he'll be hiding out somewhere. He's probably scared witless over all this—assaulting me, and so on. Do you check me on that, Nate?"

The voice said, *"Probably."*

"Well, we've got to move fast, Nate. I know it was my ball and I bobbled it, I admit that, but we've got to find that guy. Swear out a warrant, or—how would this be—suppose we tell the Health Service people he's infected with bubonic plague, or something? . . . Nate?"

The voice said, *"There's a lot of noise here."*

Wall heard a faint, distant murmur, as if a crowd of people were talking (shouting?) in the background. Then there were some underwater clicks, and MacDonald's voice again: *"What are your plans now, Gil?"*

"Plans?" said Wall, taken aback. "Well, I can either stay here—I've got a date with the local chief of police, I can keep that, if we decide to work through him— Or if you want me to come back for a skull session, Nate, I can charter a plane. But listen, we've got to get on the ball with this thing. I mean, if that maniac, Ewing, ever gets it into his head to *distribute* that thing, that Gismo—Nate, my mind just boggles. I can't picture it."

"I'm watching it," said MacDonald's voice indistinctly.

"What?" said Wall after a moment. "What did you say, Nate?"

"I'm watching it happen," said MacDonald's voice. *"What did you think Ewing was doing all this time?"*

"What?" said Wall again.

"Those things were in the morning mail delivery here. Two in a box. At least a hundred people got them. Along about

11

*ten, people started copying them and giving them away to their
friends and relations. Now they're fighting in the streets."*

"Nate—" said Wall brokenly.

*"I've got mine. Sent Crawford down for them. Packing
now, or you wouldn't have got me. I happen to know a place
in Wyoming that's built like a castle—you could hold off an
army there. Well, take care of yourself, Gil. Nobody else will."*

"Nate, give me a minute now, I just can't believe it—"

"Turn on your TV," said MacDonald. There was a click,
and the wire went dead.

Wall stared blankly at the receiver, then turned slowly.
There was a little portable TV set standing on the bench. He
walked over to it, leaving the telephone receiver swinging at
the end of its cord, and turned on the switch. The TV blurted:
*"—all down Sunset Boulevard, from Olvera Street west. And
here's a flash."* The screen lighted, showed a raster, but no
face appeared. *"Police Chief Victor Corsi has issued a call for
special volunteer policemen to handle the crowds. It's my
hunch he won't get any. The big question today is, Have you
got a Gismo? And believe me, nothing else matters. This
station will stay on the air to keep you informed as long as
possible, but no thanks to its poltroon of a general manager,
J. W. Kidder, or its revolting program director, Douglas M.
Dow, who took off for the hills as soon as they got theirs.
For my own part, I say to hell with them both. And to hell
with the Pacific Broadcasting Company and all its little sub-
sidiaries! A large ripe razzberry to Mayor Needham! And to
hell with—"*

Wall turned the set off. The voice stopped; the bright frame
shrank, twitched, shriveled to a point of light, that faded and
went out.

THREE

Ewing opened the back screen door and stepped out into the
yard. It was a still, cloudless morning; the smog was all down
in the valley. The tall dry grass was uncomfortable to walk
in, and he moved automatically down the shallow slope to
stand under the pepper tree. In the cool cavern behind the
hanging curtain of branches, the ground was bare except for
the carpet of red leaves and the hard little berries. The kids
had been building a hut in here with old lumber from the
fence, and their toys were scattered around. Ewing's ear
registered the sudden outburst of shrill voices inside the house,
and he frowned unhappily. That was not so good: you could

12

hear them half a mile away, and they were all over the mountain in the daytime. But you couldn't keep children locked up like criminals.

Anyhow, they had found a good place. The cottage stood on its own half-acre terrace more than halfway up the mountainside. Above it there was only the scrubby slope of the mountain itself, bone-dry and littered with boulders, and a row of desiccated palm trees along the irrigation canal. The one neighboring house, between the cottage and the hill road, was empty and fire-gutted. Below the house there was another terrace, where evidently previous tenants had had a kitchen garden; then the land sloped abruptly down and became an orchard of tiny orange trees. Ewing had seen the owner's name on a mailbox, down at the bottom of the mountain: Lo Vecchio, something like that. What was going to happen to him and his orchard now?

Down below, the valley lay spread out, rolling down and receding into an improbable blueness. Ewing could see the road, diminishing to a tiny yellowish thread, and the cross-hatched patterns of tilled fields. The horizon curved around him on three sides. Eucalyptus trees masked the highways; except for an occasional airplane, or a car going or coming in the residential area just below, the world around him might have been deserted.

The rattle of a laboring engine came echoing up in the clear air.

Ewing started, and peered fruitlessly off to his right, where trees screened the road. That sounded like somebody coming up the hill.

Trouble. It might be somebody from the Adventist colony down below, paying a neighborly call, but from what Ewing had seen, they all drove late-model cars. This sounded like a wreck. With his heart pumping in his throat, Ewing ran into the house, past a startled Fay and two round girl-faces at the breakfast table, and got the shotgun out of the closet. He made a second grab for the box of shells; two more jumps took him to the front porch. He was in time to see the car pull up on the road above the house.

It was a battered, dusty Lincoln coupe with its trunk bulging open. All the chrome trim was missing from the body and fenders, and the denuded strips were measled with rust. A fine spume of steam rose from the radiator.

"Dave boy!" shouted the driver, popping up on the far side of the car like a marionette. He was a dusty gray man in a faded jacket and sweater; Ewing lowered the gun and stared at him. That cracked, cheerful voice—

"Platt!" he said, in mingled relief and exasperation.

"None other! The very same! In the flesh!" Platt came stork-legged down the driveway, moving with a jerky, nervous

13

energy, elbows pumping, his long face split in a yellow grin. He grabbed Ewing's hand and shook it hard; his water-gray eyes were bright and sparkling. "Gotcha! You can't hide from me, boy! Ends of the earth! Well, hell, it's good to see you, Dave—hello, Fay, hello kids—but for God's sake"—Ewing turned to see that his family was clustered in the doorway; he turned back as Platt's stream of talk went on uninterrupted—"ask a man in and give him a drink of water if you haven't got anything better. I'm so parched I'm spitting sand. What are you up here, eagles? Hell, is this Elaine? My God, you're big! Pretty as your old lady, too. And who's this?"

Kathy, looking suspicious, retired behind her mother's skirts. Elaine, who was twelve, was blushing like a debutante. Somehow they were all moving into the living room, and Platt threw himself into the only upholstered chair with a shout of comfort. He was leaning forward the next instant, still talking, fumbling a pack of cigarettes out of his jacket, striking a shaky light, dropping the match, pulling Elaine into a one-armed embrace and winking at Kathy.

Platt was a man of galloping enthusiasms; a good experimental physicist, but a theorist whom nobody took seriously. He had a new theory every year, and believed in every one with a frantic, whole-souled earnestness. His greatest love was rocketry, but he had never succeeded in getting a clearance to work on classified projects. Platt's frustration was acute, but only seemed to wind his spring tighter. He changed jobs frequently, and popped in and out of Ewing's life: the last time they had met was in 1967.

Elaine, who was still blushing, drew away and went toward the kitchen. "I'll get the water for you, Mr. Platt."

"Call me Leroy. And not too much water, honey."

"There isn't any liquor in the house," Fay said. "We just moved in yesterday, but I can get some coffee . . ."

"No, that's OK, I've got a bottle in the car—the bottomless bottle, thanks to your boy here—I'll bring it in later and we'll have a ball, but listen, Dave—" the cigarette spilled ash down his frayed sweater—"I want to tell you, you're the biggest genius of them all. My chapeau is off to you, boy, I mean it! I wish I'd invented that! But you did it, son—you're the greatest. I mean it. Well"—he took the brimming glass of water from Elaine and raised it—"here's to you, Dave Ewing, and long may you Gismo!" He sipped and made a mock-wry face, then gulped the water down.

Ewing said, "What makes you think I—"

"Who was working with Schellhammers?" Platt cried. "You think I didn't see your John Henry all over that thing? Going to tell me you didn't do it?"

"No, but—"

"Sure, you did! The second I saw that, I could tell. I said to

14

myself, I got to find old Dave, and I'll *do* it, too, if I have to track 'm down like a bloodhound!"

Fay put in, "Leroy, how did you find us?"

"I'll tell you, honey. See, Dave and yours truly were old army buddies, and back at Fort Benning he always used to tell me how he wanted to go live in the mountains some day —wanted to be a goddam eagle and sneer down at all the flatland foreigners. So I figured, where would Dave go if he wanted to get out of sight in a hurry? Not down to L.A., because there's going to be hell popping down there. Not up the coast, because that'd take too long and he might get stuck anywhere along the way. I figured, he'd head out on route ninety-one and stop the first time he came to a high place. So I followed my hunch, and when I saw this little pimple with a house on it, I came on up. See?"

The Ewings looked at each other in dismay. Fay's hand was on the little portable radio; she must have switched it on, because a power hum came out of the speaker. But there were no voices: the last of the local stations had gone off the air yesterday evening. She turned it off, still looking stricken.

"Well, hell, you don't have to *stay* here, do you?" Platt demanded. "Not that anybody else would find you this easy, but listen, old buddy, you too, Fay, what are you going to do with yourselves, now you don't have to work for a living?"

Ewing cleared his throat. "We haven't really had time to talk about it. I'd like to build a lab somewhere, when things settle down. . . ."

"Sure you would. You will, too, boy. Hell, the sky's the limit, and that brings me to the moral of my tale. Listen, thanks to you, we can all do what we want now—and Dave, listen, you know what I want to do?"

Ewing said the first fantastic thing that came into his head. "Fly to the moon, I guess."

"Right. Good boy—smart as a razor, no flies on *you*."

"Oh, *no*," said Ewing, clutching his head.

"Sure! Dave, listen, come on with me, bring the family— I've got the place picked out, and I know ten, twenty other people that'll come in with us, but you're the boy I wanted to see first. It's big, boy, it's the biggest thing in the world!"

"You really want to build a spaceship?"

"*Going* to build one, boy. Up in the Santa Rosas—the Kennelly labs, they're made to order. All the room you want, and heavy equipment—two months to get organized, and then watch us go."

"Why not White Sands?"

Platt shook his head impatiently. "I don't want it, Davey. One thing, every space-happy nut in the country will be there by now—you'll have to elbow 'em out of the way to spit. Then, what have they got that we need? Hardware, yes, missile

15

frames, yes, but most of it is the wrong scale. We're going to start fresh, Davey, and do it right. You can't make an interplanetary vehicle out of a Viking, boy—might as well put rockets on an outhouse. Think about this, now. Really see it." He hitched closer, spreading his ungainly arms. "Build your ship—any size. Make it as big as an apartment house if you want—and all payload, Davey! Put everything in. Bedrooms, bowling alleys, kitchens—wup, no kitchens; don't need 'em. But libraries, movie theaters, laboratories—"

Ewing started. "Leroy, have you been drinking liquor copied by the Gismo? You said something before—"

"Sure," said Platt impatiently. "Eating the food, too. Why not? Just put it through twice, make sure you don't get any reversed peptide chains. Now listen, boy, pay attention—you build all that, whatever you want, get the picture? Now: put your rocket motors underneath. All you want. With the Gismo, you can have ten or a million. Now what about fuel—all those big tanks that used to kill us dead before we got off the ground? Davey, two little tanks, hydrazine and oxygen, and two Gismos. We *make* our fuel as we need it. Forget about your goddamn mass-energy ratios! I can jack up the goddamn Mormon Temple and take it to the moon! The *moon, hell*!"

He took a breath. "Dave, think about it! We can go any goddamn where in the *universe*! This time next year, we'll be on Mars. Mars." He stood up, arms out, and became a spacesuited Martian explorer, staring keenly into the distance. "What's that I see? Strange pyramids? Little men with six noses? We'll find out, but let's make it quick, because we got a date on Venus. But we'll leave behind a bunch of big Gismos as an atmosphere plant—fifty years, a hundred years, there'll be enough air on Mars to breathe without these helmets. Then *Venus*—same thing there. If there's no oxygen, we'll *make* it. Davey, a lousy hundred years from now, mankind'll own the universe. I'm telling you! We can have Mars, *and* Venus, *and* the Jovian system, just for the asking! Then what about the stars? Listen, Davey, *why not*? In that ship we can live indefinitely—we can have kids there, and they'll keep going when we kick off. Do you see it now? Doesn't it send you?"

He paused and glared incredulously at Ewing. "No?"

"No. Now look, Leroy, just to take one point—this atmosphere scheme of yours. You're going to be adding mass—billions of tons of it. It isn't like releasing free oxygen chemically, from oxides in the soil or something like that—you're going to perturb the orbits of the planets."

"Not to bother about," said Platt energetically. "Look, look —say the mass of a small planet like Mars . . ." Still talking, he hauled out a small celluloid slide rule and began flipping the cursor back and forth.

"Wait a minute," Ewing said, "you're going off half-cocked again." He produced his own slide rule from his back pocket, and they bent closer to each other, both trying to talk at once.

When she saw this, Fay got up and went into the kitchen, taking her resigned children with her.

Half an hour later, when she came back with coffee and sandwiches, Platt was just getting to his feet in an ecstasy of despair at human stupidity. "Well, hell," he said. "Well, hell. Well, *hell*, boy, I'll get the bottle and we'll have a snort to celebrate, anyway. Maybe that'll loosen you up," he added in a stage aside. The screen door banged behind him.

Ewing grinned ruefully and put his arm around his wife as she sat down beside him. "Better get the spare room ready," he said.

"Dave, no, it's just that hot little room with the water heater in it. And we haven't even got a mattress for him."

"He'll sleep on the floor—he'll insist on it," Ewing said. He shook his head, feeling a sentimental warmth for Platt—so entirely himself, so unchanged after all these years.

"Good old Leroy!" he said. "Venus!"

Shortly before noon the house was in full sunlight. The sky was clear; the heat poured down in a breathless torrent, and the dry earth bounced it back. The air over the mountainside shimmered with heat, and the palms were dusty and brittle. Ewing picked up a clod of dirt in his hand; it crumbled into brown powder. "Hot," said Leroy Platt, fanning himself with a shapeless fedora, "sure is hot." The sunlight made his pale eyes look naked and mad, surprised like oysters in the white shell of his face. He put the hat back on.

Ewing enjoyed the heat. The sun beat down on his head and shoulders as if it wanted to cook him; but his limbs moved freely, well-oiled, and tiny drops of sweat, like a golden mist, sprang out all over his arms and body. He liked his sharp-edged shadow moving crisply underfoot in the strong light. He liked thinking about the cool shade inside the house, after the heat. "We're almost there," he said, scrambling up.

From the top of the little mountain they could look down on the residential area, the Adventist college and food factory, all laid out like a tabletop village. The streets were neatly drawn, the trees bright green, the housetops blue or red.

They turned. Down the opposite slope, it was another world: naked, burned-out mountain valleys, rolling away one behind another, looking as if a drop of water would hiss into steam anywhere it touched them. Straight to the horizon, there was no sign of man.

"Now there," said Platt breathlessly. "That's it. There you have it. Thousands of square miles, Dave, mostly up and

17

down, but right next to our own back yards, and most of the time we forget it's here. Huh. You walk down a street with houses on both sides, and you say to yourself, look how we've civilized this continent in a lousy three hundred years. But, hell! We haven't scratched the surface! Dave, just think—if you can make your own water supply, wherever you want it, what's to keep you from going out there, and planting grass all over those goddamn mountains, if you feel like it? Why, hell, there's room enough to make every man a king!"

"Uh-huh," said Ewing, abstractedly.

"Of course, people being the sons of bitches they are—What's the matter?"

Ewing was staring off into the northern sky, shading his eyes. "I hear it, but I don't see it," he said.

"What?" Platt listened and stared. "A chopper," he said. A faint, distant rumble blurred over his words.

"What?" said Ewing. "Shut up a minute, Leroy."

The rumbling came rolling distantly down out of the sky. It was a voice speaking, but they could not make out the words, only a vast blurred echo.

"There it is," said Ewing, after a moment. The tiny speck was hanging over the valley floor to northward, slowly drifting closer. The rumbling words grew almost clear enough to be understood.

"Army copter," said Platt. He fell silent, and they both listened.

"Rrrr rrr rmrm," said the brassy voice in the sky. It paused and began again: *"Rrr attention plrrse. (rse.) Your attention please. (ease.) This area has been placed under martial law. (law.) All citizens are ordered to remain in their homes. (omes.) and refrain from causing disturbances. (urbances.) Stay in your homes. (in your homes.) Normal services will be restored shortly. (ored shortly.) Law-breakers will be severely punished. (verely punished.)"* The voice grew to an ear-offending shout as the copter drifted leisurely closer. Now it was almost overhead, and Ewing could see the blades whirling shiny in the sunlight, and the transparent bubble with two dark figures in it. The drab-painted machine turned as it drifted, the long curved body like an insect's abdomen. The huge voice stopped and began again. "YOUR ATTENTION PLEASE. (EASE.) YOUR ATTENTION PLEASE. (EASE.)—"

Ewing had his hands over his ears. Platt's jaws were working. He took his hands away for a moment and said, "What?"

Platt shouted, "Martial law!" He said something else, about "desertions," but Ewing couldn't make it out. The copter overhead, still shouting, drifted down toward the highway. Following it with his eyes, Ewing saw something strange. He saw what looked like a line of cars and trucks, spaced almost

18

bumper to bumper, climbing the mountain road. There was a wrecker, followed by a red convertible, two moving vans with dusty red sides, three panel trucks, two late-model sedans with glossy aluminum trailers, and a small gasoline tank truck.

He grabbed Platt by the arm, pointed. Then he was buck-jumping down the mountainside, with his heart in his mouth, catching a glimpse of the lead car turning in at the top of the road.

A round man stood up in the back seat of the convertible and aimed a gun at him. "Hold it!"

Ewing skidded, arms flailing. The irrigation canal was coming up like a fast elevator; he could see the hard white cement border, and the half-transparent minnows darting in the shadow. He couldn't stop himself, he was going in . . . He plunged back with a violent effort, and the mountain hit him hard. His ears rang. Dust rose around him. He sneezed and struggled to his feet.

The man in the convertible looked up at him without speaking. The gun was a double-barreled shotgun, sawed off short. He held it with the stock tucked under his arm. His dusty blue polo shirt was dark with sweat; his face and his heavy arms were burnt brick-color, but he wore only a shabby polo cap against the sun. A deer rifle was propped against the seat near his hand, and the butts of two revolvers stuck out of his waistband. His round face, eyes slitted against the glare, was placid and expressionless. He was chewing the ragged cold stump of a cigar.

"Stay right where ya are," he said finally. Ewing glanced to his left, and saw Platt standing there, hatless, with a bloody nose. "What was you guys running for?" the round man asked them.

Ewing said nothing. The young Negro in the front seat of the convertible was staring straight ahead, not looking up or appearing to listen. He was manacled to the wheel. So were the drivers of the wrecker and the first moving van. All three of them had the same vacant, faintly surprised expression.

The round man blinked and shifted his cigar. He nodded at the battered Lincoln up ahead. "That your heap?"

"It's mine," said Platt, starting forward. "I'll get it out—"

The shotgun came up sharply, and Platt stopped. "Just stand still," the round man said. "Okay, Percy."

The young Negro punched the drive button with his free hand, and the convertible inched ahead. Ahead of it, the links of a heavy chain rattled on the ground, while behind it a similar chain tightened with a clank and groan. After a moment, the other vehicles began to move. There were crashings and roaring engines as the motion transmitted itself down the line.

The wrecker crawled ahead. Its broad wooden bumper

19

butted up against the rear of the Lincoln, and began to shove. The Lincoln budged, trembled and bucked nearer the side of the road. Its right front wheel ran off the edge. The wrecker pushed, grinding in low gear. The Lincoln tipped downward, toward the narrow canyon between the road and the house. It hung, swayed reluctantly, and then went over with a grand smash against the side of the house. There was a startled shriek from inside. A tile fell off the roof and slid down the exposed side of the Lincoln. The dust cloud rose. The wheels spun quietly to a halt.

The cavalcade stopped, a little at a time. The round man turned his full attention back to Ewing and Platt. He did it deliberately, as if massive gears were turning somewhere inside him. He blinked, shifted the cigar butt in his mouth, and spoke. "Why did ya park ya car inna road?"

Ewing thought he had seen a face at the bedroom window. He said unwillingly, "Nobody uses this road. It doesn't go anywhere, except a ranch around the other side. They don't use it any more, there's a barrier."

The round man digested this in silence. He shifted the cigar again. "Yaa?" He chewed the cigar with an expression of distaste, removed it, spat, and put it back. "How big of a place would ya say that is?"

"The ranch? I have no idea," Ewing said stiffly. Platt was looking mournfully down at the way his car was wedged in between the slope and the house.

The round man stared at Ewing. "Ya seen it?"

"From a distance—I mean the house. I told you. I don't know anything about the ranch itself."

The round man thought about this. "Just one house?"

"That's all I saw."

After another pause, the round man nodded. He balanced the shotgun on his knee, took a soiled piece of paper and a stub of pencil out of his shirt pocket, and carefully drew a heavy line across the paper. "Okay," he said. "The heck with it." He put the paper and pencil away with the same deliberation, picked up the shotgun again, and stared at Ewing. "You live here?"

Ewing nodded.

"Who else?"

"Nobody else," said Ewing, tightly. "Just my friend and me."

"Don't tell me no fairy tales. Whatja do for a living?"

Ewing said, biting the words, "I'm an experimental physicist."

Instead of grunting and looking baffled, as Ewing had expected, the round man merely nodded. "Him too?"

"Yes."

The round man breathed quietly through his nose for a

while, staring at the ground somewhere near Ewing's feet, shifting the cigar from time to time. Eventually he said, "Come on down here—climb the chain and cross over." When they had done so, he got out of the car and stood beside them in the road. "March." They started down the driveway. "Your wife know how to shoot a gun?" he asked Ewing as they went.

"No," said Ewing heavily. It was the truth.

They walked in silence down to the shaded front porch and opened the door. In the living room, Fay and the children were waiting.

"My name is Krasnow," said the round man. "Herb Krasnow. I was a shipfitter in San Diego for seven years. I was in the Marines, too, before that, so don't make the mistake of thinking I'll be afraid to use this thing."

Krasnow's face was round and unemphatic, the nose short and wide, mouth and chin blending into his full cheeks. His eyes seemed to belong to someone else; steady, under untidy black brows. He showed his teeth rarely when he spoke; when he did, momentarily, Ewing saw that they were yellow-brown stumps, widely separated. The black hair on his arms and hands was luxuriant; his fingers were the thick, spatulate fingers, with black-rimmed nails cut back almost to the quick, of a man used to working with his hands. In his shabby polo cap and stained shirt, heavy-bellied, he might have been any workman on a street repair job, or loading a truck, or driving one. Ewing realized that he had seen thousands of men like this one in his life, but had never looked closely at one before.

Krasnow pushed his cap back, and immediately looked older; wet strands of hair straggled over his brown, bald scalp. Sitting in the straight chair beside the window, he faced the Ewings and Platt, all crowded together in a row on the couch. He held the shotgun balanced on one thigh, in a way that suggested he could aim and fire it from that position, one-handed. "See, my wife died a coupla years ago," he said. "I'm all alone inna world, so I figure, what the hell? Why shouldn' I get mine?"

Ewing swallowed and said angrily, "That's a hell of a philosophy. What about those people up there on the road—why shouldn't they get theirs?"

"You have an awful nerve," Fay said. "Who do you think you are, God? You can't do a thing like that to people!"

Krasnow shook his head. "They'd do the same to me. I take my chances, just like they took theirs. You might even knock me over and take the whole works. I'm just one guy."

Platt leaned forward over his crossed knees; he was folded up like a jackknife on the couch, all joints and bony hands. The cigarette in his fingers trembled and spilled ash. "When are you going to sleep, Krasnow?" he asked.

21

Krasnow pantomimed a bark of laughter. "Yaa," he said. "You hit it there. We been on the road a day and a half already, and all I got was cat-naps. That colored boy, Percy, he'd as soon kill me as look at me. I figure I got to get through two more nights, maybe three before I can sleep. I'm getting old; ten years ago I coulda done it easy."

"You must be out of your mind," Ewing said. "What you're talking about just isn't possible. You can't keep all those people under control forever—you have to sleep sometime."

Krasnow shook his head. "Ya gotta have slaves now," he said. He used the word matter-of-factly. "Nothing else is worth anything. Ya can't get people to work for ya any other way. How's the work gonna get done?"

"What work?" Ewing demanded. "Don't you understand, everything's free now—power, machinery, anything a Gismo will carry. Later on there'll be bigger Gismos, for things like automobiles and prefab houses. What are you going to do, build a pyramid or something? Take your Gismo, why don't you, and let those people go."

"Naa. You're talking fairy tales. Every guy goes off with his own Gismo, and that's it? Not on your sweet life, mister. There's just two ways, and you'll find that out—ya gotta own slaves, or ya gotta be a slave."

"Power hates a vacuum," said Platt. His voice was curiously subdued; he was looking with close attention at the burning tip of his cigarette. "Trouble is, though, how you going to keep them down on the farm? First chance they get, they'll cut your throat and go over the wall. Then what?"

Krasnow looked at him directly and, it seemed, curiously. "That's something I gotta work out," he said. "Like now, I got them cars chained together, and I got demolition bombs I can set off by short wave. Live bombs, one in every car. That could be better, but it works. But later on I gotta think of something else. You're supposed to be smart, you got any ideas?"

"I might," said Platt, thin-lipped. His gaze and Krasnow's met.

"Yeah. Well, meantime, I gotta find a place like you said. With a wall." Krasnow sighed. "I heard something about this place around the bend here, so I thought I'd take a look —a long shot. But I can tell from the way you talk, it's no good. I'll head up the coast, like I thought at first. There's plenty of rich guys' places up north, outa the way. Halfa them big shots are away all year. Either there'll be just a caretaker, some old geezer, or else some punks that've moved in lately. Either way, I know how to handle it."

He stood up. "Ewing, you love ya wife and kids?"

Ewing's jaw knotted with anger and fear. He said, "What's that to you?"

Krasnow nodded slowly. "Sure ya do. Okay, buster, now you listen. If ya don't want to see them killed, right here, you do like I tell ya. Understand?" Ewing's throat went dry, and he could not answer. "You're coming along with me," Krasnow went on after a moment. "I like the look of ya, and I like ya family, and I can use a scientist like you. So get used to the idea. Now come on outside—yaa, you too, everybody. I got something to show ya."

He herded them through the door. Out in the yard, blinking in the white glare, Krasnow and Platt looked sorrowfully at each other. The shadow of Krasnow's gun was a short black line on the baked ground between them. "I can't use ya, and I can't trust ya," said Krasnow. "So start runnin'."

Ewing looked on unbelievingly. He saw Platt, staring into Krasnow's eyes, shudder and stiffen. Then the tall man was whirling, all knees and elbows, diving down the slope to the terrace below—zigzagging as he made for the shelter of the nearest pepper tree—

The gun went off with a noise like the end of the world. Deafened, uncomprehending, Ewing saw his friend's body hurl itself thrashing into the weeds. The children screamed. The bitter scent of powder filled the air. Through the leaves Ewing could see what was left of Platt's head, a gray and red tatter. The legs went on kicking, and kicking. . . .

Fay's skin had turned paper-gray. She looked at him, and the pupils of her eyes began to slide up out of sight. Ewing caught her as her knees buckled.

"Soon as she comes to," said Krasnow quietly, "you and her can start loading whatever ya want on ya trailer. I'll give ya half an hour. And meantime, you can be thinking about why I done that." He jerked his head toward the body in the weeds below.

Up on the road, in the cabs and front seats of all the parked vehicles, the faces of the drivers had turned to look down on them. Their expressions had not changed, but was as if a common string had pulled them all around, like so many puppets.

At nightfall, the caravan was winding northward along the ridge highway toward Tejon Pass. The air was cool. Off to Ewing's left the sun went down behind the mountains in great tattered scarlet and orange streamers; the riding lights of the van ahead glowed in the deepening twilight.

Fay and the girls were in one of the house trailers, sharing it with some other poor devil's family. Ewing was alone with the oncoming night, in the steady drone of the engine, with his wrist manacled to the steering wheel.

A slave . . .

And the father of slaves.

23

He'd had more than enough time to think about what Krasnow had meant back there at the mountain house. Krasnow had murdered Platt for an object lesson, and because he knew Platt would never make a good slave . . . too reckless and unstable. Besides, Platt was unmarried. Platt was not the slave type.

The slave type . . .

Funny to think that there were physicist types even among the natives of the Congo, who had never heard of physics . . . and slave types, even among the physicists of America, who had forgotten there was such a thing as slavery.

And it was curious, how easy it was to accept the truth about himself. Tomorrow, after he had slept and the sun was high, he might fill up with anger again—the brittle anger, so easily broken—and swear to himself, futilely, that he would escape, kill Krasnow, rescue his family. . . . But now, alone, he knew he never would. Krasnow was wise enough to be "a good master." Ewing's lips moved: the phrase was bitter.

What about fifty, a hundred years from now? Wouldn't the slave society break down—wouldn't the Gismo become at last what Ewing had thought it would be, an emancipator? Wouldn't men learn to respect each other and live in peace?

Would it be worth all the misery and death, then? Ewing felt the earth breathe under him, the long slow swell of the sleeping giant. . . . On that scale, had he done good or evil?

He did not know. The car droned onward, following the tail lights of the van ahead. From the west, slowly, darkness scythed out across the land.

FOUR

Dick Jones opened his eyes lazily to a green-and-gold morning, knowing as he awakened that there was something special about this day. Comfortably asprawl, giving himself to the cool breeze as sensuously as a cat, he wondered what it might be: a hunt today? visitors? or a trip somewhere?

Then he remembered, and sat up suddenly. This was the day he was leaving Buckhill to go to Eagles.

He stretched and swung himself out of the big circular bed, lithe, tanned, and big for his sixteen years. His body was proportioned like a man's, broad in the shoulders and chest, but all his muscles were buried under a layer of boyish fat. There was a subtly unfinished look about him, a bluntness.

He padded across the silken carpet and into the bathroom, toes splaying on the cold marble. Taking a deep breath and letting it out, he dived into the pool. Goldfish scattered as he plunged down into the center; the tiles underwater were a blurred sea-green, lit by yellow disks along the walls. He turned upward, and broke surface. Two strokes brought him to shallow water, and he rolled over on his back, awash to the chest, dripping and blowing. He looked around, saw no one, and shouted, "Sam!"

The body-slob tumbled in, half asleep, carrying a canister and brush. He was a tall, pasty-skinned boy, a year older than Dick; they had grown up together. Without speaking, he began to soap his master and work up a lather. He rubbed emollients into Dick's hair and scalp, shaved him with a safety razor, finally brought the hose over and rinsed him down with a cold spray. Sam's heavy underlip never stayed closed, and he had big ears that stuck out. Between his shoulderblades was a design in purple ink, a stag leaping, with the word "BUCKHILL" and a series of numbers under it, enclosed by purple leaves. Still sleepily silent, he wrapped a towel around his master and began to chafe him dry.

"Sam, this is my last day at Buckhill," Dick said.

"Yes, Misser Dick. You going away by Colorado tomorrow."

"I'll be away four years. I'll be over twenty when I come back."

"Dess right. You be twenty. Dess right, Misser Dick."

Dick snorted, feeling a vague sense of outrage. All right, the boy was only a slob—or "slave," if you wanted to please Dad and use the old term—but even slobs were supposed to have some feelings. In magazines and teledramas they were always bawling when they thought about their young masters going away; so what was the matter with Sam?

Then he discovered he was hungry, and forgot the matter. "I'll have ham and eggs," he said, taking the towel himself. "Eggs over, and a plate of wheat cakes, Sam—and milk, and coffee. Tell them to hurry up, I'm starving to death."

While the slob phoned his order down to the kitchen, Dick got fresh clothing from the wardrobe and began dressing himself. In passing he turned on the wall screen: it was tuned to KING-TV in Buffalo Keep, and Dick watched the cavorting musicians with half an eye, nodding his head to the rhythm. He liked military music; it was the only kind he understood.

Sam had come back from the phone and was talking in his ear; the music drowned him out. "What?" said Dick irritably. "Turn that thing down."

Sam reached over and found the right button on the bedside table console; the music faded to a hoarse *umpah, umpah.* "Cook says," he repeated, "is too busy by banquet

25

for make you breakfas'. So you got to send me down by Stores for dupe one, or either—"

"Damn it," said Dick angrily, and paused to suck in his stomach while he zipped up the tight blue-and-saffron trousers. That wasn't just the way the suit was cut; he was outgrowing his measurement again. "Why does everything have to go to pieces around here, every time there's some damn banquet?"

"Misser?"

"Never mind. Hurry up and get out of here, and I'll go myself."

In the corridor, two slobs in light overalls were taking down the wall panels one at a time and putting up new ones, identical except that the old ones were turning blue-green with corrosion, and these were shining new bronze, fresh from the Gismo. Dick recognized the figures of the bas-reliefs as old friends; they had been in this corridor all his life, slowly changing from bright to dull in an eternal rhythm. He paused to look at a familiar hand clutching a rifle stock, and at the familiar hard-set face above it, both glittering raw, bright metal—newly reborn.

Down below, the Big Hall was deserted except for a common house slob busily scrubbing, his bare arms gleaming with sweat. The rows of tables were all bare under the lights; the covers had not yet been laid.

It was twenty-five after seven by the big electric clock. Dick's parents would still be lying abed; so would his sister Constance, who had been turning into a sluggard lately. His brothers Adam, Felix and Edward might be up, but there was no telling where. Unfeeling brats, they were probably off riding or boating somewhere by themselves, not caring whether he might want to see them on his last morning.

All this, he realized belatedly, was at least partly before-breakfast crankiness. The duped eggs might choke him, but he needed some food in his stomach.

Stores was a cooled vault, lit by islands of fluorescents on the ceiling. In one of the pools of light there was a little crowd of slobs clustering around Fossum's counter. For a while Dick couldn't even attract the old man's attention. He moved in closer, shouldering his way.

Fossum's eyes were red-rimmed and irritable; with his veined beak and the sparse fuzz on his narrow head, he looked like an angry fledgling agape for worms. "Wot, wot?" he was saying. "One crissal cennerpiece with roses and wot? Lillies of the velley . . . all right. And a hunnerd wot? Balloons? Wy dint you say so? Dont all holler by same time. Wait half a minute, can't you . . . seventeen sconces, I got det. Shettup! You got to wait. You got to wait. I can't do every damn ting by same time . . ."

26

"Fossum!" Dick bellowed.

The old man's face only turned more sour. He listened unwillingly, fidgeting, while Dick gave his order; he scrawled symbols on his pad, then made as if to turn to the next impatient slob.

"*Now*, Fossum," said Dick, moving closer. Reluctantly, the old man went shuffling back along the aisle, moving in a flickering pool of cold light that followed him as he went. He stopped under the hanging sign that said "Food." Like all the rest, the tall shelves of this section were divided into pigeonholes, each one just large enough to hold one small gnarled object. There were thousands of these, shelf after shelf all the way back into the big room. To look at them, they might have been oddly shaped pebbles, or dried-up bits of root.

Fossum's gnarled forefinger rasped down the line of pigeonholes, stopped at one, flicked out the hard little lump into his palm. Grumbling half-audibly, he went into the Gismo Room. The massive door swung to behind him.

Dick fidgeted. The lump, he knew, was something called an "arrested prototype," or a "prote" for short. More to the point, it was his breakfast in unrecognizable miniature— cooked perhaps twenty years ago and duped on the Gismo, but incompletely. The process had been stopped in the middle, so that what came out was not a plate of eggs and bacon, rapidly cooling, but a gnarled lump of quasi-matter that could be stored in a pigeonhole, and would keep forever. When Fossum put it back on the primary side of the Gismo, and removed the inhibitor, an exact copy, not of the prote but of the original breakfast, would appear at the other terminal.

To Dick, the process was boringly familiar. If asked, he would have agreed half-heartedly that the Gismo was a marvel; actually, he took it for granted, like TV, or copters. He knew, too, that he owed his own existence and that of the world around him to the anonymous inventor of the Gismo, some seventy-odd years ago; but that was history. Just now he was more interested in finding out whether the prote Fossum had chosen was the right one, or—more likely—a slipshod approximation.

Here came the old man plodding in his circle of light. There was a steaming platter on his little cart. He paused to deposit the prote in its niche; then in a few moments he was lifting the platter onto the counter. Eggs, bacon, toast, milk, coffee. The golden yolks trembled, ready to spill.

Dick choked back a shout of pure exasperation. "Fossum, I said eggs *over* . . . Oh, hell, what's the use?" He caught the nearest slob's eye, motioned him to pick up the platter, and followed gloomily to one of the eating nooks that lined the near wall.

The day was quite definitely spoiled. There was nothing wrong nutritionally or in the taste of a duped meal, of course; it was just the principle of the thing. Only slobs, generally speaking, ate duped food; people had specially cooked meals. True, most of the ingredients were duped to begin with, so the distinction was not crucial; but it was there.

He ate hungrily but without satisfaction, pushed the remnants of the yellow-smeared whites around on his plate, crunched off another bite of toast, then gave up and threw the plate, silverware and all, into the waste chute.

All the same, having eaten made a difference. Feeling gloomy but less irritable, he went out, down the corridor past the kitchens with their tantalizing odor of roast fowl and pastry, and emerged from the hillside exit. The air was fresh and cool, flower-scented, with a tang of new-mown grass. The clear *chunk*, pause, *chunk* of an axe came from somewhere below. In spite of himself, Dick breathed joyfully deep. His feet were light on the path as he turned downhill.

Ten yards or so down, he paused to look back.

Looming over him in the cool sunlight, Buckhill was gray and knobby and huge. It looked as if the mineral kingdom had tried to create a behemoth of its own, there on the hillside, and had half succeeded. The unfinished monster slept, waiting for the second spasm of effort that would give it life.

The old inn, a C-shaped mass of fieldstone, part of it vaguely Alpine, part vaguely Spanish, had been built as a tourist hotel under the democracy, in those days when the Poconos had swarmed with vacationers from the kennels of New York and Philadelphia. The first Man of Buckhill had added the fortifications and the three hideous stone sentry towers. The second Man, and the first Jones (a nephew of the famous Nathan MacDonald, whose portrait hung in the Long Corridor), had built the landing field, and a lot of underground shelters and gun emplacements; but the third Man—Dick's Great-Uncle John—had only added a few tennis and squash courts and things of that kind. And except for upkeep and minor landscaping, Dick's father, the fourth Man, had done almost nothing.

That was all right with Dick. Buckhill was perfect as it was—he would not change a stone of it when he was the Man. Let even the ugly towers stand in their places; let Dunleavy trundle out the same duped shrubs and flowers for transplanting, each in its turn, forever and ever. That, it seemed to Dick, was the way life should go.

But he was sixteen, and not yet the Man; and he had to go off to Colorado for four years.

Dick's grandfather, as it happened, had taken and held

Buckhill in the first place with the help of the MacDonald family, who were collateral ancestors of the present Boss in Colorado. As a consequence, Buckhill was still considered the leading house of the whole eastern seaboard above Charleston Manor, and Buckhill's heir automatically became a brigade officer in the Boss's army, to serve a four-year hitch at Eagles in Colorado. It was an honor, he was looking forward to it, and he couldn't get out of it even if he wanted to; so that was that.

Shadow closed over his head like water as he walked down into the gorge. The vines and mosses that covered the bank on his left were dripping; the air was full of mustiness. Just before the first bend, he came upon two garden slobs grubbing out a young maple that had fallen across the trail. The earth under the exposed roots was rich and moist; the fresh wood chips had a sharp tang of their own. The two slobs leaned silently on their axes and waited; in the dimness, their eyes gleamed bluish-white. Dick clambered over the fallen trunk and went on.

Farther down, the air was as still as if it had been poured in years ago, and left to settle. Passing, Dick reached out to the bank and idly brushed his hand over a fleshy-spined mat of club mosses, three species of them growing together within arm's reach. He had learned their names, painlessly, on many a walk down this trail with Padgett the tutor.

There was botany for you; yes, and here was petrology a little farther on, where the pages of the great stone book lay open: limestone, slate, red sandstone, marl.

Botany, ecology, forestry . . . Dick paused beneath the slanting ten-foot bole of the William Penn Hemlock. After a moment he climbed the little slope to stand above it, and put his arms around the rough, scaly bark. Looking up, he saw the enormous trunk swooping away into distance, so tilted and bare that it made him queasy to follow it: the tree seemed to be tilting, not up, but everlastingly downward into a bottomless sea of green.

He stepped away again, feeling small and apologetic, as he always did after touching the big tree. "Without permission" was the phrase that occurred to him: but of course that was ridiculous. He turned his back on it (for the last time?) and went downward again.

He had been listening for the sound of the water, and now he heard it. It grew stronger as he went down the zigzag stairway, his footsteps hollow on the boards. The upper falls, swollen by spring rains, made a thunderous white torrent, dropping short and heavy into the upper pool. The spray filled the air, almost hiding the carved-out niche in the rock wall opposite, on whose cold, slippery floor he and Adam

29

had crouched so often, playing Crusoe, or Captain Nemo, or whatever. . . .

He followed the stream down past the dark middle pool and out into the glen. Even here the sunlight had not yet reached, but there was a diffuse glow from above, like a winter dawn. The water was as clear as melting ice, and almost as cold in the lower pool and the stream, inch-deep over the smooth red stones with their startling dividing lines of green algae. He crossed the footbridge and continued down the other side, relishing the padded silence that closed in on him as he grew farther away from the nearest human soul.

This was the heart of Buckhill, somehow. All the fields above were noisy with birds at this moment—jays, grackles, crows, cardinals—but down here there was not a sound; even the falls were muffled out of hearing. This was the quiet, secret place around which all the rest turned. And he was saying his good-by to it.

When he at last got up from the weedy bank, he was aware that he had stayed longer than he meant to. He couldn't tell how much longer; time seemed to run at a different rate in the glen. Or, rather, it seemed not to run at all, until you suddenly awoke with a lurch to find that your muscles ached and your stomach felt empty.

That reminded him: there wouldn't be any lunch, on account of the banquet. He crossed the lower footbridge and toiled up the slope, quartering back to the house by way of the bridle path. Sure enough, the sun was high; in another fifteen minutes it would be flooding the glen. It was getting hot, too; he was flushed and sweating by the time he reached the kitchens.

Inside, it was hotter still; a cook's inferno of sweat-dripping scarlet noses, spattered aprons, curses, banging plates and scullions underfoot. The breathless air was thick with the smells of duck, goose, pheasant, capon, squab; of venison, beef pie, whole suckling pig, breast of lamb; of steamed oysters, clams, giant prawns, lobsters, soft-shell crabs; of cod, albacore, flounder, mackerel, swordfish, salmon; of compotes and savories, sweet-and-sours, cheeses, puddings; of breads, rolls, biscuits, lady fingers, pies, cakes little and big. Greasy kitchen boys with stuffed eyes were hurrying everywhere; oven doors were banging, dishes clattering, men at the edge of their sanity were shouting from raw throats. A steel tray went ringing across the floor with a tinkle of broken crockery behind it; there was a shriek from the smallest kitchen boy and a torrent of abuse from the cooks. Dick seized the moment to slip around behind a long table loaded with floral centerpieces (all smelling of hot grease), to the counter where the cut cheeses stood, surrounded by tiny genteel wedges. Dick cut himself a more substantial chunk, grasped a pitcher of milk with the other hand, and escaped.

That the cheese was duped, like the milk, mattered to him not at all; he had stolen his meal from the kitchen like a person, instead of asking Fossum for it like a slob. He ate under an arbor beside the bowling green, dropped the remains under a bush, and strolled down the hill past the pavilion and the tennis courts. Every yard of the grounds was thick with memories; the soil, the weeds in odd corners, the very tufts of grass were the same year after year. Everything was known and familiar, sight, sound and smell. He paused at the edge of the exercise ground, where little Blashfield the armorer was shouting at his awkward squad, "Hup! Two! Dree! Faw! By de right flank, hup! you donkeys, hup!" Sunlight glittered on the stocks of the dummy rifles; the green-striped legs rose, fell.

Here was Artcraft Row, heat waves rising from the potters' kilns as usual, an intermittent tapping from the low, cool sheds where the cobblers and carvers worked. A mongrel yawned in the dust, scratching its ear. There was a *clang! tink, clang! tink* from the smithy, that fell pleasantly into silence. High in the blasted oak over the carpentry shops, a catbird began to sing. Full-hearted, Dick passed on toward the stables.

The exercise boys were taking out the Arabs and thoroughbreds, gray coat and brown, proud Assyrian heads tugging at the bridles. Dick watched them with a connoisseur's pleasure for a while, then went on down the row to where his own favorite, Gypsy Fiddler the Morgan was stalled. The gelding had just had his morning rubdown and his coat gleamed like silk. His head came up when he saw Dick; he whinnied, and stretched his neck over the stall door. Gyp was a three-year-old, wide-chested, short and compact, the perfect saddle horse for broken country, in Dick's view. One of the stable boys came up. "Ride him dis mornen, misser?" Dick waved him aside and saddled the gelding himself.

They took the easy upland trail past the meadows and the blossoming apple orchards. Lulled by the mild air and the motion, Dick fell into a reverie of himself in a gaudy uniform, feather-helmeted, leading a troop of horse against some vaguely imagined enemy.

But four *years* . . .

Why, four years ago, he had been twelve, a mere tadpole. He had broken his leg on the ice, learned to dive from the high board, been praised by Blashfield for his small-arms shooting, grown about nine inches, started to shave, killed his first buck—all that and innumerable other things, in four years.

He imagined himself coming home, tall and fierce, thinner

31

in the cheeks and heavier in the shoulders, with a look in his eye of things unspeakable. His mother met him at the door. She had been crying. "Oh, Richard! Your father has ..."

He came out of it with a start. The gelding had carried him all the way up the trail to Skytop; the sky was a wide blue bowl around him, and far off to northward he saw a glint of light: It was a dyne or copter, lowering. After a moment he saw another, and then a third. The guests were beginning to arrive.

FIVE

The Upper Hall was crowded and stifling with noise. Women in clouds of chiffon and in bags of tweed, some with cheeks rouged in two staring disks, like dolls, others with honest country faces reddened by nothing but food, wine and fresh air, were complaining about the trip, fussing after children, nervously bowing when they encountered each other, like hens uncertain of whom to peck. Slobs were scuttling this way and that under mountainous loads of personal luggage— favorite tennis rackets, windbreakers, lounging robes, collapsible sedan chairs, all manner of unexpected and unsightly things. There were more children than ever, some with runny noses, some airsick, some running zigzags through the crowd, some sitting on the floor and howling. And the men themselves, all the lesser persons of the Poconos and surrounding areas, were stalking stiff-legged here and there with sidelong glances, conspicuously armed, pricking up their fierce mustaches, like dogs in a strange kennel.

Dick glimpsed his father in the middle of a cigar-smoking group. He edged past. "Wanted to wait for her second heat to breed her, but ..." "What do you think of this? (Here, boy, hand that case over.) Nice little needle-gun—the Chassepot design, 1870. Old Flack traded it to me for two Black Labradors ..." "... as it happens, the only copies of these particular daily strips known to be in existence. Not many people have even heard of *The Bungles,* but to my mind ..."

That was his father, bright-eyed and flushed, the way he got when he talked about 20th-century newspaper comics. Tons of them, he had, all laminated in sheets of clear plastic and filed away, each in its wall slot, in the Comics Room; he had been collecting them since he was a boy. He saw Dick, nodded absently, and went on talking. "... for ironic commentary, the real heart of that age, you have to study *The Bungles.* Incidentally, I don't suppose you know that

32

Tuthill simply quit drawing the strip one day, when he felt tired of it. It ended there and then; no other artist took it over. Remarkable, when you remember how frantic everyone was for money..."

Dick's father, the fourth Man of Buckhill, was slender and not tall, fine-featured, rather delicately made, with a fair complexion. He was strong and agile, however, and his lack of commanding height never seemed to enter his mind. He ruled Buckhill firmly and efficiently; there was no better-run estate in the East.

George Jones of Twin Lakes, the Man's younger brother, seemed to have come from another stock altogether. He was tall and heavy-boned, with a brutish jaw and brow. He had grown fatter in the last few years, and now had an imposing stomach under the green brocade of his vest. Seeing the two brothers together, at first glance you would have thought George the older. His features had a faintly MacDonaldian heaviness, which he emphasized by combing his coarse hair, already sprinkled with an iron gray, into a forelock.

"Be reasonable, Fred," he was saying as Dick came up. "You're rated at five hundred able bucks counting the guard, and I know for a fact you're at least a hundred over. It's disgraceful—you ought to have been drowning newborns five years ago, to teach 'em a lesson."

Dick's father shook his head decisively. "I would never do that, George. Not even to a slave."

"Well, then, you'd better start lopping their trigger fingers, then, that's all there is of it. I'm telling you for your own benefit, Fred, you're too soft with 'em. You may think you can just go on like this forever, but sooner or later the Boss is going to send an inspector around, and then you'll be in the s-o-u-p, soup."

Dick moved on restlessly. He had heard it all a hundred times before, and had expected to hear it all a hundred times again. A month or so ago, guest days, except for a few pleasurable aspects, had been a pain in the scut. Now he found himself listening and watching with an irritable hunger; it gave him no enjoyment, but he couldn't take his attention away.

There was a familiar shape, little Echols of Scaroon with his big stomach wrapped in a scarlet cummerbund, cigar in one hand and champagne glass in the other. He was not an esthetic sight by any means, but he turned up at every party in the district; and it struck Dick with a curious pang that he was not going to see that cummerbund any more—not for four years, perhaps not for ever.

Another figure moved toward him through the crowd: one that he recognized without pleasure. It was his cousin Cashel, Uncle George's only son. Cashel, two years older than Dick,

33

was a louring, bullet-headed youth with dusty-black hair. He and Dick had fought in childhood as a matter of course each time the families met. No friendship had come out of the fighting, as might have happened. As they had grown older they'd learned to tolerate each other, but their mutual dislike was ingrained. Dick thought Cashel sullen and malicious, as well as ugly. He was aware that Cashel deeply resented being the eldest son of a cadet line; he coveted Buckhill, for all the wrong reasons.

But as the heir, Dick shared the duties of a host. "Hello, Cash," he said, putting out his hand. "Good you could come, and so on." They shook hands stiffly, and let go with enthusiasm. "Uh, can I get you anything?" Dick asked. "Washroom's in the alcove there, if you want to go."

"No thanks, I've been," Cashel said, too promptly. His expression showed, an instant later, that he wished he had taken the excuse to leave. "I'm a little thirsty," he added hopefully.

Shackled by courtesy, Dick could only say, "Champagne? Tokay? Ale?" and put out an arm to snag a passing waiter. "Claret?" he went on, as Cashel hesitated. "Port? Riesling?"

"No Riesling, misser," said the waiter, shuffling the bottles on his cart.

"Riesling," Cashel said decisively. "Yes, I guess Riesling. Well, I suppose there's another waiter around here somewhere—" He started to move away.

The phrasing was unfortunate; Dick bristled. "I guess there are one or two," he said emphatically. "Just wait a minute, won't you?" He glared at Cashel briefly, then used the same expression on the unhappy waiter, who winced, bobbed his head, and trundled rapidly away into the crowd.

Dick and Cashel stared uncomfortably over each other's head until he came back. With him was a second waiter, pushing a similar cart. The second waiter uncorked a bottle of straw-colored wine and hastily poured two glasses, handing one to Cashel, one to Dick.

"Riesling," said Dick coldly.

Cashel accepted his. "Just what I was wanting," he said with false heartiness. He sipped at it. "This isn't bad, really."

"Only Rudesheimer," said Dick, indifferently. "I might be able to find you some of the Mohawk '75, if you want."

"No, no. This is fine."

They stared at each other blankly for a moment, holding the glasses. It was dawning on both of them that they had got themselves into a position from which neither could gracefully retreat. Cashel made a gesture as if to gulp down his wine, but checked it, to Dick's relief: that would only have meant that as host, Dick would have had to force

34

another glass on him, and as guest, Cashel would have had to drink it.

"Oh, hell," said Dick finally. "Look, Cashel, we both have our private opinion of each other, but that doesn't mean we can't stand each other for half an hour, does it? Come on, let's listen to some music."

This was a major concession: he meant Dixieland, a form of noise to which Cashel was addicted, but which made Dick as restless as a turpentined hound. Cashel brightened perceptibly. "Fair enough!"

They turned toward the inner rooms. On the way, Dick dropped his barely-tasted wineglass into the nearest glory hole, and Cashel followed suit.

The mass of people was beginning to break up and scatter. Everywhere, as they walked deeper into the house, they found small groups: some looking over the collections and trophies, some watching TV or movies, or sitting down to card tables; some eating and drinking, some chalking pool cues, leafing through books, pinching serving girls; some already drunk and singing; some talking in clusters, some amiably wandering.

Dick found the musicians he was looking for in one of the smaller lounges; they were playing 20th-century ballads to half a dozen men and women, none of them listening.

Dick caught the leader's eye. He was a grizzled oldster named Bucky Williams; like all the musicians, he had been born on the estate and trained by his predecessor. Some people considered this kind of thing a waste of time—it was a lot simpler to make a prote of whatever artist you had, and dupe another of him when the first wore out—but Dick's father had a prejudice against duping slobs.

"Dixielan'?" said Bucky. "Yes, sir." He exchanged glances with the other four. The reed men poised their lips, the piano player and the drummer unrolled an aimless little rhythm, and then, as far as Dick was concerned, the five of them began to emit independent cacophonies. There was an old-fashioned tune mixed in somewhere, but each time one of the players stumbled across it, the others seemed to feel they could safely leave it alone. Dick sat and suffered through the first paroxysm, and the second, and the third.

He was feeling thoroughly purged, but sticking grimly to it, when the most welcome of all sounds overrode the combo's music. *"The small arms competition is about to begin,"* said the room's built-in loudspeaker. "Contestants assemble at the range, if you please. The first event will be rifle, open, free style, fifty and one hundred yards."

A hum and rustle went up, all through the adjacent rooms. There were jubilant whoops and running footsteps in the hall —collisions, curses, and over everything the angry droning of scores of body-slobs' call buzzers. Dick took out his own signal box and pressed the button, but the response light did not glow. Probably Sam was too far away; the little wave-senders had a range of only about a hundred and fifty yards. . . . Or it might be that the sender had plonked out sooner than usual. This model had a bug in it that no one had ever identified, and was commonly good for about three weeks before it quit. In any case, he had a ready-made excuse to part company with Cashel, all at once and in a hurry. With a curt nod to his enemy, Dick plunged into the corridor and worked his way against the stream of guests back to the escalator.

He found Sam without any trouble, down in the Big Hall where he had been pressed into service hanging decorations. Grinning with relief, the slob went off for Dick's gun cart.

The Hall was now almost ready, the walls banked proudly with hybrid blossoms from Dunleavy's gardens; each linen-covered table with its floral centerpiece, gleaming with crystal and silver under the chandeliers. The musicians were tuning up in their alcove; the waiters stood nervously in a clump near the kitchen doors, while Perse the major-domo and two head waiters went dancing from table to table, adjusting a goblet here, straightening a napkin there. Dick's earlier meals seemed to have melted away; he discovered a hollow place inside him, and filched a handful of nuts from the sideboard to fill it.

Then Sam was back with the cart. Dick checked its contents as they went: Marlin carbine, .375 Winchester, Remington 10, the Schloss over-and-under 12—a hand-made unique, with the "do not dupe" plate in its stock—the Männlicher-Schoenauer .308, and rounds for all of them; the five-foot trophy stick; the scopes and binoculars in their padded clips; the Ruger .22 target pistol, .38 S. & W. everyday gun, Colt .45, and their ammunition. The bores looked clean, to a cursory inspection, but there was a spot of rust on the Remington's barrel. He made a mental note: time to junk the lot, except for the hand-made, and get dupes from Fossum. He buckled on the everyday gun in its holster, out of habit: he was used to the weight on his hip when he was shooting, or going to shoot with any weapon.

Nearly all the male guests were ahead of them; they passed through schools of more leisurely females, drifting in little cheerful clumps and gossiping as they went—their kindly faces aglow with liqueurs and sociability—and a scattering of stray children, dogs and mislaid servants. But there was plenty of time still: the grandstand above the rifle range was less than a quarter filled, and most of the young men were standing about in picturesque attitudes on the hillside, each negligently holding his trophy stick with its incised bands of white, yellow and red. Some of the youngest, particularly those whose trophy sticks were bare, were engaging in impromptu contests of their own—wrestling, slapping, boxing, judo, broad-jumping, spitting, tumbling, knife throwing and the like. Farther up the slope, the governesses had corraled several dozen of the small children and were trying to keep them occupied in ring-around-the-rosy, as usual without much luck: tiny voices raised in glee and anger came piping through the murmur of the crowd.

They passed the Rev. Dr. Hamper, squatting on a hillock, hands clasped below his ecclesiastical knees, head bent, smiling around his pipe as he listened to the visiting Americo-Catholic priest from Fontainebleau. It was the general feeling at Buckhill that Hamper was a mediocre chaplain, his predecessor the Rev. Dr. Morningside being remembered as a model of succinct eloquence; but he was the best natural-born Episcopalian minister Buckhill could get—so many were being duped by the big Eastern families that naturals were growing very scarce.

There was an outbreak of yelping and snarling up ahead. Through the gathering crowd, Dick caught sight of the two dogs, one a handsome collie, the other a cur—a grotesque mongrel, part St. Bernard, part Doberman, by the look of him, and part God only knew what. Pressed into the wide circle as it formed, Dick and the slob watched with interest. It was a good fight, as far as it went; but when it seemed the collie was getting the worst of it, a man in green blouse and knee-breeches stepped up and fired a handgun. The collie broke away, startled. The cur was writhing, shot through the hindquarters. The green man aimed carefully and shot him again in the head.

The body kicked once and was still. The crowd began to disperse. As he left with Sam, Dick glanced back and saw a distasteful sight: a small slob-boy dressed in the Buckhill colors, kneeling with his head on the dead dog's chest, and a tray of drinks spilled beside him on the grass.

Well, if the slobs wanted to keep pets, and let them breed at will, what could you do? Down on the flat, the band was beginning to blare "Buckhill Forever"; it was time to get on the line.

The range was almost filled; some of the other first contestants were already firing, and the bitter tang of smokeless powder drifted across. Dick carelessly took the first vacant place, and discovered when it was too late that Cashel was his neighbor. Cash looked around at the same moment, and they stared at each other with helpless distaste; then Cash shrugged and turned away, saying something to his body-slob.

The breeze was light, from nine o'clock. Sam handed him the loaded carbine. Beside him, Cash fired and a voice called, "Ten!"

Dick nodded to the slob at the TV monitor, took his stance and fired. "Ten!" called the slob.

Spah! went Cashel's gun at his ear, and the slob called, "Nine!"

Dick fired again. "Seven!" Not so good, but he'd make it up. He was a better shot than Cash, always had been.

Not today, though. Something in the noisy crowd, or maybe in the morning's frustrations, seemed to have thrown him off. Cash was lining up a good series of tens and nines, while Dick, though he squeezed off each shot with care, was shooting unevenly. "Seven," called the monitor slob. "Nine ... seven ... seven ..." There was an embarrassed pause. "Miss."

A miss, at fifty yards, with his own carbine! Mortification overwhelmed him; he wanted to sink through the shooter's stand, or wrap his gun-barrel around the TV monitor and stalk away. What wouldn't Blashfield say to him on Monday! ...

But there wasn't going to be any Monday: there, he'd forgotten again. Abruptly the sun-warmed cloth over his shoulderblades was no longer pleasant; the carbine had turned to a dead stick of metal in his hands. What was he doing here in a silly picnic shoot, when he ought to be using his last minutes at Buckhill saying good-by to the lake, or the pheasant woods, or down at the stables ... ?

"Ten!" said Cashel's monitor slob, cheerfully.

Dick glanced over involuntarily, and saw Cashel's gloomy face illuminated by an oafish pleasure. His hands began to shake and his mouth went dry. It seemed to him that the one thing that could give him any satisfaction would be to trample that face and kick dirt over it. ...

Trembling, he turned away. He knew he had a temper; he got it from his mother's family—all the Dabney men were quarrelsome and short-lived. "If y' want for die in you bed," Blashfield kept telling him, "you'll have to watch y' temper, or either be twice the man of y' guns as y' be."

Somehow he got through the first event, with a score just above the worst duffer's. The second went no better, although he took care to put plenty of distance between himself and Cash. Afterward, he went past the scoreboard with only a glance. He didn't see his own name, but Cash's was conspicuous, just under the first ten.

His bad luck still held: the pause was just long enough for Cashel himself to blunder out of the crowd and fall into step beside him. All the guests were drifting back toward the house now; with no excuse to break away, they plodded along dumbly together.

Finally Cash said, "By the way, Dick—"

"Yes?"

38

Cashel licked his lower lip, looking uncomfortable. "About tomorrow—" he said, and stopped.

Dick turned aside impatiently to pass a gossiping group of matrons. "What about tomorrow?"

"I mean," said Cash, following, "about you going to Colorado, and so on."

Dick looked at him.

"I mean," Cash said, with a final burst of candor, "about you going instead of me. I mean it's all right."

Dick stared at him speechlessly for a moment; then his fists clenched and his neck grew swollen. He closed his jaws tight. It was no good: he couldn't contain it. "Oh, go to hell!" he shouted. He made an impotent gesture, whirled and strode away.

After a moment Cashel caught up with him. His long face had turned pale. "Look, Dick, you had no call to talk to me that way—"

"Leave me alone," said Dick with difficulty. "Will you? Will you do that, old man?"

"Look, Dick—"

"You look!" said Dick, exasperated beyond reason. "Everywhere I go, I see your slobby face! Mush off! Flap!"

Cashel stood there with his white face, and his heavy hands hanging, and said, "Dick, apologize."

Dick turned away without answering. Cashel did not follow him.

The house was filling up again; some of the guests were streaming downstairs for the bowling tournament, some gathering for cards and dice. Dick prowled purposefully through the house, glancing into each game room and lounge. In the Upper Hall he ran into his mother, serenely promenading with a group of ladies in flustered hats. She saw him before he could get clear.

"Dick, is something the matter?" She put her palm against his cheek, ignoring his attempt to pull away. "You're feverish, darling."

"It's hot out in the open," said Dick.

"Ladies," she said without turning, "I think you know my son Richard."

Unmoved in the chorus of "Oh, *yes,*" "My, how you've grown," and "Aren't you a lucky young man," she fixed him with a clear, ironic gaze. Dick's mother was a tall blonde woman, majestically built like all the Dabneys. Her features were too strong for beauty—Dick and Constance both resembled her, which, Dick privately thought, was a good thing for himself, and a pity for Con—but in her bearing and manner she was the perfect embodiment of the ideal big-house wife. She was as brave as a man. In her maiden days, it was said, she had once struck down a crazed slob with a mashie,

39

and then resumed her game as calmly as if there had been no interruption.

Now she said, "Of course, if you're sure—"

Dick finished his dutiful nods and bows to her companions. Feeling acutely uncomfortable, he said, "It may not be anything. I have to talk to Dad first—do you know where he is?"

"Try the den."

Her hand touched his shoulder as she moved away, and then her clear voice was receding down the Hall: ". . . this wing, as you know, was rebuilt by my husband's father in the nineties. . . ."

Dick went on, moving faster. The elevators were all busy with guests, so he took the escalator to the top floor, and then climbed the tower stair. In the cool, leather-smelling dimness of the vestibule, he knocked at the carved ebony door, then entered.

His father was seated behind a glass-topped ebony desk, narrow head bent. He glanced up from the letter he held in his hand. "Yes, Dick?" he said. "Sit down; I'll be just a moment."

Dick sat on the broad window seat that followed the curve of the tower. From here, looking down the south slope, he could see the early sun glinting off the speedboat lake. The red stable roofs showed above the trees, and beyond that, the gray hunched bulk of the old fortifications. Vine-grown and crumbling now, they had encircled the whole estate in Dick's grandfather's time—three levels of steel and concrete, with walls fifteen feet thick in places, and a moat that once could have been filled with fuming acid in ten minutes. The first Jones had been a cautious man who believed that attack on Buckhill, if it ever got beyond the stage of small aircraft raids, would come as a mass attack of foot soldiery.

Nobody, as it happened, had ever attacked Buckhill at all. (As a child, Dick had always imagined that his grandfather must have died a disappointed man.) Most of the fortifications had got in the way of one thing or another in later years, and been pulled down; this one piece was all that was left. There hadn't been even a local war in twice Dick's lifetime. . . .

He turned to look at his father, erect in the carved ebony chair that seemed to belong to him, though its thick arms made him seem spindling. A faint, cool light played on his head from the prism in the skylight, twenty feet above; around the skylight well, tier on tier of bookshelves went up, heavy grave-looking volumes of rich red and brown leather, tooled and stamped. The windows were shut; the air was heavy with the odors of paper, leather, tobacco, polished wood. *If it were my room,* Dick thought involuntarily, *I'd open all the windows and let the wind blow through. . . .*

His father glanced at him, folded the letter and sat back, taking a thin hunting-case watch from his vest. He opened it, snapped it shut again. "All right, Dick, what is it?"

Dick said, "I think Cashel's going to try to get permission to call me out."

He braced himself, without quite knowing why; but the Man said only, "Tell me about it."

Dick did so, as briefly as he could, ending: "When I got back to the house I saw Cash once more, and I think he saw me. But he went on by. He had a kind of a look on his face."

"Yes?"

"He looked as if he'd made up his mind."

The Man nodded, looking tired and thoughtful. He spread the papers on his desk idly, then pushed them aside. "It's awkward, Richard. I suppose there's no doubt that you provoked him, not the other way around?"

Dick hesitated. "No, I guess not," he said unwillingly.

"I'm not asking for explanations, or exhibitions of penitence," said his father precisely. "Nor am I going to give you a lecture. You were armed, you provoked a quarrel. When I gave you permission to wear a handgun, I tacitly agreed to treat you as a man in matters of personal honor. I am going to do so. If this challenge is made—" The telephone rang.

The Man answered it. "Yes. Very well, send them up." He put the receiver back. "*When* the challenge is made," he said "I'll do everything I can as the head of your family ... I assume you do wish me to act for you?"

Dick swallowed hard. "Yes, please, Dad."

"Very well. If you wish any advice, I will of course give it. But I think the choice is fairly clear. You fight, or back down."

"Yes, mister," said Dick, moistening his lips. He felt bewildered and, to be absolutely honest, a little scared, but one thing he was sure of: he was not going to make the Man ashamed of him.

After a considerable time, the door opened and Uncle George entered. Behind him were his brother-in-law, Uncle Floyd Logan, and a cousin of Aunt Jo Anne's named Alec Brubaker. Uncle Floyd was older than the rest, a dark, paunchy man with bad teeth. Cousin Alec was fair skinned, wispy and nervous. Last of all came Cashel, looking sullen.

Dick's father looked them over coolly. "I think you'll find that settee comfortable, if a trifle crowded," he said. "Dick, bring a chair for Cashel."

Uncle George's choleric flush was a shade deeper when he spoke. "Fred, I'm afraid you misunderstood—this matter is private."

The Man raised an eyebrow. "So? But your son Cashel is present."

41

"Cashel is the injured party."

"If one of my family has injured him," the Man said dryly, "I don't suppose it was my wife or daughter, and my other sons are all too young to give serious offense. That leaves Richard, if I am not mistaken."

Uncle George nodded. "Well, Fred, it *is* Dick."

"Then he had best stay. And since you have brought your other relations—" The Man pressed the buzzer on his desk.

"It's a family affair, Fred," said Uncle George.

"Just so." To the slob who appeared in the desk screen, the Man said, "Go and find Mr. Orville Dabney and Mr. Glenn Dabney, and ask them to be so kind as to join us here." The picture clicked off. The Man looked coolly at his guests without speaking. The silence grew.

At length Dick's two maternal uncles came in, looking grim and wary: tall blond men both, crag-faced, with fierce blue eyes and hairy hands. Orville Dabney, the elder, was known for his habit of tossing men over his head when provoked, and worrying about protocol afterward. Glenn Dabney, who wore a thick curling mustache, was shorter and quieter, but no less dangerous. The lobe of his right ear was missing—shot off, it was said, in a duel he had fought with a visiting Cornishman in his youth.

The Man greeted them formally, invited them to sit. The little room grew crowded and hot. The Man opened the humidor on his desk and passed it around. While the men were cutting and lighting their cigars, he put his fingertips together and quietly began to speak.

After a moment, Dick realized that he was rehearsing the whole history of the Jones, Dabney and Logan families, from the Turnover up. He saw hands poised in mid-air and surprised expressions around the room as the same belated realization struck the others; then they were all silent and attentive. It was a matter of family pride to listen to that story, but not only that: as the Man told it, the story itself was fascinating.

One after another, the leading figures of all three families were sketched in—Jeremy Logan, who had fought the Morganists at Pimple Hill and Big Pocono; Fabrique deForest Dabney, the founder of the line, whom the family slobs still claimed to see on moonlit nights, riding like a demon and dressed in nothing but his famous white beard; Edward R. Jones and his single-handed conquest of Buckhill.

As he listened, although he knew the story by heart, Dick grew aware as never before, not only how proud a record his family had, but how precarious a thing it was.

The first Jones had taken Buckhill away from the former holder by what amounted to a low trick—disguising himself as a slob to enter the house, and throwing old August Boyle

42

out of his own bedroom window. That was colorful family history now, but if the same thing happened over again today, it would be a crime.

Then there was the third Man of Buckhill, Edward's brother Leonard A. Jones, who had taken over the house when Edward died in a riding accident—and whom the present Man had had to challenge and kill, in order to get his rights when he returned from Colorado. Power was a delicate thing, the story seemed to say; those who had it must hold it firmly but carefully—must cherish it, and be wise.

"And Frederick begat Richard, and George begat Cashel," murmured Dick's father. "The rest of the story, I believe, is yours, George."

Silence fell. The eyes of the company turned to look at Uncle George, who straightened, sighed regretfully, and planted both heavy hands on his knees. "Fred, and you men, here's the whole thing in a nutshell. My boy Cashel came to me a little while ago and said, 'Dad, I want your permission to fight a duel with Dick.' Well, I was shocked. I said, 'Why, what's he done?' 'Called me a slob,' he said." Uncle George looked around the room in an open, manly fashion. "Men, I tried to be fair. I said, 'Cashel, what did *you* do to provoke a statement like that from your cousin?' He looked me in the eye and said, 'Dad, I only wished him good luck in going to Eagles in Colorado.' "

Dick felt hot and cold by turns. He shifted his weight on the window seat until a glance from his father warned him to be still. Diagonally across the room, he was aware of Cashel staring miserably at his own hands.

Uncle George, gathering confidence as he went along, was saying. "I told him, I said, 'A duel isn't a thing you rush into, especially between blood relations,' but I told him, 'We'll go and talk to your Uncle Fred. I know he'll want to do what's fair.' " He leaned back and spread his hands. "So, men, here we are."

After a long moment, Uncle Orville spoke. "Let's hear the other side of it."

"The offense was given," said Dick's father at once. "We admit that, to save argument."

Orville nodded and sat back.

Uncle Floyd said, "Then there's just three ways about it. Either the one cub withdraws, or the other apologizes, or they fight."

They all chewed on that in silence for a moment. Uncle Orville and Uncle Glenn exchanged glances with each other and with the Man. As if some intelligence had passed among them, Uncle Orville turned and asked, "Will y' let your boy challenge, or not?"

Uncle George looked ruffled. "That's not an easy decision to make. If we get an apology, of course—"

"First things first," said Uncle Orville briskly.

Uncle Floyd put in, "That don't mean we can't discuss it beforehand. The question is, Fred: if our boy withdraws, will yours apologize?"

All eyes turned on the Man expectantly. To Dick's surprise, he said merely, "Ask my son."

Before Dick could speak—indeed, before he had any idea what to say—Uncle Floyd burst out, "Wait a minute, Fred. You can't put it up to the boy, he's under age."

"I can, and will," said the Man.

The Jones-Logan men seemed to consult one another with a glance. Uncle George said gravely, "Fred, you don't seem to realize. A duel is a serious matter."

"So is an apology."

There were assenting murmurs from the Dabneys, and, reluctantly, even from Uncle Floyd and Cousin Alec.

"What do you say, George?" Cousin Alec asked.

"I want satisfaction," Uncle George muttered.

Orville leaned forward. "Mean y'll let him challenge?"

"I didn't say that," Uncle George retorted. "I haven't made up my mind." He turned angrily to the Man. "You're not giving me much accommodation, Fred."

The Man did not reply.

"All right, now here's what it comes to," Uncle George said after a moment. He leaned forward to look directly at Dick. "Dick, if we should agree to withdraw, will you apologize?"

Out of the corner of his eye Dick could see his father's attentive face. The Man did not move nor make any sign, but some instinct prompted Dick to suppress the answer that occurred to him.

He said, "I'll have to wait till the time comes to decide that, Uncle George."

There was a stir as the men sat back in their places. "That puts it in your lap, George," said Uncle Orville with a grim smile.

Uncle George was scowling, and his face was dark; a vein swelled over one eye. Uncle Floyd was smiling a sour smile around his cigar; Cousin Alec was gnawing a thumbnail, his yellowish eyes turned up toward Uncle George like a hound's.

In the silence, the chiming of bells came faintly to them up the tower stair. "That will be the banquet call," said Dick's father, opening his watch. He clicked it shut precisely and put it away in his pocket. "Shall we go down, then, and leave this discussion until later?"

Uncle George glanced at his kinsmen briefly. He hesitated, then grunted and rose. "All right with me."

44

The others got up and moved toward the door. Was that all? Was it really over so quickly?

The disappointed slope of Uncle George's shoulders seemed to say that it was.

Up and down the Big Hall, in a ceaseless hum and shuffle of feet, the guests were taking their places. The orchestra was playing something bland and tuneful, with chimes in it; slobs were everywhere, guiding guests, holding chairs, serving cocktails and wine.

The narrow family table stood at the head of the room, slightly raised; places were laid only on one side, so that no one had his back to the guests. Dick found himself seated next to his father and mother, among the adults. It seemed a long way down from this eminence to his former place at the end of the table, from which Adam and the others were peering worshipfully up at him.

The other half of the table, as usual, was occupied by Uncle George and his family—as effectively concealed from Dick, where he sat, as if they had been all the way across the room.

Savory odors drifted in from the kitchen. Slobs at the service tables in the corner were pouring more cocktails from gigantic shakers. Soup tureens came down the aisles in silvery flotillas, gallons of soup, soup enough to drown a man, all fragrantly steaming.

It was, Dick discovered, mock turtle—his favorite. The whole banquet seemed to have been decently planned to suit his tastes, in fact. As he picked up his spoon, the Man's voice said, "How much have you eaten today, Dick?"

Dick stared at him. The Man's neat, small features were serious, as always. "Well, breakfast—ham and eggs—and then I had a piece of cheese and some milk around lunch time. And some nuts. Why?"

"Eat sparingly now," said the Man. "You may have a little soup and some game. No fowl, no fish, no seafood, no pastry. And no wine. Pretend to be eating more than you are. Is that clear?"

Dick's mouth fell to watering.

"Do you understand?" his father insisted.

His own mouth sounded thick. "I suppose so." This was really too much—his own farewell banquet! Oh, damn! "But Dad—"

"Yes?"

"I thought the duel was all off."

"What gave you that impression?"

Dick floundered. "Well, I don't know—"

"It may be off. I venture to hope so. But meanwhile, you will take the precautions I mentioned."

The noise was such that he could barely make out the words. Tumblers, traded for the occasion from a Canadian connection of the Dabneys', came whirling down the bare center table, pinwheels of red and yellow tights; they unwound, leaped, bowed, and became jugglers. One of them, the tall fellow, unaccountably stumbled and dropped a red rubber ball, which bounced into Mitchel Krauss's soup. Krauss stood up with a howl of wrath and flung a wine bottle at the slob. Struck fair in the ribs, the fellow toppled, off balance, and fell kicking in the aisle. Mirth exploded around him; Krauss and his crony Roscoe Burns clinked glasses, splattering themselves and their fat wives, already choking with laughter.

Off to the right, an even merrier din arose from the slobs' table, where the Rev. Dr. Hamper, Padgett, Blashfield and Dr. Scope presided over the upper servants.

The remaining two tumblers finished their act and went off. Dick noticed the one who had fallen being carried out—in pain, by the look of him. Probably he had broken a rib or two. That showed you Krauss's lack of consideration, but then, everybody knew he treated his own slobs the same way.

The soup was followed by game and Burgundy, with high-balls for those who wanted them. Under the lights, the centerpieces steadily wilted. The faces of the waiters as they hurried by were gray with fatigue, sweat-streaked. The diners' faces gleamed with grease and exertion; their mouths opened to roar with laughter, and closed around gobbets of rich hot meat, potatoes and gravy, savory Brussels sprouts, artichokes in hollandaise sauce, slices of cranberry jelly. Little Echols choked, barked, turned purple, and was heartily thumped on the back. At the younger tables there was a good deal of bun-throwing, and fencing with bunches of celery. Several small children, screaming with rage, had to be led off in disgrace by governesses.

Dick ate a little of the venison, as ordered, and put it aside; he left the wineglass untouched. The next course was pheasant, with a golden Rhine wine—probably the Mohawk, he thought bitterly. The serving slob, who was some kind of relative of the chef's, gave Dick a reproachful look as he cleared away the plates.

Then came domestic meats—duped, of course; nobody kept herds any more—with a claret. Then seafood, with a sauterne. Dick's father touched his arm and nodded toward Uncle Orville. When Dick had attracted his attention, the Man said to them both, "Cashel is not eating. He has had nothing since the soup."

Uncle Orville nodded and turned away. Dick's mouth was suddenly dry.

The meal dragged on. The room, the diners, everything

46

had taken on a dreamlike quality. Time was stifled. Course succeeded course with maddening slowness, and Dick carved the meat, chopped at vegetables with his fork, picked up his wineglass and set it down. The Buckhill Players, who in everyday life were body slobs, secretaries and the like, came on with a skit called "The Expert Eye"; Dick had seen it in rehearsal, and had thought it hilariously funny, but now it seemed vulgar and dull. Singers followed, then the magician, and then a pair of clowns—new ones; Uncle Glenn had brought them up from Newcastle. Heat waves swam under the ceiling; the sherbets began to melt almost as soon as they were set down.

Then the last of the long line of glasses was being filled with champagne; Uncle Orville, on Dick's right, rose to give the first toast.

"To the boy that's leaving us tomorrow—to spend four years away from his own fireside—learning good manners and wickedness—" Uncle Orville snorted. "May he come back none the worse for it—young Dick Jones!"

All over the room, the bright wineglasses winked as they swung up in salute. There were more toasts, endlessly, while the hot room swam in its own vapors, fumes of wine, greasy fragrance of departed meat, spices, sweat and perfumes.

Abruptly, it was all over. The guests were getting up, milling confusedly in the aisles, and slowly trickling out, leaving the sadly littered floor and the garbage-heaped tables behind them. The echoes grew hollow.

The women of the two Jones families were gone, taking the younger children with them. The last guests were out of earshot. Leaning on his elbows on the table, the Man turned and said, "Well, George?"

Uncle George's face was pale. "Fred, you've pushed me too far. I want you to understand that. I never was jealous of you—"

The Man must have made some sound, for Uncle George stopped as if stung. "No, by God, I never was!" he said. "But you think you can sit here, manning it over the whole countryside—" His voice was shaking; he stopped again, stared at the dessert plate in front of him, with its monogram and the distinctive Jones pattern, then clutched it and broke the fragile thing over the edge of the table.

Next to him, Cashel started and glanced up, his heavy face surprised.

The Man's voice seemed flat, almost colorless. "Do I understand by that gesture that Cashel is challenging Dick?"

"Unless he gets an apology, right here, right now!" Uncle George struck the table with his fist, making the silverware dance and ring.

The Man turned composedly. "Well, Dick?"

Down the table, the faces of the other men stared sullenly or angrily past him. Dick could see now, as he looked at them, what it was that was eating into Cashel and Uncle George. If he were only out of the way, it would be more than four years before Ad was sixteen; there would be a vacancy, and Cash could go to Colorado—get the training, meet the important people. . . .

For the first time he could remember, sitting there beside his father, he felt that he and the Man were completely in harmony, each knowing the other's feelings without a word or gesture.

This was what mattered, after all—not who was "right" or "wrong."

He said, "I accept." The words hung in the heavy air. Sunlight was pouring brilliantly in at the far end of the room, making the incandescents seem dim and sickly. For a long time no one spoke.

Gray-haired old Vaughan, the Man's body-slob, came at a tottering run through the doorway. The Man, Dick realized, must have signaled for him minutes ago. Leaning back casually over his chair, Dick's father spoke to Vaughan, giving him instructions; the slob went out and returned shortly with a portable typewriter. One of the secretaries, being sent for, sat down at the machine and in a few minutes produced a document which he handed with a bow to the Man. By this time, Kunkle of Delaview had showed up, redder than ever in a hideous apple-green jacket and plus-fours. Kunkle was the district's greatest sports and weapons enthusiast; he knew all the rules of every contest, and always refereed important matches. All the men, having seized the opportunity to stand up, gathered in an uneasy group to read the document—after which each sat down again in turn to sign it: first Dick's father, then Uncle George, then the in-laws beginning with the eldest.

Down in the left-hand corner, almost as an afterthought, there were two lines: "Challenge offered," followed by Cash's blunt scrawl, and "Challenge accepted," with an empty space. Dick signed, and then glanced over the paper before he handed it back: it began, "Know all men that on this 10th day of May, 2049, a quarrel arising between Richard Jones, eldest son of Frederick Jones of Buckhill, and Cashel Jones, eldest and only son of George Jones . . ." Under the last typed line, Dick's eye caught the familiar, austere shape of his father's signature, and the florid loops of Uncle George's. The capital G was small, but the J was enormous, and the last stroke of "Jones" whipped back into a descending curlicue that underlined the name.

"Well, men, it'll have to be this afternoon, if you're all agreeable," said Kunkle. "Say, in half an hour?"

48

SIX

Down the long green slope the crowd flowed in atoms of
white and scarlet, lavender, dun, sky blue. Dick moved with
it, protected by a little circle of relatives and servants: first
the Man and Uncle Orville, walking silently together, then
Blashfield the fierce little armorer on one side, and Uncle
Glenn on the other; behind him, body-slobs, porters and the
like. All around them, voices were subdued; no one shouted
or laughed. The shadows of the great oaks and maples were
heavily pooled at their roots; there was a melancholy fresh-
ness in the air. It was almost the magical twilight time of
day, when all shapes blurred into a golden mist, and the
ground seemed to glow faintly with its own light.

He was afraid.

It took all his will to conceal it, to walk steadily with his
head up, hands at his sides. His gut was like ice, his knees
were loose, his lips cold and dry.

He had played at duels a thousand times with Ad and the
others, and had thought he understood what it was like: you
drew yourself up, calm and cold; you waited for the word,
you aimed and fired, and the other man fell down. Even
when it was your turn to fall, you knew you would get up
again in a moment.

But to fall, and never get up—to disappear into that
blackness forever . . .

Now that it was ending, he could see the day as a whole.
This was what it had been leading up to, all the time, from
the very moment he had got out of bed. The frustration
about breakfast, the Dixieland, Cash and himself coming
together as inevitably as an axe and a tree . . .

He was going to *die*. His mind flinched back in horror
from that, but it was still there, grinning, implacable. His
body would rot under the ground, while delicious things were
still happening in the sunlight . . . at Buckhill, Adam would
be the Man; life would go on just the same, intolerably.

If only this feeling had come earlier, when there was still
time . . . He could never go through with it. He'd disgrace
himself if he had to, anything; but he wanted to live.

Down on the flat, a hundred yards from the rifle range,
the ground slobs had finished measuring off the distance
and had planted poles. Along both sides of the dueling
ground, the crowd was gathering; the line of fire was

approximately north and south, so that neither he nor Cash would have the sun in his eyes.

The crowd made way for them as they came up. Dick's party moved to the north end of the ground, and he saw Cash taking his place, among the huddle of Twin Lakes men, at the other end. Cash looked unfamiliar in his white shirt, more hulking and awkward than ever.

"Give me the gun," said Uncle Orville. Carrying it, he walked down to the center pole, to meet Kunkle and Uncle Floyd. They compared the guns, then conferred for what seemed an interminable time; evidently there was some troublesome point of procedure.

Dick felt the pressure of Blashfield's hard fingers on his arm. The little man was like a gray-feathered pouter pigeon; the bristly top of his head came only to Dick's shoulder. "Everybody feels same way by first time," he said gruffly. "It's all right. It's all right."

"Oh, Blashfield," said Dick.

"You'll do fine. It's just like from high board diving, firs' time. Second time, nod so bad."

Dick managed to snort. "How do you know? You can't swim, Blashfield."

The armorer's popeyed face was grave and dignified. "No, sir, but I fought for your granfadder by Pimple Hill."

Dick took a deep breath, and looked back down the line. Apparently the dispute had been satisfactorily decided; the two guns hung on the center pole, and Uncle Orville was walking leisurely back. Off through the crowd to the left, Dick could make out Dr. Scope and two white-coated house slobs working around the emergency cart. Two narrow cots on wheels were standing ready, and there was a plasma stand, and a pulmotor. . . .

Dick was thinking of the dive from the high board, the falling, and then the icy shock . . . Was that what death was like? A shock, and then nothing?

"Now, misser, det won't be long," said Blashfield affectionately. "Remember for aim by det spot right under his arm. Never de head. If you miss by head, you miss, but if you miss by heart, dere's still his liver'n lights. How's your nerves?"

"All right," said Dick, from a dry throat.

"Good." Blashfield patted his arm. "Now remember dis, too, misser. A fight is a fight, it don't madder how you got into it or wedder you're by right or by wrong. You're here to kill your man if you can. Leave de sermons to de preacher."

As he spoke, the Rev. Dr. Hamper was coming slowly forward to stand in the center of the ground. With his fine

50

white head bared in the late sunlight, the Book in his long hands, he looked around slowly before he spoke.

"Men and ladies, before that thing is done here which cannot be undone, it is my duty to ask you humbly whether this dispute may not be peaceably resolved. Men, I beg you to search your hearts. Are you determined that this quarrel shall proceed?" He turned and looked earnestly, first at Dick as the challenged party, then at Cash. No one spoke. Everyone stood around patiently, waiting for him to get it over with. Hamper faced front again and bowed his head over his joined hands. "Let us pray. O Lord, who in Thy Mercy watcheth over us, grant that we may retire from this field with hands unsullied, and with true humility in our hearts. In Jesus' name we ask it. Amen." He straightened and walked back into the crowd. There was a hum of interrupted conversations.

"Blashfield," Dick said hurriedly, "what do you think about religion? I mean—"

The little man looked at him gravely. "I dink we have all been here before, misser."

Kunkle, who had been talking to Dr. Scope, walked out to the center and raised his arms. "Folks, your attention, please. This duel is going to be fought according to the Cleveland Rules. The boys are using thirty-eights, with three standard cartridges in each gun. The distance is one hundred fifty feet. The duel will go on to the first hit, or until both boys have used up their three shots. Now, will the contestants please come down to the center?"

Dick moved reluctantly forward, watching Cashel walk toward him down the green avenue. His palms felt sweaty. Cashel looked pale as death.

They reached Kunkle at the center pole and stopped. "Now, boys," said the referee, "I'm going to hand you your guns, and you take 'em back to your positions. Just let 'em hang in your hand. There won't be any drawing from holsters. When you hear me say, 'Ready,' you take your place by the end pole, facing away from here. You understand, facing away. Then when I say, 'Turn,' you turn, and when I say, 'Fire,' you can fire at will." He glanced at each of them in turn. "Any questions? No? All right, now go on back, and may the best man win."

Dick trudged back up the line. The faces went past him, a blur. His teeth were chattering in his clenched face.

Blashfield stepped into his path, stopped and steadied him, then maneuvered him over to the end pole, beside it and about two feet away. Over the armorer's head he saw his father and the two uncles, standing silently, with set, intent faces. "Take a deep breat'," said Blashfield.

He sucked it in, held it, let it go. "Anodder."

51

"Ready!" called the voice.

Blashfield gave him a final pat and stepped away. There was a long, breathless pause. Blashfield had moved back, out of sight, with his father and uncles. His heart was pounding, hard enough to hurt.

"Turn!"

He felt himself wheeling, coming to rest on the extended right foot as he had been taught. His arm swung up, heavy as a log.

"Fire!"

Over the gun barrel, Cashel's body seemed a tiny puppet-shape; his head would have fitted easily into the notch of the rear sight. He was standing edge-on, his right arm up and almost invisible in foreshortening. Fighting the tremor in his forearm, Dick brought the sights into line at a point just above and to the right of Cashel's chest.

There was a sharp popping sound near his left ear, over-riding the distant bark of the gunshot. He saw Cash's hand flip up and come down again. His arm was trembling again and his aim had gone wide: grimly he set to work bringing it back. Now the sights were lined up again; he squeezed the trigger gently as they wavered off, held, squeezed harder as they came back. The gun bucked and roared in his hand. His ears rang.

Cash was still there, still aiming.

Bringing the gun down, he heard the popping sound again, this time on the right.

He had perhaps a second to fire before Cash's third shot. In the hush, he saw the sights drift on target. He squeezed gently, then harder. Sights and target came together with an instinctive rightness that made him think, *A hit!* The gun roared.

Under his hand, he saw the tiny doll-figure of Cashel shortening—leaning, doubling over, down in the grass.

He waited numbly, but the body did not move. The crowd flowed in on it.

As he turned away, somebody took the gun out of his hand. Somebody else tried to support him from behind, but he kept going until he bumped into a tree. Holding the rough bark, he bent over and vomited.

When he straightened, Uncle Glenn handed him a hand-kerchief. Blashfield was busy with the gun; he put in a new round, closed it smartly, reversed it and stuffed it back into Dick's holster.

Beyond him, down at the end of the avenue, he saw Uncle George standing erect in the dispersing crowd, with Cashel's body in his arms. Dr. Scope was beside him, talking, gesturing, but Uncle George paid no attention. Tears were shiny on his cheeks; he looked stunned and wild.

"Dead?" Dick asked, unbelievingly.

"Dead as mackerel," said Uncle Orville.

He remembered Dr. Scope giving him a sedative, and then a long, formless, black period, something between waking and sleeping. Once he had opened his eyes, and the room had been filled with darkness; in the open window, the cold branches were skeletal against the faint star-glow. Then he must have fallen asleep again, because when he opened his eyes the second time the lights were on and his father was bending over him.

"What's the matter?" he asked dizzily.

"Get your clothes on," his father said. "Padgett, where's that coffee?"

The gray-haired tutor came forward with a silver pot in his hand. "Drink this." said the Man, shoving a filled cup at him. He gulped it; it was scalding hot.

The lights in the room seemed sickly and thin. The blinds were drawn. "What time is it?" he asked.

"Just before six," said Padgett. "If we hurry, we'll get away before dawn."

"What?" said Dick, sitting up. Sam came up with garments in his hands. He put a shirt over Dick's head, and Dick held up his arms automatically.

"We think it best for you to leave early," his father said. There were pouches under his eyes and he was wearing yesterday's linen.

Dick stood up, swaying. The image of that falling body leaped into his mind, unbidden; he said, "Oh . . ."

It had rained during the night and all the lawns were slick and sodden; but now the early sun was out, golden against grayness, and the sky to the east was clear. Up behind the house, on the field leveled by Dick's grandfather, there were two planes on the runway: a slim, two-engined Lockheed passenger-fighter, and a dumpy, gray Lippisch aerodyne. To Dick's faint surprise, there was no activity around the Lockheed; Blashfield and a squad of the House Guard were standing near the open door of the dyne.

Still thinking it was a mistake, he kept walking past the dyne toward the Lockheed; but his father stopped him with a touch on the arm. "That one's going later, as a decoy," he said. "This is yours."

Dick looked with distaste at the squat shape. The aerodyne was a dependable but ungainly old boat, built to a design that had been only half developed at the time of the Turnover, when all technological work had stopped. It was stable and strong, and about as safe to operate as anything but a Cub; but it had no style at all. Dick felt rebellious; it was as if he had been given the wind-broken old mare to ride.

"Couldn't you pick something funnier-looking?" he demanded.

His father merely cocked an eyebrow at him, and motioned to Blashfield to get his men aboard.

"Well, what are we afraid of?" Dick demanded. "Uncle George? Listen, Dad, if it's all the same to you—"

The Man turned. "Yes?"

"I'm not a baby," said Dick.

"Richard," said his father slowly, "you have led a somewhat sheltered life. I agree that you are not a baby; but being a man means more than fighting one duel. Do you understand what I mean?"

"I suppose so," said Dick.

"Meaning that you don't. You'll be on your own soon enough, and able to make your own mistakes. Perhaps you should have had that freedom earlier. But until then, you will do as I suggest. Here comes your mother now; go and say good-by to her."

Dick looked up; she was just emerging from the covered passage. The light scent she used enveloped him; her kiss was cool and undemanding as always. "Good-by, *dear* Dick."

After her came Adam, burning-eyed, with Constance and Felix breathless beside him. Ad was carrying something square wrapped in silk; he pressed it into Dick's hand. "It's a present," he said. "A memory book. Padgett helped us pick the quotations, and Litts bound it—we thought he'd never finish in time."

"I told him what designs to make," said Constance. "Dick, I hope you like the binding, and everything. Will you send me some enamels for my collection?" Her color was high; she looked about to burst into one of her meaningless fits of tears.

The Man urged him toward the gangway. The dyne engine was warmed and idling; the wash from its underjet steamed out around them. "I know how you feel," the Man said in his ear, "better than you think. When you get to Eagles—" he pressed a thin envelope into Dick's hand—"give this to a man named Leon Ruell. Have you got that?"

"Ruell," Dick repeated.

"That's right. He'll explain things better to you than I can." To Dick's astonishment and discomfort, there were signs of emotion in the Man's face. They gripped hands; then the Man pushed him up the gangway. Stooping, he entered the cabin. Padgett had left room for him next to the door; Blashfield and the guards were ranked behind. The pilot, a stolid young slob named Otto, turned in his high seat to wait for orders.

The gangway was being trundled off. Looking through the open doorway, Dick could see his father standing erect, his

54

clothes rippling in the jet-wash. Around him the family stood waiting; there was Miss Molly, late as usual, with Edward in her arms; too bad, he had wanted to say good-by to Eddie—; and the Rev. Dr. Hamper had turned up from somewhere, and Dr. Scope, and Sim the stableboy. . . .

With the low sun gilding their faces, they all looked like strangers. It was as if there were a wall of colored glass beyond the doorway, and they had all got on the wrong side.

Otto was looking questioningly down at him. Dick raised his hand; Otto turned, and the door closed. The sighing rush of the jet grew heavier; there was a whine and racket as the internal props cut in. Slowly and steadily, the dyne began to lift.

Looking now through the cabin window, Dick saw the ground drop away. The people grew foreshortened, their heads craned upward, hands went to brows. The landing field slipped aside. The lawn had a new, thick greenness as it opened out, spread itself like a carpet; now he could see all the familiar corners at once, as if by some unlawful and magical vision. There was the little strip of lawn between the house and the bridle path, with the old sundial and the birdbath in the middle: how many long afternoons had not that sundial and birdbath bounded his universe! Looking down, he could see every familiar unevenness in the ground; it was like looking into the past, and he stared, fascinated and uneasy.

Now the rooftops of the house itself drew back; he could see the bluish sheen of the slates, drying under the sunlight, and the birds' nests in the gutters; he saw the soot-blackened mouths of the chimneys gaping to heaven, and the towers' empty heads. Now the house fell away, the earth opened out around it, and for a moment Buckhill lay spread nakedly below him: the stables, the games courts, the glen, everything, all in its hidden proportion. Dwindling, dimming, it was a relief map, a model of a country he had dreamed about. Those tiny dots of color were people, standing on the lawn; he could not even guess which. Then even the dots winked out, the house was swallowed up, and there was nothing but the wooded hill, streaming with violet shadow, receding.

SEVEN

A little before six they were crossing the Allegheny Plateau south of the ancient city of Pittsburgh—detouring, Dick judged, so as to stay out of sight of the great houses that clustered more thickly to northward. Once into the plain, they turned still more to the south, more than seemed sensible; but Dick let the matter go. He ate without appetite from the tray Padgett served him; he felt numbed and listless. The one burst of anger had been his last. The image of Cashel's falling body was still with him; he worried at it absently, as if it were an old sore tooth gone dead at the root.

Past the Mississippi the wild country began, thousands of square miles of nothing but grass, rippling in the wind like an endless yellow-green sea. It was hypnotic and disturbing; Dick found himself overwhelmed by the sheer brutal size of the world. From their height, the great plain had a perceptible curvature; clear and bright in the sun, it looked as if they could reach down and touch it; and yet he knew that those clustered black dots, almost invisible, must be men or animals . . .

"Bison," said Padgett with interest, peering down through a pair of binoculars. "Quite a good-sized herd. And there's the hunting party—Comanches, probably."

He passed the binoculars to Dick. Staring down at the suddenly magnified scene, he could see the dusty brown backs humping along like a living avalanche; flights of birds exploded ahead of them from the grass, and an occasional frantically tossing head of deer or antelope zigzagged away to either side. Behind them came the hunters, round black heads over the manes of the horses. Dick saw two or three rifles; the rest of the party were armed with bows. The bobbing forms were tiny and doll-like, unreal in their silence: for one moment Dick could almost imagine himself astride the plunging body, dust hot in his nostrils, the drumming of hooves in his bones . . . then it was gone. The tiny figures raced backward, lost in another dimension.

The sun rose with torturous slowness; the morning seemed to take forever. Unused to sitting still so long, Dick felt his muscles beginning to cramp. Padgett sat placidly beside him, eyes bright with interest. He was too well trained to speak when not spoken to, but Dick could tell that the stream of informative comment was running along just the same in his neat gray head. If they passed over a ruined city, visible like a pale scar through the earth that had mounded it over, Padgett would know or conjecture which one it was, and could tell you who founded it, and many curious and edifying incidents in its history. He knew the names of mountains and rivers, where the old state lines had run, which half-visible tracks were railroads, which highways.

"Padgett," said Dick, "do you think there's going to be a feud?"

The tutor looked at him gravely. "There was a similar

case," he said, "I remember, in the Carolinas, some thirty or thirty-five years ago. One cousin was said to have drowned the other in Port Royal Sound; of course, the elder branch claimed it was an accident. The following year, there were three or four more deaths from duels between the two branches of the family, and I believe one man shot from ambush. The Columbia House Bretts, and the Pamlico Bretts. I don't suppose you ever heard of them; the male line is extinct, if I am correct." When Dick was silent, he added, "Of course, that was some time back, but I would say it could happen. Your family has a certain reputation for hot-headedness."

Dick felt a flush warming his cheekbones; he almost welcomed it as a relief from the numbness. "I don't care what you think," he said. "I'd do the same thing again."

"Oh, well," said Padgett, unabashed, "it may very well have been the best thing you could have done. For the time being, at least; in the long run, no one can say."

Dick looked at him curiously. "How's that?"

"Reputation is everything in a place like Eagles. I imagine the rumors will be flying ahead of you; it isn't every youngster who comes to Eagles fresh from his first mankilling. And of course, while you're there, you'll be *relatively* safe from reprisals; however, at the same time, a young man with a reputation has to maintain it. On the whole," said Padgett, leaning back in his familiar summing-up attitude, "I'd say your chances have been widened, in both directions, by the duel. . . . Ah! There they are; aren't they beautiful?" He leaned forward again, gazing raptly out the window. "I've always wanted to live in the Rockies."

Floating toward them from the horizon, the first phalanx of mountains stood up bare-headed; not like Pennsylvania's gentle hills, they sprawled peaked and blue-violet, with patches of late snow on the upper slopes. Dick stared, fascinated. Closer, he could see the black parallel lines of burnt tree-trunks against a slope of bluish white snow, like stubble on a pale chin. Closer still, the mountains grew steeper and more desolate until they were flying through a high gorge between two ranges of cloud-veiled peaks. The river, serpentine down below, was a thin silver ribbon in the softness of the green valley; the crags above were majestic, naked rock keen in the wind. And as they flew, at the head of the valley loomed the tallest peak of all, with a gleam and glitter of buildings at its summit.

There were striations of ivory and blue, knife-edges of brass, glints of jade green, saffron, cocoa brown. Level after level rose to cover the peak, like a many-colored hat on a giant's head, and at the top it blossomed into pure fantasy—pinnacles, minarets, domes, and one incredible shape, a skeletal golden tower that disappeared in the turbulent clouds high overhead.

"Eagles," said Padgett, and fell silent again.

The mountain loomed higher still; the fantastic city tilted its face upward. They were losing altitude, dropping toward the foot of the mountain, where Dick could see a scattering of buildings, like something spilled from the heights. "Why aren't we landing at the top?" he asked.

"It's the updraft. They heat the whole mountain top, and I suppose they're not too careful about insulation; anyhow, at this altitude, it makes quite a powerful ascending current of air. Notice the clouds, how they break and boil up just overhead. You couldn't land a plane there—or drop a bomb, either, for that matter. You'll go up by the funicular." He pointed, and Dick for the first time noticed a line of suspended cables that swooped up the mountainside. One car was crawling up as he watched, another descending.

Up forward, the radio was muttering at Otto. They leveled off and hovered until a flock of small copters got out of the way, then lowered to one of the small landing areas that were clustered on either side of the central runway system. The almost inaudible howl of the jet and props cut off, leaving a ringing silence.

An armed, uniformed man boarded the dyne almost as soon as the door was open; his speech was so good that Dick answered a whole series of mildly insulting questions, taking him for a person, before he noticed the green tattoo on his forehead, half hidden by the visor of his cap. The fellow was a slob; and he had coolly demanded—and received—Dick's sidearm. Sputtering with indignation, Dick was about to demand the gun back, but the cautionary pressure of Padgett's hand stopped him.

Other places, other customs, Dick remembered. "Come on, Padgett," he said, getting up, "you can say good-by to me at the cable-cars, anyhow."

"I would not advise it," said the uniformed guard. "They would stop him at the next check point, and then there might be a little trouble. He could not accompany you as far as the funicular, in any case. These, incidentally—" he waved toward Blashfield and the rest of the guard, sitting glumly silent in the rear of the cabin—"being armed, must stay in the dyne."

"Good-by, misser Dick," called Blashfield gruffly.

"Good-by," said Padgett, pressing his hand. Dick saw with surprise that the old man's eyes were moist; "God guard you," said the tutor, huskily, and stepped back.

"Now if you will, young mister—" the guard was saying.

Dick stepped down. Slobs in white coveralls were unloading the dyne's luggage compartment, trundling the bags away

58

on handcarts. The guard led him away in a different direction; two others in the same uniform, armed with semi-automatics, fell in behind.

"Where are they going with my things?" Dick asked, pointing.

"To inspection. Everything will be returned to you in good order. Now if you will step in here—"

"Here," was a low stucco building in which Dick was fluoroscoped, fingerprinted, examined by a dentist who tapped all his fillings, and given an identity bracelet, which, he later discovered, was locked on and could not be opened.

Sobered and with much to think about, he found himself half an hour later standing on the glassed-in platform of the funicular railway, waiting for the down car to arrive. On the platform were three of the omnipresent, gray-uniformed airport guard, plus half a dozen people—sunburned men in big, gold-trimmed white hats, two pretty women in flimsy dresses, a bearded man in a turban, carrying a briefcase.

When the car came down—an archaic-looking thing, painted black and gold—only four passengers got out of it. Three wore a scarlet uniform. As far as Dick could see, they were armed only with light wooden cudgels. The fourth was a man in black, with a white face. The three marched him over to the waiting airport guards, left him there, and marched back into the car. When Dick looked back over his shoulder, the man in black was trudging away in the midst of the gray squad—going where? What had he done?

The car was narrow and stuffy; the seats, set one above the other like chairs in an auditorium, were upholstered in stiff crimson plush. After an interminable wait, the car jerked, throbbed, and began to rise.

Dick leaned across the aisle toward one of the men in white hats. "Pardon. Is this the *only* way to get up to Eagles?"

The man looked surprised. He was lean and stringy, burnt the color of copper; his eyebrows and lashes were almost invisible. "No," he said mildly. "They's an express tube, comes out down the valley. Depends how much traffic, whetha they let you use it." After a moment he asked, "Your first time up?"

Dick nodded. The sunburnt man squinted at him confidentially, lowered his voice still more. "Don't ask too many questions," he said, and leaned back.

The trip took forever. Bored, half suffocated, Dick got out eventually on a broad glassed-in platform that seemed to overhang the valley. He stared down, fascinated; down at the bottom, where the converging lines of the cable railway disappeared, the valley was a cup of gold, the snaky line of the river was intolerably bright, even through the tinted glass. Wisps of cloud vapor rushed upward past the window; the big panes bowed inward, trembled, straightened, bowed in again. . . .

All his previous life seemed to be down there in that improbable cup of gold somewhere, silent and stifled. Voices echoed behind him, footsteps; a hand plucked at his sleeve.

He turned. People were crossing the platform in all directions, a glitter of color, a babble of voices. He saw three different uniforms, two beautiful women, a gang of slobs with a handtruck piled high with boxes. There was a man in a gorgeous garment of peach satin, the sleeves padded and puffed until they swelled him to twice his size; chain around his neck with a golden pendant; beard on his chin, rings on his plump fingers. He passed leisurely, leaving a wisp of perfume in his wake. Here came two women in big white headdresses, walking together, close in conversation; their black skirts swished to the ground. There strolled a boy, not more than twelve, resplendent in red-orange tights, eating peanuts from a cloth bag.

Nearer, an ugly face was peering up into his own, as good-humored and misshapen as a bulldog's. There was barely room on the fellow's forehead for his green slobmark; his ears were enormous and hairy, his nose flat. "Your firs' time at Eagles, Misser Jones?" he said hoarsely. "If you would condescend yourself to come this way with me, jus' for a minute now—" He backed away, showing a mouthful of tusks in what was meant for an ingratiating grin.

Dick followed, across the platform to an open booth where another slob sat, this one a bored, sallow-skinned fellow with mournful brown eyes. "Here we have with us now Misser Richer Jones," said the gargoyle, slapping his palm on the counter. "You take good care of him now, and no nonsense, you mind?"

The bored slob, with a look of distaste, reached below the counter and produced two articles, a belt with two thin chains dangling from it, and a slender wooden staff about a yard long, knob-tipped at either end.

The gargoyle, grunting with satisfaction, seized the belt and began to fasten it around Dick's waist. "What's this?" said Dick, resisting. For the first time, he noticed that both slobs were wearing similar belts, with the chains attached somehow to their sleeves just above the elbow. "This is what we call the elbow check, Misser Jones," said the gargoyle, deftly threading one of the needle-tipped chains through the slack of Dick's right sleeve. "All the men got to wear them at Eagles, and the buck servan's too. You find before you know it that they won' bother you at all." He threaded the second chain through the other sleeve in the same way, removed the needles, and snapped the ends of the chains to

60

studs on the belt. Moving his arms experimentally, Dick found the chains prevented him from raising his hands higher than his head.

Looking around irritably, he saw that it was true: sure enough, everyone in sight was wearing some version of the belt and chains. He still didn't like it. "I don't understand. What's this for?"

"Jus' to keep the men from disagreeing so much among theyselves," said the gargoyle. "An' it protecks the ladies a little, too. Now this is the stick, what we call the swagger stick—that's the only weapon you can have in Eagles, but I jus' show you that now; no use you to take it with you before you learn youseff how to use it the proper *and* correck way." He handed it across the counter to the other slob.

"But I do know how to use it," said Dick, reaching. "Damn!" The chain brought him up short; he couldn't extend his arm fully.

The gargoyle doubtfully put the stick in his hand. "You sure now, Misser Jones? With the chains, an' all?"

Dick balanced the weight of the thing across his fingers; there was about an ounce of lead in each of the padded knobs, he judged. The ones he had used at home were heavier; otherwise there was no difference, except, of course, the handicap of the chains. Evening after evening, ever since he was twelve, he had got his knuckles bruised and his nose bleeding—to his intense disgust, since nobody ever fought with sticks—down in the gymnasium with his father. Engage, thrust, cover, parry, chop, backhand, retire . . . it was in his bones, and he had never suspected what it was for until now.

"I can handle it," he said, and thrust the stick into a spring clip at the side of his belt, where it seemed to belong.

The slob behind the counter had produced a thick loose-leaf book and was turning the pages. "Jones," he said, "let's see . . ."

"Nev' mind!" cried the gargoyle. "You don' have to tell me, I know where Misser Jones belongs. Come right this way, misser—we fix you up in one, two, three time!"

The archway under which they passed was a single huge sheet of some white metal, intricately hand-chased in a design of running deer and oak-leaves. Silver light spilled down it from a trough-shaped reflector at the ceiling. Beyond that, the hall was brown translucent glass, lit from behind; the floor itself was heavy glass, under which water ran in a shallow channel.

They climbed three ivory steps and threaded their way through a gossiping crowd that half-filled a large hall. A peacock strutted across their path, tail-feathers spread like a many-eyed gossamer fan. Music murmured from somewhere,

61

broken by the harsh shrieks of cockatoos, caged in a brilliant line down the farther wall.

Dick looked around disaprovingly as he walked. There were too many people—all, to his way of thinking, ridiculously overdressed—; the place was too big and too gaudy, and in spite of the sickly sweet overtone of perfume, it smelled bad. Here they went down another shallow flight of steps and under another scrolled archway: the place seemed to be built on half a dozen levels, without plan or purpose.

Now they were in a narrow corridor whose golden walls and floor were as irregularly curved as a natural tunnel dug out of the earth. Down one side of it, swift and deep, flowed what must be the same stream he had seen before. Here it had no floor over it, and no guard-rail either. A dark shape flickered past, a young trout perhaps, but it was gone too quickly to see. Dick looked back over his shoulder; at the end of the corridor, the stream dived out of sight.

Just ahead, a young man was kneeling with one hand in the water, while a little knot of people—two girls, another young man, a handful of slobs in wine silk—looked on. As they approached, another dark shape hurtled down the stream; the kneeling young man moved convulsively, exclaimed, "Ha!" and held up his hand in triumph. In a soaked cloth bag of Kelly green—his hat, evidently, since it matched his costume—a fish squirmed and flopped. Laughing, he shook it out onto the floor. The spilled water splattered Dick to the knees.

Still kneeling, the young man looked up with a glint of humor. The fish, a speckled trout, arched itself once, twice, and toppled into the stream; it splashed and was gone.

"Good shot?" asked the young man, still smiling easily. He was blond and handsome; the fanciful lace-trimmed collar of his tunic was open over a strong brown throat. Behind him, the others watched silently.

"Misser," said the gargoyle, taking Dick's arm, "this corridor is too trafficky today—better we go round by the South Promenade."

"Leave him alone, Frankie," said the young man without turning his head. "I asked him a question."

The cold water was soaking through Dick's trouserlegs to the skin. "It was a good shot," he said.

The gargoyle, Frankie, was whispering in his ear, "That's Jerry Keel, misser, be careful—" Ignoring him, Dick leaned swiftly, scooped up a palmful of water and flung it at the other's face.

The blond man, Keel, was up instantly, nose and chin dripping, knobbed swagger stick in his hand. His smile was tight over his teeth. "Now, then, let's see," he said.

62

"Jer, he's a green calf," one of the girls murmured.

"He's wearing a stick, isn't he? Come on, you, don't keep me waiting."

Dick drew the staff free of its clip and closed his fist around one of the knobbed ends. Cautiously, he and Keel advanced toward each other, toeing toward the edges of the puddle of water. Dick found the elbow chain a little disconcerting; he would have to try to remember he couldn't make a full lunge. . . .

They engaged. Keel had a curious, negligent stance; he held the stick palm up, rapped it against Dick's with offensive gentleness. Angered, Dick feinted right, left, and swung for the other's knuckles. Wood met wood, jarringly; Keel's stick whirred with motion, grazed Dick's wrist, then hit his staff so shrewdly on the backswing that he nearly dropped it.

Both drew back for a moment, staring eye to eye. Then Keel stepped forward and Dick met him, each treading dangerously on the slick wet metal. Keel engaged with a flurry of beats, ending with a straight thrust which Dick answered by a back-parry and lunge. Keel made an assault on the elbow and hand; Dick double-parried, shifted his grip and cut over, narrowly missing Keel's face. They stepped back again, breathing a little heavily.

Dick's wrist was numb, and the inside of his elbow chafed from trying to lunge farther than the chain would permit. Keel grinned at him, swung his stick twice with a *whit, whit,* and stepped forward again.

They engaged a third time; Keel feinted twice, parried Dick's counter-thrust, and lunged. Dick saved himself by leaping back, but immediately closed again with a strong beat, chop and thrust. Keel parried; when his guard was high, Dick stepped across the puddle and closed in. Keel staggered, off balance; Dick hit him solidly with a body check. They lurched, grappling together; Dick fended off Keel's clutching hand and shoved again. With a wild yell and a splash, Keel went into the stream.

The crowd ohh-ed. Dick heard a thump; he turned in time to see Keel's head and one arm appear, haloed in spray, where the water arched down under the wall.

There was a scurrying of footsteps. "Fair play! Fair play!" boomed a sudden voice. Keel's friend and two or three slobs, hurrying toward him, stopped and drew back. Standing inside the corridor entrance was a stocky man in green and russet silks. His hair was iron-gray under a foolish, lemon-colored hat, but his eyes were black and brilliant. "You know the rules," he said, and turned to Dick with an ironic salute of his stick.

In the water a yard away, Keel's body was spread-eagled against the narrowing sides of the channel. The passage, Dick

63

saw with horror, had no bars or grille across it: the only thing that kept Keel from being swept down with the current was the pressure of his hands and feet against the smooth metal. The elbow chains prevented him from taking a secure hold; the force of the falling stream was tremendous. He could not move, or he would lose his grip. Water and spray covered him above the chin: he was slowly drowning where he stood.

Dick's involuntary motion was checked. "Jones?" said the stocky man quietly, with the stick he held resting lightly on Dick's arm. His voice was deep but breathy, with the suspicion of a lisp. His face was an unhealthy paper-gray, his nose beaked, his mouth firm and thin.

"What?" said Dick. "Yes, but—"

"My name is Ruell. *Ruell*. Take my advice—let him go. He would have done it to you."

The man's dark, wet head had dropped a little farther forward. The muscles of his back quivered and seemed about to relax. Dick had a sudden incongruous vision of another body falling, leaning head downward into the bright grass.

His mouth was dry. "Get out of my way!" he said hoarsely. He flung his stick away, careless of where it went, and kneeled on the brink with one foot precariously braced against the side of the entrance. He got his hands around Keel's wet, cold wrist, and pulled.

A giant's hand was tugging Keel the other way. Dick went down on one side, still hanging on. He was sliding toward the edge, helplessly; the lights in the ceiling were a bewildering glare.

Arms went around his waist. There was a clatter of sticks on the metal, voices babbling; another giant's hand began to pull him backward. Dick's arms threatened to come out of their sockets; he hung on grimly. Keel's arm and lolling head came reluctantly over the brink, then the other hand, feebly groping; then the rest of him.

It was not Keel's friend, as Dick had imagined, who had held him by the waist, but the gargoyle, Frankie. The friend, a man with a dark forelock and a sullen lip, was looking on from the background. Rolling to his feet, Frankie bent over Keel, then straddled him and began to push rhythmically at his ribs. A little water dribbled out of Keel's mouth; he stirred. "He be arright," said Frankie cheerfully. "If you wait for me jus' a little minute now, Misser Jones, I take you to you' rooms."

The stocky man (Ruell? Why was that name familiar?) had bent to retrieve his swagger stick and was delicately dusting his hands. He must have been the third man, then, on the human chain that had dragged Keel to safety. "I'll take him," he said, with a stiff little bow to Dick. "If the mister doesn't object. What suite?"

"Number H 103—in the rosewood court aroun' by the Old Fountain."

"I know where it is. Come along then, Mister Jones; you've done quite all you can do here."

As they passed, the sullen young man made a sudden face and gesture: "Jerry won't forget you!"

"Nor will he," murmured Ruell, strolling on at Dick's elbow. "You made a mistake; Keel is not a grateful man, he's too vain. I now warn you again, and then I'll drop the subject: you had better kill that man if you can, the first chance you get."

They were crossing a huge, paved courtyard, glassed in fifty feet above, with beds of geometrically planted geraniums and phlox, dogwood, asters, delphiniums, tulips. Dick felt bewildered and weak from reaction; he said, "Why did you help me pull him out, then?"

"It was your choice," said Ruell, indifferently. "On your left," he went on, "the Winton Number One." He was pointing to a hideous object on a flagstone dais, a four-wheeled golden carriage with lucite wheels and an embroidered canopy over the open seat. Every inch of surface was chased, engraved, jeweled, elaborately ornamented. "One of the first automobiles sold in the United States," Ruell said. "A reconstruction, however—historically valueless, but the only one of its kind." He pointed again. "On your right, an early Packard—the first with a wheel instead of a tiller. Beyond that, of course, is the Stanley Steamer."

"Is that what the Boss collects?" Dick asked. "Autos?"

"Ha!" said Ruell, explosively. His nose twitched and his eyebrows went up. "Ha, ha! Oh, ha, *ha, ha, ha!* Ah, my dear boy—" He hugged himself with one arm, with the other clapped Dick on the shoulder.

Dick moved away. "What's so funny?"

"Now here," said Ruell, recovering instantly, "we have the famous Old Fountain." It was as a waist-high flagstone pool, twenty feet across, with a thin jet of water in the middle. "The eel-like fish," said Ruell, "are lampreys. Quite unpleasant—they cling to their prey with that toothed sucker, then rasp a hole in it with their tongues, which also have teeth. A Roman of the time of Augustus kept lampreys in his fishpond, and threw slaves to them for trivial offenses. Vedius Pollio was his name; that was twenty-one centuries ago. *Plus ça change, plus c-est la même chose.*"

Dick stopped and turned to face him. "My rooms can't be far from here," he said. "I imagine I can find them myself. Good-by."

Ruell stopped him, looking contrite. "My dear boy, I didn't

65

mean any offense. I laughed, impolitely, at your ignorance. You asked if the Boss collects cars—well, I can't just at the moment think of anything the Boss does *not* collect. He collects collections. He collects interminably and insatiably. This whole mountain, in fact," he said persuasively, taking Dick's arm again, "is little more than a thin shell, over a bottomless pit of the Boss's collections. Now. Your suite is just here."

Dick allowed himself to be led again, thinking it the quickest way to get rid of the man. There was something he profoundly disliked and distrusted about him; perhaps it had something to do with the nagging familiarity of the name Ruell— He stopped suddenly, feeling for the thin envelope he had stuffed into his breast pocket. It was still there.

"Yes?" said Ruell, alertly. "Have you something for me?"

"If you're the man my father—I mean, if your name is—"

"Leon Ruell; of course; I thought you knew. But don't let's talk here—one moment." He leaned, opened a carved rosewood door, urged Dick inside.

The ceilings were immensely high, ending in peaked, prismed skylights from which a multicolored radiance spilled down the walls. The walls to a level above Dick's head were of carved rosewood; the rest was blue plaster. From beyond a doorway came the sound of hammering: the rooms had a musty, untenanted air.

"You'll be comfortable enough here," said Ruell, sniffing disparagingly, "for a day or so, until we can find you more suitable quarters. Now, then, if you please." He held out his hand; Dick put the envelope in it.

Ruell, with an apologetic nod, turned half away, slit the envelope with his thumbnail, opened a sheet of flimsy paper and read it slowly. When he was done, he creased the paper thoughtfully once, twice, and began to eat it. He smiled at Dick's astonishment. "Rice paper," he said, swallowing. "Haven't you ever used that trick? Well, you will, you will."

The hammering had stopped. From the other room came the gargoyle, Frankie, dressed in a blue overall like a show dog and carrying a box of carpenter's tools. He nodded cheerfully to Dick. "We fix you up, one, two, three, Misser Jones." He went out; there was a brief colloquy at the door, and he came in again, dressed in a yellow coverall and carrying a painter's kit.

Dick stared at him with his jaw unhinged. "All done pretty quick, Misser Jones," said Frankie, grinning happily; he disappeared into the other room.

With a muttered exclamation, Dick followed to the doorway. A section of the paneling in the inner room had been removed and replaced with raw, newly carved wood. Frankie was taping sheets of masking paper around it, with his cans

66

of stain and shellac, his brushes and spray gun neatly laid out around him. His coverall was definitely yellow, an unequivocal, almost offensive yellow, and it was a different garment entirely from the blue one he had worn a moment ago.

Ruell was at his elbow, looking amused. Remembering the exchange at the door, Dick said, "There are two of them—is that it? Are they twins?"

Ruell went off into one of his choked explosions of laughter. "Are there two!" he repeated. "Twins!"

Frankie looked around—if it was Frankie—with his grin broadening. "Don't you feel bad, Misser Jones," he said "We surprise mos' people, don't we, Misser Ruell?"

Ruell's laughter was trailing off into a series of little sighs: *Ahuh. Ahuh!* Finished with these, he asked solemnly, "Exactly how many are there of you at the present moment, Frankie?"

Frankie's expression grew equally serious. "This morning," he said, "they was two hun'red forty-three of me exackly. You know las' month they was only two hun'red twelve, the mos', but this month we doing so much work to build up the Long Corridor where it fell down, they need us bad. We the bes' servan' in Eagles, Misser Ruell. Nex' nearest is Hank the carrier, and I think they only a hun'red, a hun'red ten of him. Well, Misser Jones, you never see a fellow so many, eh?" He laughed with pleasure.

They turned away. "There used to be some fabulous number of him," Ruell said, "I don't recall, three hundred fifty or so, and Frankie's one ambition is to beat his own record. He counts himself every morning, and if he's lost any, he goes around with a long face for the rest of the day. Is anything the matter?"

"It doesn't seem sensible," said Dick. He started to sit, then, remembering that he was technically at home, offered Ruell a chair first. "How do you tell which one you've sent on an errand? Or suppose you want one of them to remember something for you, how do you find him again?"

"Oh, Frankie tells himself everything," said Ruell, sitting gracefully upright, legs crossed, hand on his stick. "That's why he's so useful—he knows everything, goes everywhere; besides which, if you have a useful servant, why experiment?"

It was the fifth or sixth time he had heard the word "servant" that day. "Don't you call them slobs here?" he demanded irritably. "Or even slaves?"

Ruell shrugged. "My dear boy—" His ironic glance sharpened. "Let me see now. You ride well, your small-arms shooting is just fair, your swagger-stick work is quite good, as you have demonstrated; with coaching, you might become exceptional. You swim, no doubt, dance, I suppose; know nothing, want to know nothing . . ."

Dick stood up.

"Don't lose your temper," said Ruell evenly. "It's your worst fault, except for ignorance: sit down, I have something to tell you. I say, sit down."

For some reason, Dick sat. "You are of a prime age," Ruell went on in the same tone, "strong, well set up and not bad looking. Above all, you are a new face. I think that will be our best line of attack."

"I don't understand you," said Dick.

"Don't you? Let me put it this way. At Eagles, everything is power; orbits and spheres of power, tides of power. As you have none yourself, you must have a protector: the question is, which? Now, nothing is ever given for nothing, at Eagles; what have you to offer? Let's see: no particular talents nor skills, no connections at Eagles except myself—and nothing to expect from me but good advice, incidentally—no supporters, no special information, in short, nothing but your person. Now let me think." He paused, two curved fingers at his chin. "If only you had let Keel drown, there would have been an opening. Keel is Randolph's boy, and you could hardly ask for anything better than that; Randolph is the Boss's secretary of entertainment. Very nice; it's too bad. However—" he scanned Dick's face more closely—"I don't believe you're the type; curious, I had rather expected . . . Well, that leaves us just one alternative." He sat back. "We shall have to make a ladies' man of you. It's a shorter career as a rule, and a chancier one—the dear ladies are capricious —but we'll see what we can do. I'll introduce you to one or two of them; I assure you, some of them are not bad-looking at all; and if nothing happens, or if it doesn't last, well, we'll try again."

Dick had a baffled feeling that anger would be out of place; he felt half disgusted, half incredulous.

"Are you serious?"

Ruell's eyes narrowed slightly; he frowned, and did not answer.

Dick stood up. "Ruell, I listened to you because, well, my father mentioned your name—"

"Yes?"

"—but there's a limit to that. I don't like you, and I don't want your advice. So you can get out."

Ruell stood up slowly. His paper-gray face was shut and still. Dick felt his heartbeat accelerate. Ruell's thin hand, on the knob of his stick, tightened and relaxed. "For the sake of your father," he said, "I'll let this pass—just this once. You are a very foolish young man; you had better learn wisdom, and learn it soon." At the door, he turned briefly. *"Au revoir."*

Dick let out the breath he had been holding, and sank

down in the chair. He felt suddenly tired again; his head was beginning to ache and his eyes burned.

Duped slobs, and hand-carved paneling that had to be finished on the spot. Lampreys in the fountain; what had Ruell meant by that sentence in French, 'The more it changes, the more it's the same thing'? The horrifying implications of the things Ruell had said so calmly, sitting there across the room: "protectors"; "Randolph's boy"; "ladies' man." What if it were all true?

But there: it couldn't be.

EIGHT

For ten days, he had been walking the corridors of Eagles, jostled by slobs pushing chair-carts, stared at and (he was sure) laughed at behind his back. The Colorado-style clothes he was wearing were clumsily cut, but the best he had been able to get; the fabrics seemed dull, too, although they had looked all right when the tailor brought them to his rooms. He was beginning to get the feel, now, of Eagles "style," and becoming acutely aware that he didn't have it—the richly folded garments, the ornaments, the touches of color, the odd feather or rosette, the whiff of perfume; the manner, the angle of the cocked elbow, the walk, a thousand things.

He passed a scaffolding that covered half a wall. From the next corridor came the stuttering roar of jack-hammers; Eagles, it seemed, was constantly being rebuilt, redesigned, redecorated.

He had gotten himself lost innumerable times, in spite of the map one of the Frankies had given him, but the manifold sights of Eagles were beginning to pall on him. He was sick of his narrow rooms; there was no gymnasium in them, no library, not even a decent pool.

He knew not a soul in Eagles except Ruell, unless you counted the Frankies and other slobs; and the devil of it was, he couldn't seem to get to know anybody else, either. He had not even succeeded in meeting Colonel Van Etten, the Army officer in charge of commissions. Twice he had cooled his heels in Van Etten's cream-and-gold outer office, the first time to learn that you needed an appointment to see Van Etten, the second time, having got an appointment, to find that Van Etten had been called away. When you telephoned Van Etten, he was not in.

From the corridor in which he was walking, broad, curved steps fell away into the cool green dimness of an antique cocktail lounge. The bottles and glasses behind the bar were aglow with spectral colors; the bartenders were only silhouettes. Hungry for company, he paused and looked in; at a nearby table, a woman glanced up at him and stared incuriously for a moment before she turned back to her companion. Dick hesitated, then drew back: the place might be a private preserve of some kind, he had no way of knowing. He passed on.

The corridor curved and twisted obliquely down a row of little artisans' workshops (coral jewelry, wooden bookbindings, batiks, painted gourds) and emptied onto the main corridor again. Now he was in territory he knew; this was the main artery at mid-level. It was always crowded, always colorful day or night. Here came a man in purple robes with a miter on his head, trident in one hand and censer in the other. Dick had seen him before and asked about him; according to Frankie, he was a priest of Eblis—whatever that might be. Here came a chattering group of girls, all young, most of them pretty—slobs, worse luck; he had hardly seen a young freewoman since he got here. Behind them walked two swarthy fellows in black, with truncheons and scowling faces; he knew them, too, by the uniform—Gismo Guards.

Here was the little refectory where he had eaten once or twice before; it was only a few yards from the door of Van Etten's office, but there was no use going there, since his new appointment wasn't till day after tomorrow. Eating alone in public was a hard thing for him to get used to, but eating by himself in his rooms was worse. Glumly, Dick settled himself at one of the tables and ordered a light snack—squabs, pizza with anchovies, tartar steak; he wasn't really hungry.

Halfway through, on impulse, he beckoned the waiter.

"Yes, misser? Something else?"

"No, not right away. I was just thinking—do you know Colonel Van Etten when you see him?"

"Oh, yes, misser."

"What does he look like?"

The waiter blinked nervously. "Colonel Van Etten? Oh, very tall man, misser, looks like this—you know, *stern*—and a scar right across here over the eye."

"I see. All right, that's all."

The waiter bowed and went away. Dick moodily ate the rest of the pizza garnished with raw hamburger, thinking, Well, why not? What did he have to lose? He might waste a day, he supposed, but then he was sure to do that anyway. He left the refectory and took up his station in an arcade just opposite Van Etten's door. People went in and out, some in Army uniform, some not; none fitted the description. Probably Van Etten had at least one private entrance, but then if he found that and watched it, out of pure perversity the man would be bound to use the front door. When he grew bored, Dick went down the arcade to a telebooth, turned off the movie that was playing, and punched "Private."

"Yes, misser?" said the likely-looking blonde girl who appeared on the screen.

"A scramble call to Buckhill in the Poconos. I'll talk to anybody."

"One moment, misser." The screen dimmed, glowed again. "I'm sorry, misser, all the channels are busy. Will you place your call again, please?"

Still busy. Dick turned the machine off and went back to his vantage point. He had tried to call home every day, and the channels were always busy. At first it had been merely a matter of duty, but now he was beginning to get worried about it. If he could only ask the Man what to do . . . He could write a letter, but he had no one reliable to send it by. There was no telling who might read it if he entrusted it to somebody else's courier, or even if it would be sent at all.

An hour passed, then another. Bored and weary, Dick stuck grimly to it. He wondered what Ad and Felix were doing at this hour—riding, or swimming in Skytop Lake? An astonishing wave of homesickness came over him; the smells, the air, the very tiles underfoot were hateful. He stiffened his spine, and stayed.

Toward mid-afternoon three officers came out of the doorway, deep in conversation. The one in the middle was a head taller than the others, lath-thin, white-haired at the temples under his scarlet helmet. Dick moved closer, uncertainly: yes, no, yes, there was the scar.

"Colonel Van Etten?"

The three looked up. "Yes?" asked the tall man.

"Colonel, I'm Dick Jones from Buckhill. I'd like to talk to you for a moment; it's about my commission."

Van Etten blinked at him slowly. "Your commission?" he asked in an absent-minded tone. "Is there something wrong with your commission?"

"I haven't got one yet, Colonel—that's what I wanted to talk to you about."

The two officers flanking Van Etten exchanged glances. Van Etten said, "Your name again, was—"

"Dick Jones, Colonel."

"Jones, I conduct Army business in my office, by appointment. Talk to my secretary."

He started to turn away. Dick said loudly, "Colonel, you don't understand. I've been trying to see you the usual way. I've been here ten days, your secretary keeps putting me off—"

Van Etten stopped, looking amazed. "By heaven!" he blurted. One of the other officers rose on tiptoe to mutter

71

something in his ear. "Yes, certainly," said Van Etten. "Crump, make a note to remind me later—Jones is not to be received in my office, not even to apply for an interview, until one month from date."

"Yes, mister," said the youngest officer, getting out a notebook.

One month! Dick felt himself shaking with anger.

"And if you don't like it," the Colonel went on inexorably, "you can go back to Dunghill, or whatever you call it."

"Colonel, the name is Buckhill," said Dick, raising his voice; he saw people in the corridor turn to stare.

"*Two* months!" snapped Van Etten. He faced Dick challengingly for another moment, then looked at his watch and turned away. "Late—come on."

The youngest officer snapped his notebook shut. "You young idiot," he muttered to Dick, "you'd better get a friend —and fast." Then he followed the other; the crowd closed around them.

Dick carefully unclenched his fist; the nails had bitten into his palms. Some of the faces in the corridor were curious, some amused, some indifferent. His vision blurred; he turned blindly away and went where his feet took him.

After a while he found himself on the Upper Promenade, the highest level of Eagles proper except for one or two cupolas. The day had turned dirty outside, and the gray light from the transparent wall made the fluorescents look sickly and dim. Dick walked over slowly and pressed his forehead against the cool glass. Out across the valley, the farther mountains were purplish-gray masses; the clouds behind them were moving fast—sooty thunderheads shot with pale light, but so dense that they made it look like twilight in mid-afternoon. Veils of vapor shot up past the window, ghost-like; the big pane buckled inward, hurting Dick's forehead, and he drew back. The lower levels of Eagles were threads of light; he couldn't see the floor of the valley, it was too dark.

It had been spring outside when he first entered this place . . . ten days ago. Looking to the left, he caught a glimpse of the unfinished Tower glinting brass-color against the gray. The sky grew still darker; a flurry of hail beat against the windows, then another; then a rushing, rustling torrent that closed in the Promenade as if with a cold silvery curtain.

This couldn't be the way every applicant for a commission got treated. Why was he having so much trouble? It was like a barrier across his path, whichever way he turned. The Colonel hadn't seemed to know who he was at first, but then one of the other officers had said something in his ear . . . One month, and then two when he protested. If he

spoke again, he supposed, it would be three, or four . . .
they could keep him like this as long as they liked. And
would the channels stay busy between here and Buckhill,
too? Until he gave in, did as he was told? But that would
be never.

Head down, he went slowly toward the elevators. People
passed him in murmuring groups; when they got in his way,
he detoured around them without looking up. Crossing the
floor, he met a pair of legs in green tights that sidled to the
left when he did, to the right when he did.

He stopped and looked up: red-trimmed, black tunic,
belted with a chain of bronze medallions; froth of lace at the
throat, paper-gray face. It was Ruell, smiling easily.

"Well, young Dick? Why so pensive?"

Behind him, Dick was aware of others watching, but he
dismissed them as unimportant. "Ruell, I want to talk to
you."

"Excellent! My young friend, let's go downstairs where
we can be more private."

"No, here," said Dick, not moving. "Did you tell Van
Etten not to give me my commission?"

"My dear boy—have you been having trouble with Van
Etten?" Ruell scratched his long jaw, lazily, with a faint
smile. "These things can be so easily smoothed out; you
should have come to me." Behind his head, the pale rain-
light wavered on the metal ceiling.

There was a suppressed murmur of laughter in the background.

Dick heard himself saying, "I can't fight everybody in
Eagles. But I can fight you." He drew his staff free of the
clip. His heart was hammering wildly; he knew he couldn't
defeat Ruell, but there was nothing else to do. He thought
fiercely, if he beats me now, I'll come after him again. And
again. I won't let up till he does.

"Since you are so insistent," said Ruell slowly, with his
hand on the knob of his stick. "But wait. One last word,
before we descend to desperate measures. I like you, young
Dick; I knew your father. Though it's all against my judg-
ment, I'll get you a different sort of protector if you like.
What do you say to an ambitious upstart who merely wants
a following of well-born young men? Bodyguards, flatterers—
a little fetching and carrying, a fight now and then, perhaps. Believe me, Dick, I'll be losing my time on the deal,
but at least, you won't be wasted. Yes? Shake hands on it?"

Dick hesitated. He could feel his resolution slipping away
while Ruell talked; it was hard to nerve himself up again,
and his voice came out harsher than he meant. "Put up your
stick."

Ruell's face took on that closed, hard look that Dick

73

had seen once before. His eyes glittered under half-closed lids. Behind him, the ring of onlookers drew back a little, with a shuffle of feet. Ruell stepped back with his left foot, bending his knees a little; his right hand dropped slowly and the stick came up in a blur of motion. Before he had even seemed to touch it, it was leaping in the air between them like a live thing; Dick's staff shuddered in his hand to a series of beats; left, right, left . . .

Recovering belatedly, Dick chopped for the shoulder. Ruell parried without seeming to move, feinted high, cut under Dick's guard and thumped him solidly in the ribs. "That's one," he said woodenly. He stepped back on guard.

Dick attacked with fury and skill, and found himself unwillingly dancing through a sort of fencing-master's exercise: Ruell parried every blow without countering, or merely leaned out of the way and let the stick whistle through the air. *Thwack, thwack, thwack,* grunt . . . Ruell was making him look ridiculous, as if his best efforts were no more dangerous than a baby's. "Fight!" he grunted, and heard the laughter ripple up around him.

Infuriated, Dick lunged. The elbow-check brought him up short; Ruell parried with a contemptuous tap, closed in and swung a numbing blow to the temple. Dick tottered, dazed and off balance. "That's two," said Ruell dimly, and hit him again in the pit of the stomach. "And that's three."

Dick went down; the spinning floor slapped him hard; he lay where he fell, fighting for breath.

Voices echoed indistinguishably; footsteps jarred the floor under his cheek, and then went away. The iron grip on his chest finally eased a little. The first breath he drew was pure agony, but he had to have it or die.

Somebody lifted his head, which was no help; he struggled weakly, and the hand disappeared. A minute later the hands were back, more of them and rougher—the first one, he realized dimly, had been a woman's. They hauled him up but he couldn't stand; they got his arms around two brawny necks and dragged or carried him across the floor until, by the echoes, they got to one of the alcoves in the rear wall. They lowered him and laid him out on the sofa; he let them do it; he was feeling too sick even to open his eyes.

"The poor kitten," said a woman's voice. It was a low voice, musical but husky. "Who is he, do you know?"

"Name of Jones," said a man. "Frankie says he's been here almost two weeks without making a connection."

There was a murmur and a gone-away feeling; then footsteps coming back, and somebody put a wet handkerchief over his forehead. "Just leave him, if you ask me," said the man's voice. "You know Ruell."

"Yes, but what's going to happen to him?"

74

"No use worrying about that, Viv—nothing much you can do." The man sounded deferential and a little stilted, as if he were saying not what he thought, but what was expected of him.

The woman said, "I could always adopt him myself."

"Viv, you know you can't. You've got six too many people on your list already. Dear, you owe it to *yourself* to be sensible."

"Oh, I suppose you're right. You usually are, Howie."

Opening his eyes, Dick got a blurred glimpse of a man's red-velvet sleeve and a woman in white—clouds of white or cream-colored lace, and an enormous white hat. The woman was looking down at him, one gloved hand at her chin; behind her he could see a little group of dark-uniformed slobs.

"Well, at least," she said, "we can take him home and let Dr. Bob look at him. Then we can decide. Saul, run and get a chair."

One of the slobs bowed and said, "Right away, Miz' Demetriou." Dick closed his eyes again, not much caring if he lived or died, and in a few moments he was hazily aware that they were lifting him into a chair-cart. The next thing he knew, he was in a bed somewhere, and a man with gray whiskers was bending over him, exhaling rum. There were silver birds in the dark-blue canopy high overhead. "Ow," he said, turning away from the fingers that prodded his temple.

"Um-hm," the gray-whiskered man remarked, and straightened up with a rustle of silk. "No bones broken. Just a little concussion, maybe; nothing serious. Keep him quiet for a day or two, say, and he'll be all right." He began packing something into a box, looking down with a serious expression, breathing in little grunts.

From the yellow glow of light beyond him, an ironic voice said, "Just a day or two, eh? Viv, I give up."

When he awoke again, he had a little trouble remembering where he was and how he had got there. He sat up, and a girl in yellow came over immediately from the other side of the room. "Feeling better?" she asked, smiling pleasantly. "Like a little breakfast?" She was young and not bad-looking, if you could overlook the green slob-mark in the middle of her forehead.

"No, I'm not hungry." Under the coverlet, he discovered, he was wearing some kind of elaborate sleeping garment with a drawstring throat. He started to swing his legs over the side of the bed. "Just get me my clothes."

The girl looked anxious, and pressed him gently back. "Oh, no, please, Mister Jones. Lady said you must stay in bed until you feel better. Please, now."

75

His head was throbbing abominably, and he was in no mood to argue. He pushed her out of the way and stood up. His legs were weaker than he had expected. He had to catch onto the bedpost to steady himself.

The slob girl was backing away. "Oh, dear. *Miz' Demetriou!*"

The door opened and a woman came rustling in with quick, determined steps. "Now, really. Get back in that bed, do you hear?"

Rather than fall and make a spectacle of himself, Dick sat down on the bed. The slob girls helped him put his legs up, and tucked the coverlet around him. "That's all," the woman told her, and sat down gracefully in the bedside chair. "We haven't been properly introduced," she said; her throaty voice dwelt mockingly on the next to last word. "I'm Mrs. Charles Demetriou; you're Mr. Richard Jones: how do you do?"

It was the first chance he had had to see her clearly. She was a slender woman, dressed this morning in a full-skirted violet negligee, with a toque of the same color perched on the brown, glossy waves of her hair. Her face was lean and brown, hollow under the cheekbones; she had great dark eyes, heavy-lidded.

Dick was feeling short-tempered. He only half remembered the conversation he'd heard the day before, but there had been an argument about whether to help him or leave him, he recalled; and anyhow, this woman had been a witness of his humiliation.

"I'm glad to know you," he said shortly. "Nice of you to help out, and so on, but I'm all right now. If you'll just send a message to my body-slob to come and get me—" When she did not speak, but continued to look at him unsmilingly, he felt uncomfortable enough to add: "I can rest up just as well in my own place. I don't want to seem ungrateful or anything, but—"

"But you do," she said. "Very." She stood up, slender and erect, and put her hand on a old-fashioned French phone that stood by the bedside. She posed there as if she had forgotten what she set out to do. "Is your valet reliable?"

"I don't know," said Dick. "They sent him around from the bureau. I guess he's all right."

"What's his name?"

"Albert."

"Oh, *dear*," she said earnestly. "A gawky sort of thing, who always looks as if he needs a haircut?"

"Yes, that's him. Why?"

"But he's the worst servant in Eagles; they give him to overnight visitors—couriers, and people like that. Dear Mr. Jones, couldn't you do any better?"

"I don't know what you mean," said Dick; the headache was worse, and it was hard to listen. "They told me you can't bring your own slobs into Eagles."

"Well, of course, that's true, but still—" She took her hand away from the phone and stood by the chair, looking down at him. "Does your head hurt?"

"Some."

"I should think it would. Here." She took an ice bag from the table and laid it gently on his swollen temple. Her scent when she leaned over him was unobtrusive and fresh, something like sandalwood, not cloyingly sweet like most women's. "Why did you pick that fight with Ruell, anyway? Didn't you know this would happen?"

"I thought I might as well," said Dick, defensively. "I'm not much worse off this way, but if I'd won—"

She sniffed delicately. "He happens to be the best stickman in Eagles; but you didn't know that, did you?"

"No," said Dick, feeling belatedly foolish. Well, but what else could he have done? If it came to that, what could he do next?

Whatever he did, he mustn't seem to be asking for sympathy. "I really had better be going," he said. "If I could just have my clothes—"

"Don't be foolish," she said, unsmiling. "Maybe we can help you. Tell me, what did you think would happen if you did beat Ruell?"

"I don't know. It was a loony idea, I guess, but I couldn't think of anything better. I thought I could make him call off his dogs."

"His dogs?"

"He's got Van Etten and I don't know who all else working with him. I can't get my commission, or make a call home—"

Her fists clenched. "That lizard! That just makes me furious, to hear—" She turned. "Howard, come in and listen to this; you won't believe your ears."

"No?" said a voice Dick recognized. A tall man came leisurely toward them across the room, broad-shouldered in a plain yellow shirt. He was young, only a few years older than Dick; he had a pleasant, narrow face and a narrow mustache, and he was smoking a lean, long cigar.

"Richard Jones, Howard Clay. Now tell us the whole story, Richard, because we're all friends together. Howard, listen to this."

"I'm listening." Clay perched himself on the end of the bed and leaned back against the bedpost; his brown eyes were friendly but ironical.

Seeing no way out of it, Dick told them everything that had happened to him from the first day. When he had finished, Clay whistled softly. "I admire your spunk, any-how," he said. "But you went about Ruell the wrong way. He's provoked now; he'll never let you go unless you give in."

Dick's hands clenched into fists on the coverlet. "There must be some way out. Is that what you have to do here, to get along—let somebody barter you off like a slob, or an animal?"

There was an awkward pause. "I wouldn't put it just like that," said the lady, with marked coolness. Clay leaned over and stubbed out his cigar in an ashtray; his eyes were narrowed.

"Well, I'm sorry," said Dick; "but that's how it seems to me."

"Tell me," Clay began, "have you thought of appealing to the Boss?"

Dick hesitated. "I don't know. Do you think that would work?"

"No; but it's the only fool thing you haven't done yet. Now look here, Mister Jones, my advice to you is this: Find yourself a protector, don't wait for Ruell to do it for you. Get somebody to your liking, and if possible somebody a cut above Ruell, so he won't dare make too much trouble. Let your friend barter him off, or frighten him off, or whatever, and you'll be all right. Otherwise, Ruell will make you eat dirt. He'll keep you cooling your heels until you're ragged, and then he'll put you in the Misfit Battalion, and that only for a beginning. It's the truth." Clay rose gracefully, turned his back, and strolled off across the room, hands in his pockets.

The woman looked after him thoughtfully. "Howard."

"Yes?" he said over his shoulder.

"I think I'm going to do it."

He swung around. "I knew you were going to say that. You're insane, you know. You might as well take on the Magyar Corps de Ballet; you can't feed them, either."

"Charles will have to give me a larger quota," she said.

Clay sniffed. "Yes, but will he?"

"He'll have to." She turned to Dick. "Would you like me to adopt you, Richard?"

Dick hesitated. For some reason he did not feel that he would like it at all, and yet reason told him that he couldn't afford to let any honorable opportunity slip away. "What would I have to do for it?" he asked.

"Do for it?" she repeated wonderingly. "Oh, I see. Richard, how old do you think I am?"

The sudden question did not appear to surprise Clay; he came nearer and put his foot up on the arm of the chair, and they both watched Dick with silent enjoyment.

He looked at her: her skin seemed firm and unlined, except for a trace of crepiness around the eyes. There was no loose flesh under the chin and her hands did not seem wrinkled or heavily veined; those were supposed to be the telltales. Her figure was as slim as a young woman's. There was nothing about her that seemed old, except perhaps the confident stare of her eyes and the determined mouth. And yet there was none of the softness of youth about her anywhere: her very slimness was almost skeletal, and the fine bones showed through her face.

She was probably at least forty; he had better lop off a few years for politeness. "Thirty-five?" he said.

They both smiled. Her smile made her seem girlishly delighted; she said, "Much more than that. I'm—well, I'm old enough. I have a grandson almost your age. Haven't I, Howie?"

"Mm," said Clay, biting off the end of a fresh cigar.

"Let me understand this," said Dick. "You'd clear up this trouble about my commission, and using the TV, and so on?"

"And feed you, and clothe you decently," said Clay. "You've been on a visitor's quota, I expect, haven't you? Well, Vivian will have to do better for you than that; how, I don't know, but if she says so, I suppose she'll do it." He glanced at her out of the corners of his narrow eyes.

She put her hand on his arm. "Don't worry, Howie," she said quietly.

Clay seemed reassured. "And for all this," he told Dick, "you won't even have to carry a parcel . . . unless you feel like it. Vivian demands nothing—she's a philanthropist."

The woman gave him a look which Dick could not interpret. "Oh, *you*," she said, and turned with a smile. "Then it's all settled—yes?"

Dick was remembering Ruell's matter-of-fact voice: "Nothing is ever given for nothing, at Eagles." Across the bed, these two strangers were looking at him with something unspoken in their eyes.

But how could he say anything except "yes"?

The screen flickered and blurred, out of synch.

"Dad? Is that you?"

"I'm here, Richard. You're coming in clear and strong; what's the matter at that end?"

"It's—Oh, it's all right now." The blurred streaks of color coalesced into his father's face, greenish in the shaded parts. Dick touched up the red control, turned down the blue; the face took on a more normal appearance. "How is everybody?"

"We're all well, here. Richard, we've been trying to get

in touch with you ever since your arrival. Your mother has been—"

"Dick, dear!" His mother's face came into view; her voice sounded strained. "We've been so *worried*. Why haven't you called?"

Dick heard himself saying, "There's been a jam-up with the scrambled circuits." He had had no conscious intention of lying, but he saw now that the truth was impossible, it would have involved too many explanations.

"Well, at least you're all right," she said, staring earnestly at him out of the screen. "It's so good to see you, dear. You look a little tired."

"No doubt he's been busy," said his father. "Your commission came through, I take it?"

"Yes, Dad. I'm in the Fifth Horse, under General Myer." Clay had taken him around to Van Etten's office the day after his drubbing, and Van Etten, his demeanor changed as if by magic, had settled the whole matter in five minutes.

His father nodded approvingly. "That's a good outfit. You spoke to Ruell?"

"Yes."

"And did he arrange a connection for you?"

"Well, not exactly, Dad." He hesitated: here, surely, he had to explain the whole business; but where was he to start?

His father's expression sharpened. "No? Do you mean you haven't got a connection?"

"Oh, yes, I've got one—Mrs. Demetriou; she's very nice. But Ruell and I had a kind of a disagreement. . . ." His voice trailed away.

"A woman?" his mother asked. "Fred, I'm not sure I care for that. Dear, what kind of a woman is she? How did you meet her? Is she—"

"I've heard of her," his father said. "It's all right." He looked steadily at Dick. "You haven't made an enemy out of Ruell, I hope?"

"Oh, no, Dad." An outright lie.

"Very well. Richard, the children want to say hello to you, and then we'll talk again."

His mother moved reluctantly away from the screen. "Dick, be sure to write as soon as you can . . ." He realized with a curious shock that she looked older than she had when he left.

Ad and Felix tumbled into view, shouting, "Hello, Dick!" followed by Constance looking oddly grown-up, with her hair done on top of her head, and young Edward in Miss Molly's arms, all beaming and babbling at the same time. . . .

His father shooed them out of the room after a few moments, and stood with his head turned, waiting to be sure they were out of earshot; then he turned and looked at Dick silently.

"How are things," Dick asked, "at Twin Lakes?"

"As well as could be expected," his father answered. "The decoy plane we sent returned safely, you may be interested to know."

Dick started; he had forgotten about it.

"However, that's a small matter," his father continued. "What I wanted to discuss with you, Richard—" He hesitated, uncharacteristically, and began again with a frown of distaste. "You may possibly remember the juggler who fell and was injured during the banquet."

Dick thought a moment. "Oh. Yes, I think so."

"We found some filth concealed in his clothing—pamphlets. Directions for making weapons out of kitchen knives and garden implements. Worse things."

Dick felt himself paling with shock. "You mean *our slaves*—?"

"Some of them must have received copies without reporting it. We don't know which ones. We've never used manacles here, Richard, but I think under the circumstances we have no choice."

"Yes, of course, Dad." He moistened his lips. "But; I mean, I can't believe—"

"No, neither can I. Our slaves have always been loyal. But there's something in the air this year, Richard; I've felt it in Richmond and other places. I think it's best to be prepared. Well, Richard, that's all, then, I think."

"Yes, Dad. Good-by."

The picture rushed toward its center, a streaky whirlpool of color, twitching, dwindling, gone.

NINE

After a month he was beginning to feel almost at home in Eagles. There were some things about it that he didn't like, some that disturbed him, some he couldn't understand, but on the whole, there was no denying that it was a fascinating place to be. Eagles was inexhaustible; it covered the whole south and east faces of the mountain-top in dozens of bewilderingly split levels. There was an underground games arena where football and baseball were played by team of slaves; there was a library, housed in an area bigger than the main building at Buckhill; there were collection halls, gardens, observatories. There were whole sections that

Dick had never seen, and was not likely to without special permission; even leaving these out, the place was forever changing, always full of new things. No one ever seemed to let well enough alone; you might awaken to find that the corridor outside had been repaved in slabs of turquoise, or that the little Moorish courtyard just this side of the Grand Promenade had vanished and been replaced by an aquarium full of incredible fish—frilled, golden, stately fish that made you want to stand and stare at them.

But there was never time to pause very long anywhere. Something else always beckoned, or there was an appointment to keep, or clothes to be fitted for a party—clothes alone took an astonishing amount of time—or if not that, then girls, or Vivian. On the whole, he had to admit that he didn't see much of Vivian, she disappeared sometimes for days; but there were times when she wanted to be escorted somewhere by four or five protégés, and then it was only common courtesy, considering how much they all owed her.

He frowned. His valet, Alex, who was certainly ten times better trained than the one he had had before, or Sam at home, either, for that matter—although Dick was rapidly learning to accept his unobtrusive deftness as a standard—Alex immediately stopped finicking at the folds of his neck-cloth, stepped back, and with his head a little on one side examined the effect.

"Alex, we haven't anything on with Mrs. Demetriou today, have we?"

"Not that they've told us about, mister. We haven't seen the Missis this week."

"That's right, good. I was thinking of the opera, but that's Friday. Is Mr. Clay here yet?"

"I see, mister." Alex stepped to the door, glanced out. "Just arriving, mister, this minute."

"Well, are you through with this damned neck-cloth?"

"Dick!" came Clay's voice from the outer room. "Let's go—we're late already."

"I haven't had breakfast!" Dick protested.

Clay popped his head in the doorway. "It's almost one o'clock, you fungus. Come on, do you want to see the Tower or don't you? Make up your mind."

"All right." Alex was holding out his new morning jacket; he slipped his arms into it. It was hand-loomed, watered silk, in a pattern that gave him height. "Are Thor and Johnny coming?" he asked.

"No, just the two of us—I could only get two places." Alex was fastening the belt and chains; Clay picked up the striped silk cap from the dressing table and clapped it on Dick's head. "Come on," he said, dragging him toward the door. "I tell you, we're late."

Clay had a chair waiting. As soon as they got into it the chairboys started off at a trot; but they were hardly well into the main corridor when they slowed down again. There was some sort of turmoil up ahead; people were drawing back to either side of the corridor, chairs and pedestrians alike. They followed suit. Down the wide empty avenue came a little group of men at a walking pace. In the lead was a heavy man of about fifty; he moved slowly and ungracefully, bloated and stiff under a gray mantle. On either side and a little behind walked a Household Guard with a holstered pistol, the first firearms Dick had seen in Eagles. Behind came an empty chair pushed by two slobs, and trailing on either side were four or five men in formal dark morning dress.

The man in the lead had a sallow face, jowls loose and shapeless, a blob for a nose. There was a dead cigar clenched in his wide, lipless mouth. He did not turn his head, but glanced from side to side as he walked. His little eyes passed incuriously over Dick and Clay; his gloomy expression did not change; he walked on.

The crowd was beginning to flow back into the corridor, "Who was *that*?" Dick demanded.

Clay gave him a sidelong glance. "You don't know? That's right, you've never seen him. That was the Boss."

The crowd flowed along, brilliant, glittering, with a cloud of scent and a murmur of laughter. Here were half a dozen East Indians in turbans, hawk-nosed and dark, with flashing eyes; here came a priest of Eblis and a gypsy mountebank, disputing, arm in arm; there was the famous Mrs. Wray, whose intrigues were the talk of Eagles; here came a work detail and a cart loaded with monstrous slabs of flooring. The corridor boomed, clattered, rippled with echoes: this was life. The owner of all this must be a fortunate man; what more could anyone ask in the world?

But if the end of it was nothing but that gray frog-face, and that expression of settled gloom? . . .

They passed a doorway guarded by an ape-faced fellow in black; the door had a familiar G and crossbones symbol —a Gismo Room. Dick understood now perfectly well how Eagles was organized, and why it could be no other way. All the Gismos in Eagles belonged to the Boss, just as all the slobs were his; that was an elementary precaution. There was an elite guard that watched the Gismos, and an even more select corps that did nothing but watch the guards, with an elaborate tradition of rivalry and hatred between them.

There were hundreds of Gismos in Eagles, pouring out a wealth of things all day and all night long; but even here, there was a limit to their number. There had to be a quota system—so much for a casual visitor, so much more for a Secretary's favorite, so much more again for the Secretary himself. That made sense of the whole tumultuous, unrelenting struggle for position that went on in Eagles: position to command more luxuries and pleasures for yourself, and to dispose of them for others. Then there was the danger, too, that made it a game fit for a man to play: with each step up the pyramid, your position became more exposed, there were more people who would like to pull you down. It was danger that put the spice in it, that made eyes sparkle and lips gleam red.

Crossing one of the wide plazas at mid-level, Dick happened to glance up and see a familiar figure leaning over the balcony above. It was only for an instant, then the bright red tunic was gone into the crowd.

"Someone you know?" asked Clay, following his glance.

"Keel, I think. He's out of sight now." He and the blond young man had met in the corridors several times since Keel's ducking, but each time they had only nodded distantly; Keel's crowd and Dick's did not mix, and so far there had been no further trouble.

But there had been something in Keel's expression just now, or the tilt of his head: a hint of that good-humored mockery which was somehow more disturbing than malice. . . .

"He won't bother you," said Clay absently. "No gang feuds; that's the rule, and the Boss enforces it."

"He could challenge me," said Dick, and grinned self-consciously. He had been working out under old Finnegan the stick-master, and his natural aptitude for the stick had so far improved that none of Vivian's other protégés could stand against him.

"Well, you're not worried about that, are you? Forget it."

They had ridden up a ramp and through a doorway where Dick had never gone before; now they were in a long glass-roofed esplanade which paralleled a sunken railway track. Below them, two cars were standing idle, one loaded with sheets of burnished golden metal, the other empty. The tracks dwindled almost to a point; beyond, through the glass, Dick caught sight of a slender peak of metal, bright against the pale sky.

A nervous fellow in the fur jacket and shako of the Household Guard was fussing about on the platform, superintending a small flotilla of chairs, twenty or twenty-five of them, which he had got jammed up against a V-shaped barricade. He came bustling over with a list in his hand: "Clay? Jones? All right, then we can start. Just a moment." He turned; there was some sort of disturbance up at the point of the V. Standing, Dick saw a red-faced man in the lead chair striking at the face of a slob who was holding the gate closed. The stick rose and fell deliberately; the slob, vainly trying to protect his head, fell out of sight, but another one instantly took his place. There was a muffled roar from the red-faced man, who raised his stick again; but the nervous Guard officer shouted, "All right, open!" The gate swung back; the chairs began to move. The officer pushed by toward a chair of his own, muttering and gnawing his mustache.

Once past the bottleneck, the chairs spread out into a scattered flock. Dick recognized two or three people he knew slightly, but most of the group seemed to be visitors; there was an elderly lady in a hideous, flowered mantle, two middle-aged couples, a lank young man in a Western hat. The red-faced man was still in the lead; Dick saw his head go back as he tipped up a bottle.

He transferred his attention to the Tower, which became gradually more visible through the glass roof of the passage. As they drew nearer, he could see that its lower stages were cross-hatched with scaffolding, a little like a tower built of matchsticks, from the center of which the metal tip protruded . . . and it was only with that thought that he began to realize how huge the Tower really was.

The passage was very long, the Tower farther away than it seemed, and the closer they got, the more incredibly, monstrously big it appeared. The huge buttresses began to loom over them; the distant, sunlit tip of the tower grew tiny by comparison, glinting up there like a half-fallen star. Dick felt a curious shrinking of his own person, which he did not like: instead of the Tower growing larger, it was as if he and all the rest of the human beings had grown small —small as grasshoppers.

"We leave the chairs here," called the nervous officer. He was standing at the end of the passage; beyond him, through the glass doors, they could see a dark space in which trucks moved and loops of cable hung out of vacancy; there was a muffled roar of engines and a clatter of riveting hammers which made the officer's voice almost inaudible. The guests were getting out of their chairs and converging on him; the boys were wheeling the empty chairs away.

"We are now about to enter the Tower of Eagles, the tallest man-made object in the entire world," said the officer's high voice. "One thousand, six hundred feet in height. The Empire State Building in New York was one thousand, two hundred and fifty feet in height, the Great Pyramid at Gizeh was only four hundred and eighty-one feet in height when intact. The Eiffel Tower in Paris, France, is nine hundred eighty-four and one-quarter feet high, or less than two-thirds the height of Eagles Tower. The Tower has a triangular cross-section and is constructed of a unique ferro-platinum alloy throughout. The engraved plates of the exterior are of fourteen-carat gold, and each represents more than eighty hours of hand labor by skilled craftsmen. Kindly step this way."

They passed through the dorway into a vast space of confusing shapes and sounds. Near at hand, the interior had a finished appearance and was brightly lighted; farther away, there was a gulf of darkness broken only by shafts of dim sunlight, and the occasional blue flare of a torch. "This," shouted the officer over the din, "is the Grand Staircase which when completed will rise the entire height of the Tower." Floodlights illumined the bottom of the distant staircase; it swept in a graceful curve up around a central pillar, and was lost in the darkness of the staging above. Every second step had a niche, in which a ten-foot statue stood. The marble of the steps themselves, as well as the banister, railings and walls, seemed to be intricately carved and inlaid.

"To the left of the Staircase," the voice went on, "you will observe the Edmond Cenotaph, erected in memory of Edmond Crawford, second Boss of Colorado." This was an enormous wedding cake of granite and white metal; there was an inscription, which they were too far away to read, and the whole thing seemed to form a base for what Dick guessed was a heroic figure of some kind, but only the feet were visible.

The group was straggling off to the left, into a large and temporary-looking open elevator. There was room for them all, and to spare; a small truck could have been driven onto the car. With nothing but a flimsy folding gate between them and vacancy, the car jerked and slowly rose.

Above the first stage, the interior of the Tower revealed itself as a dim, hollow shell of scaffolding in which tiny figures were at work like bees in a honeycomb. Some portions of the inward-sloping framework had been covered with great arabesques of wrought-metal, intricate figures that curved and looped back upon themselves; others were being faced with what looked like all enamel or ceramic tiles. "Each and every square inch of the Tower," said their guide, "inside and out, at completion will be ornamented with unique works of art by Eagles craftsmen gathered from all over the world. Here you see one of the fifty cineramas which will be set in motion throughout the Tower." This was a floating platform, almost invisibly suspended, on which gigantic bright-colored automatons knelt stiffly—a man and two boys, all with jointed snakes wrapped around them. "Mythological scenes are represented," the guide added.

At the next stage the car came to a halt, and they all

trooped out across a clattering floor to another and smaller elevator. This took them into twilit gulfs above, where the sounds of labor echoed but dimly, and then into a sudden and dazzling glow of light. They had risen above the area of scaffolding into the sun again, and in rows of tall windows they could see the sky.

The second elevator also stopped short of the summit, and they climbed a narrow echoing stair, beyond which the wind whistled, to reach a triangular platform under a domed roof.

Dick paused at the nearest window and looked down. He could not see the base of the Tower, but down there, directly below, lay Eagles like a many-colored carpet dropped on the mountain top. From this giddy height the mountain itself dropped away into distance; the window frame trembled under his hand to the wind's buffeting, and the wall seemed about to tilt over into emptiness.

Clay's hand at his elbow roused him. "Come on, don't daydream or you'll miss it."

The rest of the group was crowding around the center of the platform, where a railing surrounded a circular open shaft. This must be the central pillar around which the stairway was built, Dick realized; for some reason, it was hollow. He found a place next to Clay and peered down.

The shaft was about ten feet across, perfectly circular and smooth, and dropped straight down until the successive rings of light from recessed lamps melted into one. The bottom was a dot, a mere mathematical point. A cool air breathed up the shaft, carrying a faint, unpleasant odor. Dick found himself trembling.

"Sixteen hundred feet down," said Clay, beside him. He took out a handkerchief, tied a knot in it, and dropped it over the rail. The winged, white shape floated downward, drifted, diminishing, crawled endlessly toward the center of light, and was gone.

"No metal objects, please," said the guide. Across the shaft, the red-faced man was about to drop a metal flask. "Cloth, paper or wooden objects may be dropped," the guide said, "but you are asked not to drop metal, glass or plastic."

The red-faced man dropped his flask in. It struck something protruding from the wall of the shaft with a sharp *tink,* glanced off and receded, whirling.

"Mister," said the guide, advancing, "I asked you not to drop metal objects."

The red-faced man turned unsteadily, fishing a cigar lighter out of his pocket. "Don't tell *me*," he said, and threw the lighter in. He scowled into the officer's face. "Are you a man, or are you a slob?" he demanded. "Don't no slob

87

tell me what to do, by God. Here——" He struggled to get something out of his pocket.

The officer signed to the two guards, who were hurrying up. They seized the red-faced man by the elbows and started to manhandle him toward the stair. He resisted, shouting obscenities, and managed to kick a middle-aged lady in the hip as he passed. The lady fell with a shriek; the officer, biting his mustache, stepped up and hit the red-faced man on the temple with a little, leather-covered blackjack.

The blow did not look hard, but the red-faced man slumped instantly and was carried off like dead meat. After a moment, the rest of the crowd began to straggle after; the injured lady was helped to her feet and left with the rest.

Following, Dick stumbled against a stack of paper bags, heavy and solid; a dusting of white came off on his shoe. Curiously, he paused and bent to read the label, half obscured by white powder: UNSLAKED LIME.

He caught up with Clay halfway down the stair. "That Guard officer *is* a slob," he said. "I saw his mark. But he hit a man—hit him hard."

Clay nodded. "He had his orders."

"But you can't have slobs hitting people," Dick said. "What's going to happen to him now?"

Clay glanced at him with a faint smile. "What do you think?"

They entered the elevator and rode down in silence. The Guard officer, who was pale, looked straight ahead. The red-faced man hung, breathing heavily, between the two guards who supported him. At the ground floor they propped him in a corner while the officer telephoned; that was the last Dick saw of either of them.

TEN

Melker's reception, as usual, was crowded and colorful. Melker himself was there for a wonder, a gnomish, unpleasant little man with a really repulsive beard. His rooms were big but rather shabby; Melker had vague Army connections but was nobody himself, as far as Dick could determine: why everybody seemed to come to his Saturday night receptions, he couldn't tell; but since everybody did, he went too. The entertainment was good—two accomplished dancers tonight, and a comedian who had once been attached to the Household. Towards eleven o'clock, though, as always, the evening turned unaccountably dull; all the pretty women began to go home, the waiters with the drinks disappeared, some old gasbag like Colonel Rosen would take the floor and start fighting the War of Establishment all over again—people would be yawning all over the suite, and at this point, Dick always drifted out with a gang of acquaintances who were looking for something livelier.

Tonight, however, Clay drew him aside as he was moving toward the door. "Going so soon? Wait a while."

Dick nodded toward Colonel Rosen, who was holding forth in a parade-ground voice at the other side of the room. "And listen to that? No, thanks."

Clay didn't release his arm. "There's a reason. Wait."

Puzzled and intrigued, Dick found a seat and watched more alertly. For a while, if anything, the assemblage merely got more desperately dull. Then, after one incoherent drunk was helped out, the atmosphere miraculously changed. Colonel Rosen shut up and poured himself a neat drink; waiters were again moving among the chairs; there was a murmur of talk and laughter; even the lights seemed brighter but less glaring.

Dick looked around him. Most of those present were men in their prime; there was a sprinkling of young men and oldsters, and only three women—two dowagers who had settled themselves close together, each with her own body-servant at hand, and a youngish but very plain woman in the far corner.

Melker, who was seated near the fireplace, now rapped for attention with a wineglass. "Men and ladies," he said, "the subject for tonight is 'Slavery.' Colonel Rosen, will you oblige us by opening with the traditional view?"

Dick groaned, not quite inaudibly. Rosen, a florid, nearly bald man in his fifties, cocked an eyebrow in his direction as he began. "Slavery is an institution of every civilized society, from the most ancient times to the present. Using the term in the broadest sense, there never has been a time when civilized arts and sciences, to such an extent as they existed, have not been founded on forced labor, that is, on slavery. We may distinguish—"

"Objection!" said a vigorous-looking, dark-skinned man, pointing his pipe at Rosen. "Do you maintain that the peasant of the Middle Ages was a slave?"

"I do, mister."

"He was not, he was a serf, and there's an important difference. A serf was attached to the soil—"

("—Like a pumpkin," murmured an ironic voice in Dick's ear.)

"—and could only be sold with the soil, whereas a slave was absolute property and could be sold at any time."

"The chair rules," said Melker, "that Colonel Rosen may

call the serf a slave if he wishes. Colonel, please continue."

Dick twisted around; Clay had moved over unobtrusively and was sitting close behind him. "What is all this?" Dick whispered.

"The Philosophers' Club—shut up and listen, you may learn something."

"We may distinguish," Rosen was saying, "between systems of individual slavery, slavery of classes, and mechanical slavery. The latter, an invention of the so-called Industrial Revolution, put an end to the formal practice of individual slavery in Europe and America, but introduced a new form of the slavery of classes, that is, industrial slavery. In more recent times—"

"Just a minute, Colonel," cried the plain young woman. "Those people were free. They had a democracy, on this part of the continent—they could move from job to job, just as they wanted."

"But they had to work?" asked the Colonel.

"Well, if you want to put it that way—under the monetary system they had to work, yes, to get dollars—but they could *choose,* don't you see—"

"They could choose whether to work or starve," said the Colonel positively. "The difference between—"

"Oh, now really! Colonel, those people were the best paid workers in history—They had cars, they had television sets—"

"My slaves have television sets," said Rosen; "they don't need cars. If they did, they'd have 'em. The fact remains, they can't dispose of their own time. That marks the essential difference between your slave and your freeman, whether you call 'em slaves, serfs, cotters, villeins, factory workers—"

"Or soldiers, Colonel?" asked one of the dowagers, in a penetrating voice.

Rosen stiffened. "Lady, I'm a housed man, serving freely. I can resign my commission at any time—"

"Mrs. Maxwell is out of order," Melker interposed smoothly. "Miss Flavin, the chair rules that the Colonel may call industrial workers slaves, under his own definition. Colonel, I believe you were building up to a point?"

"I was. Now, mechanical slavery, the slavery of the machine, was hailed as the great emancipator; it was supposed to eliminate the need for human slavery and make everybody a gentleman. The more work performed by machines, the more leisure for humans." (Half a dozen people had their hands raised; the chairman ignored them.) "Well, I give you the Gismo, the last word in mechanical slavery—"

"In mechanical *production,*" began Miss Flavin, heatedly,

but Rosen waved her to silence. "One minute. The Gismo does everything any of the Industrial Age machines were supposed to do, to eliminate human labor—it generates power, it manufactures everything from jet planes to toothbrushes, it replaces parts, and all this at zero cost for materials, and the absolute minimum of human supervision. *But—*" He paused. "The Gismo won't clean a room, make a bed, comb your hair or carry a gun. And the more leisure you've got, the more demand for personal service. So you see the result—mechanical slavery *makes* human slavery, and the proof is, we've got the highest proportion of slaves to free men in the history of the world—over fifty to one. Three hundred to one, here in Eagles. You moralists can argue all you like, it couldn't have happened any other way." There was another hooker of spirits at his side; he picked it up, drained it with a little ironic salute of the glass, and set it down.

"Very good," said Melker, rapping for order, "very good, Colonel, now since you've made such a kind invitation to the moralists, as represented by Miss Flavin, let's hear them argue."

"Well, in the first place," said the plain woman, looking indignant, "we're not moralists as Colonel Rosen calls us, we're humanitarians. That's an ethical position, and if the Colonel doesn't know the difference between ethics and morals, I won't take the time to instruct him now.

"Colonel Rosen has just explained to us how inevitable slavery is," she went on, "and of course there's just one little thing wrong with his argument. It took five years of brutal war, and the *extermination* of hundreds of thousands of people, to impose this so-called inevitable system that we enjoy today—a system that, as the Colonel admits, was actually obsolete nearly a hundred and fifty years ago. And, of course, the Gismo is the end-all of all scientific progress, why, yes, we've seen to that, because there hasn't been a single, important, scientific development in the last fifty years —not one! But that's sensible, of course, because we saw what just one little invention, the Gismo, did to the world, and we're afraid one more might upset our *inevitable* system!"

Dick looked around at Clay, open-mouthed with astonishment. He had never heard such talk, never imagined anything like it. But Clay was leaning calmly back in his chair with his cigar cocked at an interested angle, for all the world as if he were listening to some moderately novel opinion about the weather.

"Question," called a scholarly-looking man from the opposite side of the room. He was white-haired and wore

91

old-fashioned nose spectacles. "Does Miss Flavin assume that war, itself, is not inevitable?"

She turned to face him. "I most certainly do, Doctor Belasco. Like all apologists for brutality, you no doubt believe that history proves your point—there have always been wars, therefore wars are inevitable. Adopting your own puerile argument, I could say that there have always been periods of peace, therefore peace is inevitable."

"Intervals between wars," grunted Colonel Rosen. "Man's a fighting animal, woman's a species of talking bird."

"We are a trifle off the point," said Melker. "Miss Flavin, if it's agreeable to you, I think we should all be interested to hear something of the alternative system your group proposes."

"Certainly," said the woman, with a hard look at Rosen. "We humanitarians, as our name suggests, believe that man has an ethical duty to man. We believe that the value of any system is measured by the consideration given to all human beings, not just to a favored class: and by that standard, our present system is a miserable failure."

"Oh, well," said Rosen loudly, "if we're going to use that kind of logic, down with horses—they don't lay eggs." There was some laughter.

"Colonel, we have given you considerable latitude in your definitions," said Melker. "Miss Flavin, if you please."

"Our first objective," she resumed, "is the abolition of slavery and a return to free, democratic institutions. No progress, either moral or material, can be made in a world which is frozen, like ours, into a rigid mold of suppression of liberties. Once this objective is attained, in an orderly way, then our other problems—and they will be many—can be dealt with as they arise. We do not believe that the only stable society is one that crams forty-nine fiftieths of itself into a degrading servitude."

Several hands were in the air; Melker nodded to a pale young man in a puce jacket. "Mr. Oliver?"

"Of course, I'm no philosopher or anything," Oliver began jerkily, "but it seems to me—you talk about consideration and so on. Well, suppose you let all the slaves go. I can't quite see it myself, but what I want to know, suppose you had a lot of little families scattered all over, instead of the big houses we have now, well, how do you know there'd be any more consideration then? I mean, wouldn't all the families be fighting with each other, where now, at least, we've got 'em under control, so they can't fight."

"A very valuable and interesting point," said Melker, smoothly. "Mr. Collundra, did you wish to answer that question?"

The dark-skinned man said, "Well, in a way. Mr. Oliver,

of course, as you point out, it's difficult to measure consideration. Or happiness, or anything of that kind. But there is a standard that can be used, and that's the efficient use of land. Seventy-odd years ago, there were a hundred and eighty million people living on the North American continent; today, there's no census, but probably there are about one-eighth that number. Now, I merely offer that as a scale on which you can compute one way of living against another; I think we might profitably debate that point."

"Good; now we shall see some fireworks," said Melker, rubbing his hands. "Mrs. Maxwell?"

The old woman's expression was amused under her mask of cosmetics. "Well, Mr. Collundra is absolutely right, although I doubt that he knows it. Efficient use of space *is* the test, and I can add some figures to the ones he gave. When the white men first came to this continent, I understand, the place was about half forest. In five hundred years they got that down to one-third—cleared the rest, made it into farms, and towns and cities. Then we came along, and in less than a hundred years we got it back pretty near to half forest again. We ought to be proud. There isn't but about a hundred thousand square miles that we actually use; I mean improved land, land that looks some way different from what it did before we got there. One good epidemic could carry us all off; the Black Death in Europe, I understand, buried more people than there are in North America now. Then the cougars and coyotes could take over; there's plenty of *them*."

She seemed to be finished; Melker nodded to a white-bearded man who sat vigorously erect. "Commander Holt?"

Holt cleared his throat and said mildly, "I don't know if I understand the lady, but it seems to me if it's density of population you want, the best civilization was pre-Gismo India; they had about two hundred to the square mile there. Now, it may be that there are too few of us at the moment; that's an unusual situation and we're growing fast; I understand most of the country families are running to four and five children apiece. I hope we never get to two hundred to the square mile. But I suppose we'll get somewhere near it, and then we'll have to have another war of the character Miss Flavin describes." He cleared his throat at length, and began again, unexpectedly, "Now this question of population is, it seems to me, one that Miss Flavin and her supporters have consistently refused to face. Miss Flavin, let me put this question to you. You believe, do you not, that it was a primary, ethical mistake to limit the number of Gismos?"

"Of course it was," she answered. "It was the one original injustice from which the rest inevitably followed. But as for population increase—" a thin flush appeared on her cheeks

—"there are ways and means, as you perfectly well know, Commander—"

"No, if you'll pardon me, there aren't," said Holt. "Voluntary birth control methods only work on the people who choose to use 'em. A population check that doesn't work on everybody, doesn't work at all, because it simply breeds out the ones who use it. The only population check that really works is one that affects everybody, like a limit of space or food. Now, Miss Flavin, with Gismos freely available, there wouldn't ever be a shortage of food, would there?"

"No."

"No, there couldn't be. And we would hope that people wouldn't go to war and kill each other off, merely because there was getting to be a lot of 'em, isn't that right?"

"If you like to put it that way."

"All right, then that leaves a limit of space: and, Miss Flavin, there wouldn't've been any end to our natural increase until there was one of us for every square yard of land surface on the planet."

Melker beamed. "Taking advantage of the privilege of the chair, may I say that your picture of the future gives me gooseflesh of delight: one enormous pile of refuse, with people standing in rows, each beside his Gismo. No trees, no competing animals or birds, no room for lakes or streams —and, for that matter, why waste the oceans, Commander? I suppose we could build rafts . . . Yes, Mr. Kishor?"

A lantern-jawed young man, perched on one arm of the sofa, had been scribbling in a notebook. He held up the results. "I thought you might be interested to know just how many people the Earth could support, at the rate Commander Holt mentioned—in round numbers, sixty-one trillion, nine hundred forty billion people."

"Of course, we could build a second story and double that," somebody called.

Melker was rapping for order. "Seriously—seriously—" a heavy, blunt-featured man kept saying.

"Yes, Mr. Perse."

"Seriously, there really is an answer to this ridiculous problem we've been tossing around. I refer, of course, to space travel. Now I know some of you think of space travel as a kind of twentieth century frenzy, like the stock market or swallowing goldfish. But I assure you it is not. Space travel is an art completely worked out, in the most thorough detail, more than a century ago, and lacking only an adequate fuel—which the Gismo provides! If it were not for the unfortunate moratorium placed on scientific progress at the beginning of the present era, we would be in space now —and indeed, this isn't generally known, but we have some reason to believe that one or more spaceships may actually have got off during the War of Establishment. If it's standing room you want, there's the Moon—there's Mars, Venus and all the other planets of this system just for a beginning. True, we are sadly limited on this poor little planet, but there's no need in the world to talk about reducing our numbers. Men and ladies, I ask you to consider that in our home galaxy alone there are more than thirty billion suns."

Dick's head was swimming. His first idea, that these people were talking treason, was obviously wrong, or else an old warhorse like Colonel Rosen wouldn't stay here and listen for a minute. No, this was what he had been looking for without knowing it: knowledgeable talk that didn't have the taint of slobbery. These were the people who really knew things. Dick conceived a sudden determination; he thought, *I'll be like them. I'll talk that way too!*

Going home afterwards through the blue-lighted residential corridors—walking for the exercise, with Clay striding along beside him—Dick felt elated. Through the narrow clerestory he could see the stars, sharp and bright in a sky flooded with moonlight. Life rolled on, after all: here or at home, it made no real difference; he was Dick Jones of Buckhill, and the world was his oyster.

All the servants had gone to bed except the valet; Dick dismissed him, too, poured Clay a nightcap, and flung himself down on a divan. The room was spacious and warm; the shaded lights glimmered from the polished surfaces of tables and bookcases; there were fresh camellias, tastefully arranged, in the vases. "Howard," he said, "how long has that been going on?"

The scrape of Clay's match was loud in the stillness. "Not very long, actually." The fragrance of the cigar drifted across. "There was a Philosophers' Club here that lapsed about twenty years ago; Melker revived it. I had an idea you'd fit in." He smoked in silence for a while. "Of course," he added, "they'll expect you to speak up, eventually. I'll lend you some books if you want."

"Yes—about space flight?"

Clay's answer came after a pause. "Better stay clear of that, Dick. I know Perse has a way about him, but that's a dead end."

"Why? It sounded pretty logical."

"That's not settling anything, to run away into space. Our problems are right here. Besides, when he tells you it's all worked out, he's lying. Half the art has been lost; I know." Another pause. "Who do you think is the most important person you heard there tonight?"

Dick thought about it. "Well—Melker?"

"No, not Melker."

"Rosen, then, or Holt."

"No, not either of them, or any of the Humanitarian crowd, either. Mr. Oliver."

Dick twisted around on the divan to look at him. *"Oliver?"*

"That's right. You're moving in exalted circles now, my boy. 'Oliver' is Oliver Crawford—he happens to be the heir to Eagles. Some day he'll be the Boss—and if you're his friend by that time—" The glowing tip of Clay's cigar made an expressive, upward gesture. "He leans toward the conservative side, naturally, but he's squeamish; wants to keep what he's got without hurting anybody." Clay rose. "It's getting late; we'll talk again tomorrow."

Dick sighed; he felt peacefully tired. "Howard?"

His friend turned, a silhouette in the lighted doorway. "Yes?"

"When I first came here, that snake Ruell told me nobody in Eagles ever does anything for nothing. He was wrong, wasn't he?"

Clay looked at him quietly across the room. "Get some sleep," he said gently, and closed the door.

ELEVEN

The Boss awoke out of a smothering dream of darkness. His heart was hammering; he came upright in the bed with a panicky motion that left him trembling and dizzy.

But the lights all around him were burning as before; nothing was wrong, no one was in the room. The alarm had not sounded. The wide carpet was empty on every side; he could see the domed ceiling, no one was clinging there.

He leaned back against the cushions, closing his eyes for a moment. A horrible dream. Horrible. Even now, his heart was still thudding and leaping in his chest; he could still see the gray corridor, and his son Oliver stooping to unfasten the round metal hatch cover in the stone floor. He had been paralyzed, unable to call out, until the cover moved, and he saw an edge of darkness underneath. Then the shadows swooped in, and he turned, shouting for help: and then he woke up.

It was not possible to trust anybody. Perhaps if he had someone he could trust in these rooms at night, watching over him, he wouldn't have these nightmares so often . . . very likely indigestion caused them, however. He massaged his slack stomach, groaning, until he forced up a loud belch, and felt a little better. He blinked. His heartbeat was slowing down, the dream was fading. But he was awake now; it was six o'clock. There was no use in trying to get to sleep again.

What could have been under that hatch cover to frighten him so?

It reminded him of the pit under the Tower; there was a cover on that, to keep the stench in. . . . He sniffed, brooding, hunched in the bed like a great gray lizard, with his hooded eyes gone milky and dull.

After a moment he roused himself and thumbed over the communicator switch at the bedside.

"Boss?"

"No alarm," he growled. "Get a party ready in the Tower —about ten."

While he waited, he opened the safe and made himself a snack from the private Gismo and protes inside. It took about ten minutes; then the communicator buzzed softly. "Yes?"

"Ready in the Tower, Boss. Ten—all bucks. We can get you some females if you prefer."

"Doesn't matter." The Boss tore the last mouthful of meat off his chicken drumstick, and threw the bone into the disposal box. Wiping his greasy hands on his gown, he waddled over to the TV chair and sat down. His heartbeat was thudding faster again, with a sullen, angry tension. He scowled, pulling the lapboard to him.

His fingers stiffened as he touched the controls. The resentment, the buried anger that was always with him, that had no object and no outlet of its own, boiled up and he let it come. He pressed the selector for "Tower."

The screen opposite flared into life. The Boss punched the second button in a row of six.

The screen flickered. The telltale read, "Shaft One."

He was looking up a smooth, dark bore to a circle of light, at an apparent distance of ten or twelve feet; he could see the underside of the little gangway, and the brace that supported it. Above, the yellow-painted ceiling glittered in the floodlights.

He punched the next button. The top of the shaft leaped back, diminished to a tiny button; this second camera was located a hundred feet down. Hooded lamps at intervals of about ten feet made flares and then rings of light up the length of the shaft, as if it were the inside of a great annular worm.

His lips pulled back over his teeth; he heard himself grunt, an unwilling sound.

He punched the fourth button. Now the view was almost the same, but the top of the shaft was invisible; the rings

97

of light seemed to melt together as they converged. This camera was four hundred feet down.

He punched the fifth button. The shaft looked the same; this was at the nine-hundred-foot level.

He punched the sixth button. His breath was beginning to come short and heavy, rasping in his throat. The screen showed a light grid of iron, half-inch rods criss-crossing five inches apart. Above the grid, he saw the same diminishing perspective. This was the lowest point, sixteen hundred feet down; under this, there was nothing but the pit.

He punched the first button: the telltale read, "Platform." The camera was located at eye level across the shaft opening from the gangway. On the far side, across the railing, a small crowd was gathered. There were the ten slaves in white shirts, and half a dozen guards. They were all waiting in silence, heads down, as if the glare hurt their eyes.

The Boss's throat was dry. He touched the audio key and said, "Get the first one out."

All the heads jumped, turning toward the loudspeaker. The guard corporal pointed to one of the slaves, and two guards hustled him out, white-faced and slack in the knees. He was a thin man with a ragged mustache. They forced him out to the end of the gangway, with vacancy under his feet, and held him there. The Boss could see his Adam's apple work convulsively as he tried to swallow.

The Boss poised his heavy fingers over the buttons. His jaw and throat were tense, brow knotted. "Get ready," he said. In the screen, the doomed man's mouth opened, his body went rigid all over.

"Go," said the Boss, leaning forward avidly.

TWELVE

Dick was half undressed, and more than half drowsy, when there came a cautious rapping at the door. Rather than wake up one of the servants, he went to answer it himself. "Yes? Who is it?"

But no answer came, and the Judas window was empty. Dick heard a faint rustling at his feet, and looked down in time to see a white envelope sliding under the door.

He bent and picked it up. The envelope was blank; inside was a single sheet of paper. He stooped under the nearest light to unfold and read it:

Dear Enemy:

Seeing you today reminded me how anxious I am to renew our acquaintance. The grille, which some wag removed from the Trout Brook, before our first meeting, has since been welded in place, so I'm afraid I can't offer to drown you there. In fact, it would be awkward if I were to leave your corpse anywhere in Eagles. I suggest, therefore, that we meet for a game of follow-the-leader *outside* Eagles. If you use the maintenance exit at the north end of the Upper Promenade within the next half hour, you will find me waiting on the roofs. Bring warm clothing and climbing gear. I trust you as a man of your honor to burn this note beforehand, and not to tell anyone.

Sincerely,
A Friend

P.S. If you don't happen to feel well enough to come, I'll understand perfectly; I wouldn't dream of calling you a coward the next time we meet.

Dick crumpled the paper. His hands were cold; his heart was thumping with anger and apprehension. Coward, was he? Keel was the coward, ducking a fair fight for a crazy thing like this. Probably he wouldn't even be there himself; it was ridiculous . . . even in daylight, the thought of those dizzy heights was unpleasant; it would be twice as bad at night, in the cold, with that wind rushing up the mountain.

He turned. No, he'd be a fool to walk into such a trap. Besides, it was late, and he was tired, and not completely sober. . . .

Reluctantly, he halted. That was all true, but it didn't make any difference: of course he'd have to go.

He picked up the wadded paper where he had dropped it, and burned it in an ashtray. It went up with a mocking *whoosh,* as if it had been soaked in some inflammable solution. Nerves jangling, Dick went back to his wardrobe to dress. He chose the warmest clothes he could find, heavy riding pants, a fleece-lined sweat shirt, loose and comfortable, worn over a turtle-necked jersey. He hesitated between warm gloves and thin ones; finally chose the latter. It would be bad to have numb fingers, but worse, probably, to have a clumsy grip. He put on a pair of his Army riding boots; they were strong, but as flexible as chamois. He clipped his stick to the belt, but removed the elbow chains. As an afterthought, he filled a small flask with brandy and stuffed it into his pocket. He cast a last glance around the apartment, at the warm bed waiting and the rich disarray of the wardrobe. Then he slipped out into the corridor.

The Upper Promenade was deserted under the stars. Dick found the maintenance door, an unobtrusive gray-painted square of metal, under the ornamental scrollwork on the north wall. It had a stout latch, hanging open.

He slid the door open against its spring and cautiously put his head out. It was a bright, cold night, the blue of gun-metal. High in the starred dome hung a crazy, three-quarter moon, and here below, all things were flooded with an eerie whiteness: roofs, copings, cupolas, and the upper slopes of the mountain itself, all silent and bare in the night.

A few yards away, standing at ease on the ribbed metal roof, was Keel. His breath puffed white. Under the shelf of his brow, his eyes glittered.

Dick moved forward, letting the door close behind him.

The wind was chill on his face; the stars in their vast dome seemed to crackle with cold. He looked around. Beyond the bulk of the Promenade, from which he had just emerged, Eagles showed itself as a forest of peaked roofs, domes and minarets. Every window was a dark eye; only the Tower itself, looming like a mirage beyond the sea of roofs, sprayed yellow light from its peak.

The wind howled steadily, beyond the short roof on which they stood. Keel's voice rang hollow: "Well met by moonlight!"

Dick kept advancing until he was only a few paces from Keel. The blond man was dressed much like himself, in leather jacket and whipcord trousers with high laced boots. With the moon behind him, his face was in shadow, lit only by the faint reflection that came from the polished roof. Behind a puff of vapor, his teeth gleamed. "I thought I had suggested that we come without weapons?"

Dick pointed to the long-handled pickaxe that protruded over Keel's shoulder. "What about that?"

Keel glanced toward it. "Climbing equipment . . . very useful, but let's start even." He unslung the axe, together with the coil of light rope that was clipped at his shoulder, and flung them together toward the edge of the roof. They fell into silence.

Dick shrugged and removed his stick. It clattered briefly on the roof, then a gust took it and he saw it whirling end over end, receding into the void, before it dipped downward again and was lost.

Keel was waiting with an ironic smile. "Ready, then? Let's go." He turned his back and started off diagonally across the roof. At a corner of the Promenade there was a steel ladder. Keel grasped the rungs and clambered quickly up. Dick watched him a moment, then followed. The rungs were icy cold in his hands, and he wished he had chosen the other gloves. Keel's white, foreshortened form was silhouetted a moment against the sky, then it disappeared. Dick climbed, with the wind fluttering and pawing at his back.

At the top of the ladder, he found himself facing an unsuspected slant of metal roof, rising steeply to a peak high over his head. Keel stood up there, in silver and black, waiting.

The ladder continued in widely spaced steel rungs up the slope of the roof. There was nothing for it but to keep on climbing. As he ascended, Keel made him a mocking salute and moved on out of sight again.

The peak of the roof turned out to be one end of a long ridge that ran straight away into the distance and then made a sharp turn, ending in a blocky tower. Tower and roofs were washed in clear white; below them, everything was one inky gulf of shadow, without a gleam to tell its depth.

The ridge itself was flattened, forming a sort of catwalk perhaps eight inches across. On this precarious perch, a few dozen yards away, Keel was standing with his arms akimbo, waiting.

By stretching upward from the last rung, it was possible to plant one foot on the ridge, and then, raising the other, to bring yourself up in an awkward, crouching position. With the cold wind whipping unpredictably against one side and then the other, it was all he could do to steady himself with hands and feet; but shame drove him upright. He stood, with his heart thundering, fighting for balance.

There was a long moment when he was certain he would fall; then that passed, and he could stand without windmilling his arms. The distant figure of Keel made him another ironic salute, and, turning, made off toward the bend in the ridge.

He followed, planting one cautious foot after the other, in an unreal stillness. Except for the wind, and Keel's distant figure moving, there was not a stir of life anywhere in the world; they had left all that down below. The thought of the warm, lighted, busy corridors gave Dick a curious pang: how many times had he walked by down there, without ever suspecting the existence of this lonely world a few yards overhead?

His moon-shadow glided along ahead of him. He could make out the Little Bear, low over the rooftops, and a little higher, the Big Bear, upside down. The Milky Way sprawled in a gigantic arch high above; he hardly dared glance at it, for fear of losing his balance. Imperceptibly, as the minutes went by, he was growing light-headed from the height and the cold, and the theatrical white glare of the rooftops. Up the low tower he went, following Keel, and down the other side into a bewildering maze of roofs and walls. They climbed ladders sometimes, and sometimes scaled crowstep

101

gables where the pitch of the roof was too steep to walk. Dick's ears were singing with the cold, his fingers and toes numb with it, but he followed wherever Keel led; his sense of danger was muted, almost inaudible, like a familiar sound droning away somewhere in the distance.

After a long time they paused to rest, each astride the ridge of a steep roof; Keel turned and they sat facing each other, a dozen yards apart. All around them was the sky and the silent sea of rooftops.

Keel's breath puffed frostily over his head, and his eyes glittered. From somewhere he produced a leather-covered flask, raised it in salute. Remembering, Dick took out his own flask and unscrewed the top. They drank together. The brandy was cold and smooth down his throat, spreading fiery inside his body.

He saw Keel's teeth glitter. "Sorry you came?"

"No!" he called; and in a strange way it was true.

Keel nodded and turned, holding himself precariously with his hands on one slope of the roof while his legs dangled down the other. Then he was hitching himself forward again, and Dick followed.

Now their way was along cornices, clinging by fingertips while the wind lashed them from below; along copings, so weathered that they could not stand but must embrace the frigid stone with legs and arms; down rabbeted quoins and along the gutters of roofs, inching, spread-eagled.

The moon was high when they reached what might have been the end of the world: a steep curb roof, slanting down almost vertically to a curious, wide ledge nearly twenty feet below. Beyond that and on either side there was a chasm which even the rays of the high moon did not fill; it went down and down, and ended only in black shadow.

Standing at a wary distance from Keel, Dick glanced at him uneasily. This was a dead end; there was no way to go on from here. But Keel was turning his back on the gulf, lowering himself carefully until he hung by his hands from the coaming, his body flattened along the lower slope. His face shone pale, upturned in the moonlight. Then he was gone with a sliding rush, and peering down, Dick saw him safe on the ledge below.

For the first time since the beginning of the adventure, Dick felt foreboding strike his heart. Were they going down into that endless moonlit canyon—over the ledge and down?

"Afraid?" Keel called up softly.

Dick set his jaw. He turned and gripped the curb as Keel had done, then let himself down. The smooth leads were clammy and cold against his body. He swallowed hard; he couldn't see anything below him, and it was hard to make his hands let go. But there was no going back; his fingers re-

laxed, then gripped frantically as the slope rushed upward.
His feet struck the ledge with a jar. He came upright, dizzy
and shaken.

Keel was standing a short distance away, staring across
emptiness to the closed and shuttered building opposite. Directly across from him, there was a little iron balcony which
Dick had not noticed before. It looked deceptively close. It
was set a little lower than the level on which they were
standing. But the two buildings, as well as Dick could judge,
were at least fifteen feet apart.

"This is where the tackle would have helped," said Keel,
without turning his head. Dick saw what he meant. There
was a projecting cornice above the balcony; if you could
catch a hook on that, you could swing across quite easily.
But without a rope, it was out of the question. It was fifteen
feet or more—a standing jump, in heavy clothes, and with
that chasm under you. You would have to jump headfore-
most, as if into a pool; it would take more nerve than most
men had.

Keel was removing his gloves, with jerky motions. He
wiped his palms on his jacket; Dick saw that there were
beads of sweat on his forehead. He stepped back until his
heels met the base of the roof. He steadied himself with his
hands on the leads, and looked across at Dick. His face was
strained; there was something like appeal in his eyes.

Dick watched, unable to speak.

Keel straightened, swung his arms, and stepped forward to
the front of the ledge.

"Keel, don't!" said Dick suddenly, with his heart at his
throat.

Keel shook his head and stepped back again. He took a
deep, painful breath and let it out. He breathed in again, held
it, with his eyes still fixed on the balcony across. "Shut up,"
he said suddenly. "Oh, God." His eyes closed; his teeth
showed in a grimace.

"Keel, listen—we'll bang on the roofs—attract somebody's
attention."

"Never," said Keel. He breathed deep again, hesitated,
then with a curious grunt he started forward. His foot struck
the front of the ledge: he launched himself out in a hard, flat
dive.

Watching, Dick felt the blood drain from his head. The
other man seemed to hang in midair, arms outstretched.
Then Keel's hands struck and clutched at the iron bars. They
slipped; Keel's body went reeling under and hit the wall with
a thud. There was a horrible moment when he seemed to be
hanging there, unsupported, half in shadow below the balcony. Dick heard a gasping cry, and then Keel was falling,
silently, past stage after stage of the moonlit masonry wall,

dwindling: the darkness swallowed him silently up, and then, after another long moment, there was a distant slapping sound that echoed and died away.

THIRTEEN

Dick pressed his back against the leads to keep from falling. His knees had turned to water; he was breathing in great gulps that hurt his chest, and the rooftop world was swinging slowly, nauseously around him.

When it steadied, he looked out across a desolate sea of roofs—angular, flat, sharp-peaked, blunt, set at all angles; here a church-like spire, there two twin minarets, yonder a flattened dome. In all that expanse, not a warm light showed; even the glow at the top of the Tower had gone out. He was alone.

Now he understood what Keel had hoped to do at the end of this journey—reach that balcony and disappear through the door behind it, to leave him here on the ledge, afraid to make the jump and unable to get back the way he had come. It would have worked; it *had* worked . . . Dick turned his eyes away from the balcony. Whatever happened, even if he died here of cold and exposure, he knew he could never bring himself to jump.

What other choice did he have? The roof was sheer at his back, impossible to climb. That left the three sides of the ledge itself, and kneeling down cautiously, hating himself for the effort it took, he peered over each of them in turn. On the right, there was sheer masonry, unornamented; not a fly could get down that wall. Straight ahead, letting his head hang over, he could just make out the dim gleam of some ornamental stonework a dozen feet down; below that, nothing that offered any hope, and even that far it would be impossible to descend without climbing tackle.

On the left, the building abutted the gable-end of a somewhat lower roof, set back ten feet or so. The next building was of the same height and had a pyramidal roof; then there seemed to be a gap. Both roofs had stout gutters, and it looked to Dick as if he could make his way around that pyramidal roof on either side toward the east. It would be something, a beginning—if only he could get from the ledge to the first roof.

But the wall on this side was as sheer as the other; only a faint continuation of the front wall's ornamental ridge—a mere toe-hold, and that too far down to be of any use.

No, Keel had known what he was doing; there was only one way to get to this ledge, and only one way to get off it. He was trapped.

He stood erect, looking and listening. Nothing had changed; there was no movement and no sound, except the faint, far-off singing of the wind. He forced himself to turn slowly, inspecting with minutest care every visible wall and roof: there might be some small thing he had missed that would save him. But everything was the same as before; every window was shuttered and barred.

Now that he was standing still, the cold numbed his body. He realized suddenly that this was the beginning of his death.

At that thought, his heart began hammering again; life ran thickly at his throat, impossible to deny. He dropped down on his knees again at the left side of the ledge, staring at the distant roofs and then at the blank wall below him—concentrating fiercely, as if by an effort of will he could create a way across.

Moonlight was slanting down the wall, picking out every tiny irregularity. The more he stared, the more it seemed to him that some of those dark spots were actually pits in the masonry. There was a cluster of them directly below, and then a few more at random intervals to the left. About halfway to the next roof, a shallow groove began; if he could reach that, with his toes on the narrow ridge— It began to seem remotely possible; but that first five feet of wall, with emptiness yawning under it: that was a horror.

The moonlight was deceptive; it was impossible to tell how deep the pits might be. The darkest ones were out of reach; Dick leaned over and probed the nearer ones with his fingertips, but found them disconcertingly shallow, mere hollows in the stonework.

Sitting with his legs crossed on the cold ledge, he stripped off his gloves—another reminder of Keel—and then, after a moment's hesitation, his boots and socks as well. The boots were too unwieldy to carry, but he would need them again if he managed the crossing, whereas if he didn't— He slung them one at a time across to the adjoining roof, where they slid to the gutter with an unpleasant slithering rattle.

He knelt, then lay down with his legs dangling over. It was easy enough to find the crannies with his bare toes, although they already ached with cold; it was harder to let himself down with his weight on his forearms, searching for lower toe-holds; then the moment came when he was clinging by toes and fingertips, and could get no farther down without releasing the top of the wall: and that was impossible.

Somehow he did it, with one hand and then the other. Gripping with fingers and toes, he pressed himself to the wall. Once, when he took one hand away to hunt for another hold, the fingers of his other hand began to slip. A cold dizziness took him; he clawed for the same hold again, found it and hung panting, while the salt sweat stung his eyes.

After a time he gathered up courage to try it again, and this time succeeded. Now his toes were on the masonry ridge, and the worst was over. In a few cautious steps he reached the groove at chest level. When the groove ended, the roof was tantalizingly close. He inched toward it, straining as far as he could from his last hold, then jumped. He landed flat on his chest, knee and one hand in the gutter.

It would have been pleasant just to lie there, with the roof solid under him. But he still had a long way to go. He found his arms and legs astonishingly weak, but contrived to get his boots back on, and climb to the ridge of the roof.

The pyramidal roof was set as a corner-piece between two gable roofs forming an L; it was too steep to climb safely, but it gave him only one nasty moment as he swung across the corner from one gutter to the next.

From the ridge of the third roof, far down, glimmering distantly, he saw a glow of yellow light.

It was a glass-roofed courtyard, and the light came from a row of antique city street lamps that lined the ornamental pathway, three levels down. Dick knew the place well; Vivian's suite overlooked it at the back, and he even thought he could tell which was her bedroom window.

He had been over an hour reaching the spot across the roofs; he was tired and half frozen, and there was no more sensation in his fingers. He had fallen, coming down the lightning rod to the sunken glass roof, and bruised his shoulder; now he crouched on the glass, feeling the warmth from below while his breath steamed around his head. There was a maintenance door in the corner of the roof; from here he could see the ladder and the little platform that led up to it; but it was locked.

The lights, down under the glass, seemed to swell and contract as he looked at them. His head was clear, but everything he saw had an unreal vividness and beauty: the lamps, the flagstones glittering, the very stones of the façade held him with their unusual shapes and textures. He could see each leaf of the plane tree to his right, silhouetted, yellow-green intermingling with a mystery of darkness.

He was out of the wind here, and the slow warmth from the glass relaxed his limbs. He had no desire to be elsewhere, or even to get up from his knees; his body seemed almost to belong to someone else.

A vague idea came to him that he ought to make an effort now, while he still could. He got one foot up and stamped with it half-heartedly on the glass pane. He stamped harder:

the outer pane broke, and a rush of warm air came up around his ankle.

He stepped down with both feet, pushing the slabs and splinters of glass aside. He stamped, with one foot at a time and then, holding onto the framework, with both. The inner pane cracked; he felt himself falling, and clutched hard at the framework. There was a wrench at his shoulders, then the balcony of the topmost window was coming up to meet him. He fell, and lay where he fell, looking up incuriously as a dim light came on inside.

Someone came to the windows and opened them; he saw eyes staring and heard exclamations. Then he had the notion that he was being carried, and some time afterward, looked up to see Vivian Demetriou bending over him, her dark eyes depthless in the lamplight.

It was a different bed, and a different room, but the impression was very strong that he was back in that bedroom after his fight with Ruell; he had a curious feeling that Clay had been here only a moment ago, but he was certainly not here now; there was no one in the room but Vivian and a servant girl moving quietly at the sideboard. She came across with a tray now, and Vivian took the ruby wineglass from it, dismissing her with a turn of the head.

With a rustle, Vivian moved to the bed beside him and leaned over to raise his head. She held the glass to his lips: it was tawny port, rich and warming on the tongue. His head rested in the curve of her arm; he could smell her scent, dry and fresh, like sandalwood.

"Was it a walk on the roofs?" she asked softly.

He closed his eyes briefly in assent.

"It must have been terrible," she said in the same drowsy half-whisper. Her brown satin negligee was open loosely down the front, lace-edged, and in the opening there was a shadowed gleam of flesh that moved liquidly when she moved. The rim of the glass touched his lower lip again; he shook his head.

She set the glass down behind her and let his head fall gently back to the pillow. "And the other man? . . . Was he killed?"

He nodded, conscious of the warm curve of her side that pressed against him as she breathed. His lips were sweet and sticky with the wine.

Slowly she leaned nearer; slowly and deliberately her mouth descended on his.

FOURTEEN

On a fine morning in July, the Boss and some men of his inner circle were standing, dressed for the hunt, waiting to board the express car that would take them to the valley floor. The men of the circle had been scrupulously early; the Boss had been even later than usual, but now he seemed in no hurry. He stood at the edge of the terrace, a little separated from the group, staring out through the glass at the clear, bright arch of the sky, palest of blues, with a few high streaks of cirrus visible. A con-trail was slowly prolonging itself from left to right in the middle distance; the Boss watched it, absently pulling one glove tighter and then the other.

The white line of vapor suddenly bloomed at the end: petals of gray sprouted and spread. There was an exclamation from someone in the group; heads turned.

Seconds went by; then the glass rattled suddenly and fiercely to a rushing *whooom* of sound that passed overhead. "My God!" said someone. The gray cloud was diffusing; there were some descending streaks of vapor. The con-trail was still etched across the sky, ending now in a round blur. Lower down, three or four small craft began to converge toward a spot on the ground.

The Boss turned his head slightly and asked a question; one of his secretaries scurried forward and answered it. Nothing more was said. The Boss signed for the car to be opened, and they all trooped aboard.

Half an hour later, by chance, two of the men met beside the body of a freshly killed buck. It was in a stony clearing in the foothills south of Eagles; the airport was only a quarter of a mile away, invisible over the rise. The Boss's helicopter, from which he had shot the buck, was hovering not far away. Two foresters were working over the body, poisoning it for the vultures that wheeled high overhead.

"Those carrion eaters are getting to be a problem," said Palmer, casually, reining his horse nearer. He was the Boss's Transport Secretary, a choleric man with deceptively mild blue eyes.

"They are," said Cruikshank, stroking his red-gold whiskers. Both men glanced up, not at the vultures, but at the hovering copter.

"Do you know who was on that plane?" Cruikshank asked.

"Certainly. It was Rumsen, on his way back to Ischia."

108

"I was afraid of that," said Cruikshank. He was the Secretary of the Army. "The question is now, what will the Duce do?"

"Send another messenger next time, I suppose: that much is all to the good."

"No." Cruikshank turned to look at him directly. "It's a bad business, Gene. I've seen them go like this before. They're like old rogues; they get the taste of it and can't stop."

Palmer took out a cigarette and lit up, blinking at Cruikshank over the pale flame. "He'll never kill anybody in Eagles. That's an obsession with him."

"No, but are you safe *now*?" He saw Palmer glance up involuntarily toward the dark shape in the copter. "Will you be safe tomorrow, or next month? You know he's tired of slaves, Gene—he wants bigger game."

Palmer said, "I've got to think about it."

Cruikshank sat his horse quietly. The sun was warm on his shoulders; beyond Palmer, the buck's filmed eyes stared up at him. It was a good buck, an eight-pointer. Flies were clustered on the spot of blood that had welled from one nostril. It was a duped buck, of course; plentiful as game was in the surrounding country, they had to stock these few hundred acres for the Boss's hunts. It even seemed to Cruikshank that there was something familiar about the buck; after all it was possible; how many times, he wondered, had this same buck died here in the sun?

Palmer said, "If I thought there was any alternative—"

Cruikshank said with gloomy satisfaction, "But there isn't."

"I wonder if we'll like the next one any better?"

Cruikshank smiled grimly, gathering up the reins. The foresters were finished and walking toward their horses; the copter was drifting off to westward.

"Julius, Augustus, Tiberius," said Cruikshank under his breath, "Caligula, Claudius, Nero . . ."

FIFTEEN

The patrol slogged down the stony mountain trail. The sun was burning overhead in a bright, clear sky. Bringing up the rear, Dick looked with distaste at the bobbing heads of the six foot-soldiers, and the rumps of the two pack animals. His throat ached for water, but there was no use risking another rebuff by asking Lindley to halt the column while he refilled his canteen.

The transport had dropped them with what seemed to Dick very short supplies. There was a rule, of course, against carrying a Gismo into hostile territiory; they were "roughing it," Lindley said.

Up ahead, a voice was lifted in nasal song: "*A girl who played poker with Tucker, was deathly afraid that*—" Lindley, who looked frail as a pipestem, was enjoying himself.

Two days ago, Clay had come to him with an air of suppressed excitement. "Dick, something big is about to happen."

"You mean the turnover?"

"Hush! Yes, that's what I mean. How did you know?"

"You've been building me up to it for weeks, haven't you? I wondered when you were going to say something."

"They wouldn't let me be more definite till now. All right, look, this is your chance to get on the right side. There's a man named Lindley in your regiment who's about to be sent out on a routine mission. When he comes back, he's going to get a promotion and a new assignment, to the Chief Armorer's office. Now, we have to have a man in that spot, and it can't be Lindley—he's untrustworthy. So we're going to get you assigned to that mission under Lindley. All you have to do is . . . make sure he doesn't come back."

There was no question in Dick's mind which side he was on, in spite of the traditional loyalty of Buckhill to the Boss's family. Such considerations did not bother him at all. What was bothering him was this business of Lindley. It wasn't that he liked the man, either: Lindley was a pale-haired, pink-skinned, popeyed man with an intensely irritating condescension of manner, and a really reptilian irony. It would actually be a pleasure to kill him . . . and that was the trouble.

Whenever he thought about Buckhill—infrequently, nowadays, there was so much else to occupy his mind—he was sobered to realize how deeply he had changed in a matter of a few months. He could still remember the anguish and horror he had felt, that afternoon on the lawn, when Cashel fell.

Now, that image was all blurred and mixed up with the memory of Keel's body dropping into the moonlit canyon. Two duels, two deaths, and now he was being asked to bloody his hands again.

What if he found he liked it? . . .

Toward noon they stopped and broke out duped rations, watering the horses from a tiny stream that rushed down the valley side. Lindley, reclining at ease with his pack for a pillow, examined the hill above them through a pair of binoculars. "Ah," he said suddenly. "Sergeant, take two boys and see if there's anybody home up there—right there, above that big gray boulder."

The slob saluted, motioned to two others; in a few moments they were out of sight in the thick second growth of hemlock and spruce. Dick trained his own binoculars on the spot Lindley had indicated. All he could make out was a tangle of dead branches, like a heap of deadwood washed down in the spring floods, or like an impossibly big bird's nest.

After a while he saw the soldiers' mottled green uniforms appear among the trees. Lindley's squawk-box came to life and said, *"Nobody here, misser."*

"Anything inside?"

"Just some junk, misser—couple of skins, bones. Garbage."

"All right," Lindley said indifferently, "photograph it, leave a trap and come down."

Dick looked with puzzlement at the two Polaroid snapshots the sergeant brought back: they showed a man-high tangle of sticks, rudely interlaced, matted with dead leaves and mud. The interior view showed a few well-gnawed bones, probably of deer and rabbit, and a small heap of stiff-looking skins. There was a shard of pottery in the litter.

"Ever see a lair like that?" Lindley asked, taking the pictures.

"No, never. What kind of animal is it?"

"Human animal," said Lindley, scribbling on the backs of the snapshots. "Worst and most vile scavenger in the world. Poisonous bite, too. Well, we'll surprise this one if he comes back. Probably he won't."

"Are you saying that somebody *lived* in that pile of branches?"

"House, if you please," said Lindley, with his ironic pop-eyed stare. "Don't they have anything like that in your part of the country?"

"No. There are a few colonies of fishers in the swampland, but they live in something that looks like a house, at least—some even have chimneys."

"That's because you keep the Indians out," Lindley commented. "A mistake, if you don't mind my saying so. Give me a nice clean Comanche any time, over those lumps of dirt."

Dick was staring up the hillside. "What do they do in the winter?"

"Oh, starve. Freeze. They've forgotten how to make fire, you know. Some of them last through, eating all the grease they can get. There's plenty of game, of course, but they can only catch cripples. Very bad nutrition. They have scurvy and rickets, not to mention lice, fleas, ticks and mites." He looked at his watch. "Time to be moving. Sergeant, saddle up."

A few hours later they were filing into a steep little valley, past hillsides blue and fragrant with lupines, down to the foaming stream that sparkled under the cottonwoods. Dick saw a fish leap, a clean arc in the sunlight; the air was full of the thunder and spray of the water, the rocks in the stream glistened with it. He swallowed involuntarily, feeling an itch to dismount and clamber down among those stones.

To his astonishment, Lindley gave the signal to halt. In a few moments, the horses were pegged out under the trees, two soldiers were scrambling for firewood, and Lindley himself was squatting tailor-fashion beside the stream, rummaging in his pack.

"What now?" asked Dick, coming up.

"Now," said Lindley, fitting together the sections of a fly rod, "we wait. We are at the agreed spot, at the agreed time. Our contact may please himself to turn up today, or he may not. In the meantime—" he handed Dick the rod, and began to assemble another—"we fish."

Dick chose a colorful, wet fly from Lindley's collection, and cast upstream with care, but little finesse was needed: the stream was swarming with trout. Between them they had landed a dozen in less than half an hour, all of the same species, unfamiliar to Dick, with red-spotted sides and a yellow dorsal fin.

After dinner they lay at ease on their sleeping bags, watching the sky darken and the first stars come out. Crickets were thrumming in the fields above; a fresh, cool air drifted up from the stream, invisible now behind the dark tree-trunks. The dying fire glowed red. A little distance away, one of the tethered horses stamped and nickered. Lindley rolled over on one elbow; Dick saw his eyes glisten in the half-light.

From up the slope came a hail: "Halt! Who goes there?"

The answer came in a low, guttural voice: "Friend."

"Advance and be recognized, friend."

Lindley had his revolver in one hand; with the other, he stubbed out his cigarette in a shower of tiny red sparks. Dick sat up. At first he could see nothing, then he made out two shadowy forms descending the slope. At Lindley's command, one of the other soldiers threw a handful of branches on the fire. The dry twigs blazed up; in the wavering light, Dick saw the approaching man's face. It was flat and brown, the nose wide, the hair coarse and black under a dirty felt hat. Gold rings glittered in the man's ears; he was dressed in a leather jacket and blue Levi's that clung to his bandy legs.

"Hello, Johnny," said Lindley, rising. "That's all right, Pierce; go back to your post. Sit down, Johnny—you like coffee?"

The Indian grunted and sat down. "This is Johnny Partridge," said Lindley. "He's a Klamath; his people were chased out of Oregon by the Arapaho about fifty years ago. Not many of them left; Johnny does odd jobs for us now and then, don't you, Johnny?"

"Do good job," said the Indian, taking a steaming mug of coffee from one of the soldiers. He sipped it noisily and handed it back. "More sugar."

"That's right, four spoons for Johnny," said Lindley. His pink face was keen and cruel in the firelight. "And plenty sugar, plenty tobacco for Johnny, if he gives us good information."

"Two rifle," said Johnny, raising his hand. "Hundred box cartridge."

"One rifle and ten boxes of cartridges," said Lindley, "*if* the information is good enough, Johnny."

"Plenty good. White man big medicine cross. Plenty trouble." With his hand he sketched a Gismo-shape in the air, so accurately that Dick was half convinced. How could anybody out here in the wilderness have got hold of a Gismo?

"Heaven only knows," Lindley had said the day before, "but it's just possible, and of course we have to be sure."

Now Lindley was saying, "You see big medicine cross yourself, Johnny?"

A vigorous nod. "Plenty big medicine. You come now, I show you."

"Think there's anything to it?" Dick asked Lindley as they were mounting.

"Oh, probably not. Johnny's never seen a real Gismo, only pictures. He's an incorrigible liar, anyhow; all Indians are." The column was forming; Lindley chirruped to his horse and trotted off to the head, leaving Dick to bring up the rear as before.

The roar of the stream fell behind them; the darkness closed in. Dick could barely see past his horse's head, except when they were mounting a rise and the rest of the column was silhouetted against the stars. There was no sound in the world except for the plodding of the horses' hooves and the faint jingle and creak of harness.

When the moon rose, low in the south, they were picking their way around the shore of a quiet lake, one sheet of dull silver beyond the jagged shapes of the pines. They rode, with brief rests, most of the night; the moon had set again when they came to a halt at last near the crest of a ridge.

"We rest here until dawn," said Lindley in low tones, gathering them around him. "No fires, no smoking, no loud talking. Sergeant, post two guards; the rest of you sleep if you can."

There was frost on the ground, and the air had turned bitter chill. Dick dozed fitfully in his sleeping bag, and woke to feel Lindley shaking him.

113

The sun was a faint greenish glow on the horizon; he could see the shapes of men and horses only as flat cardboard cutouts in the gray half-light. "Come with me," said Lindley.

They climbed to the top of the ridge, and lay down on the needle-carpeted ground, facing across the canyon. Beyond Lindley, Dick could make out the flat-hatted shape of Johnny Partridge. The other side of the canyon was a gray blank between the trunks of the pines. "Johnny claims he can see them already," Lindley remarked in an undertone, "but I think he is lying. Keep your eye on the skyline over there."

The sky insensibly brightened; there were silvery streaks, pale and cold, over the eastern horizon. Shadows could be distinguished, and a little color crept back into the world. Somewhere behind them a coyote was barking, a sleepy, lonesome sound. Dick could see now that the opposite crest was heavily wooded in small evergreens, with a few towering lodgepole pines. He blinked. At one moment the scene was absolutely deserted; the next, the shadows under the branches of the trees opposite were full of oval shapes—dozens of them, all at the same height above the ground. As he watched, he actually saw a doorway appear in one of them and a tiny man-shape clamber down an invisible hanging ladder.

"Ah!" said Lindley beside him. There was a click and a rustle as he brought his rifle up to firing position. Dick saw him squinting through the scope; then he lowered the rifle again with a sigh. "Nice target, but we must have patience. Did you see him, Jones?"

"Yes."

"They're something new in this district—weren't here when I came through two years ago. According to Johnny, they're a mixed crowd, half-breed Arapaho and Sarsi, escaped prisoners and that kind of thing, all interbred with degenerate whites. A cut above our friends of yesterday, though; they've got up to the monkey level."

The bottom of the canyon was a dry watercourse, choked with deadwood; the opposite slope was steeply eroded. "What I want you to do," Lindley said, "is to get across there as quietly as you can, but don't take all day about it. I'll give you three boys and Johnny for an interpreter; the rest of us will stay here and snipe."

The shadows were just beginning to darken when Dick and his squad reached the top of the trail. Somewhere a cur began to bark, and then another. One of the tree houses shook abruptly, and a head popped out of the doorway.

Behind them there was the short, sharp bark of a rifle.

Splinters flew beside the primitive's head, and he ducked back inside with a shrill cry. Other tree houses began to shake; there was a confusion of emerging bodies, dogs barking, voices calling urgently back and forth in the morning air. Back on the other ridge, the rifles spoke again and again: a body fell thrashing into the brush at the foot of a tree.

At Dick's gesture, the soldiers had spread out along the edge of the village. He looked around for Johnny Partridge; there he was, to the right. "Tell them to bring it out," said Dick.

The Indian nodded. He threw back his head and uttered a short burst of guttural syllables, high-pitched, that made his throat pulse like an animal's.

After a moment, a hidden voice answered. Johnny Partridge listened, then turned. "They say no white man medicine cross here. Big liars."

Dick shrugged. "All right, we'll do it the hard way. Tell them—"

He was interrupted by a shout of warning from across the canyon. He caught a glimpse of a dark figure in the doorway of one of the huts, one arm raising a stick; then the hut erupted in a shower of splinters. The guns across the canyon were firing almost continuously; every shot was going into the same hut. The primitive's body leaned out, and Dick had time to see the long bow in one hand before it toppled and crashed below. Something dark began to drip from the woven bottom of the hut.

Dick turned distastefully away.

"Tell them," he said, "the same thing will happen to any of them that try that again. Tell them to stay in their huts till we say to come down."

Johnny Partridge translated, in another high-pitched gush of syllables. There was silence.

Dick pointed to the nearest hut. "This one first."

The Indian moved nearer, shouted again. After a moment the curtain moved and a timid, hating face peeped out. The primitive tossed down a rope-and-stick ladder, climbed down it and stood empty-handed, looking from face to face with a feral alertness. Dick gestured to the soldier on his left. "Up you go."

The soldier saluted and scrambled up the ladder. There was an instant howl when he disappeared inside; the hut shook violently, and after a moment the soldier reappeared, struggling with another primitive. They toppled out, but both saved themselves by clutching at the doorway. The soldier, uppermost, gave the primitive a boot down, and she—it was a female—sullenly descended beside the male. Like him, she was black-haired and yellowish-skinned; she had broad shoulders

115

and pendulous breasts. Neither wore anything but a strip of bark, fore and aft.

"Anything up there?" Dick demanded.

The soldier hesitated. "I didn't have time to look good, misser."

"Up you go, then." The soldier climbed, disappeared, put his head out. "Nothing here, misser." He came down.

"All right. They can go up again. Tell them we don't want their women."

When the Indian translated, the two primitives looked incredulous. They glanced at each other, then slowly climbed the ladder.

There was a struggle at the next hut, and the next; then it grew easier. Every hut in the village was emptied and examined.

The Gismo was not there.

Johnny Partridge barked a question at the last hutful of primitives, a male, female and a half-grown boy. The male answered briefly. Johnny Partridge asked another question. The male said something short and pithy, and then spat.

The Indian's eyes were glittering as he turned to Dick. "I ask him, where white man big medicine cross. He say he don't know. Then I ask him where old holy man. He say old man dead. Big liar. Find old man, find big medicine cross!"

Dick peered into the forest beyond the village. There was nothing to be seen; they might waste days beating around these woods.

"Big cowards," said Johnny Partridge. "Little bit hurt, they talk, okay?"

Dick hesitated. "Go ahead."

Johnny Partridge stepped forward, seized the boy and jerked him away from his parents. The boy stumbled and fell to his knees. Holding him by the hair, Johnny Partridge put a knife against his throat.

The parents came forward a step, with cries of alarm, then stopped, looking at the soldiers' leveled rifles. Johnny Partridge asked his question; the boy said something in a high, strangled voice. The Indian asked again. The knifepoint nicked the skin; the boy felt blood running down his chest. He spoke again in a terrified gabble.

Johnny Partridge looked pleased. The parents uttered sounds of horror; guttural questions came from every side of the clearing, and the parents shouted in reply. In a moment the village was in an uproar.

"Come on," said Johnny Partridge, jerking the boy to his feet. "We go quick, he show place."

Dick saw angry faces glaring down from the hut doorways in every direction. A gun barked from across the canyon,

116

and a warning shot splintered through one of the huts. The gabble of voices grew louder.

As Johnny Partridge pushed the boy forward, the parents fell on him. They swayed together in a tangle of limbs. At Dick's motion, one of the soldiers stepped up and clubbed them with his rifle butt, one after the other. Johnny Partridge was streaming with blood from a torn ear and a scratch over one eye, but he had kept his grip on the boy's arm. They moved on.

The boy was sobbing, almost doubled over with his hand held by the Indian in the small of his back. He led the way past a muddy spring into the forest. After a few yards they came to another clearing, rudely planted with stunted corn. Beyond that, an almost imperceptible trail led deeper into the trees.

The clamor behind them swelled again. They heard a fusillade of shots, then a crashing in the forest on either side. Running footsteps came up behind them. Turning, Dick saw the soldier beside him swing up his rifle, heard the crash of the shot, loud among the trees, and saw the running primitive pitch forward.

Voices were calling on either side. "Better hurry it up," said Dick to Johnny Partridge. The Indian nodded, and they swung off at a trot. The firing had stopped.

The trail bent and ended suddenly in front of a sandstone cliff. In the cliff was a cave opening, closed by a hide curtain. The curtain twitched aside and a primitive leaned out, bow in hand. One of the soldiers went down with a feathered arrow in his shoulder. The other two fired together and the primitive fell, bringing the curtain down with him. Dick heard a long wail of despair from the woods.

Inside, the cave was dark and smoky; it smelled of excrement, rotten meat, garbage and other things. On one side, the floor was heaped with skins, ugly, earth-colored pots and jars, and a clutter of smaller articles. From a pole jammed across the roof of the cave hung a green side of meat, swarming with flies.

At the rear, the cave narrowed and there was another hide curtain. In front of this stood an old male.

He was emaciated, dirty and unkempt: his wild eyes stared out of a tangle of grayish hair. He was dressed in a garment made of cloth, that might once have been magnificent by the primitives' standards, but it was frayed and tattered now, gray and greasy and stiff with dirt; his bony chest showed through it and it hung in festoons to his knees. He waved his clawed hands at them, mouthing something toothlessly. His mad eyes rolled; he did a little shuffling dance, back and forth in front of the hide curtain.

"Crazy man," said Johnny Partridge, respectfully. "Very old, very holy."

"Get him out of the way," Dick said.

The nearest soldier made a pass with his rifle butt; the old male leaped nimbly back and disappeared through the curtain. At Dick's gesture, another soldier ripped the curtain down.

In the dancing light that came from a wick in a little pot of oil, the old male was grimacing and gibbering with fear, flinging out his arms and then drawing them back. There was not much else in the cave: just a kind of rude altar scooped out of the sandstone, and on the altar, standing upright, a cross of wood.

Just that. Not a Gismo.

Two pitiful crossed sticks, bound together by sinew, with a snakeskin dangling from either side.

SIXTEEN

As it turned out, the primitives' arrowheads had been poisoned. They had extracted the arrow from the soldier who was hit, without any trouble, but an hour later the fellow died in tetanic convulsions. That offered an opportunity.

They made camp when night fell, on an elevated slope which would be hard to attack without warning. The sky was clear. Dick felt the earth swinging ponderously under him; the air was still fresh with the powdery smell of sage. In the darkness and silence, Dick felt himself paradoxically close to Buckhill. Remembered scenes came vividly into his mind: the green lawns; the early-morning shadows under the stable eaves; the sparkle of sun on the lake. He thought he understood now for the first time how much Buckhill was worth—how much his father had willingly paid, and *his* father before him.

Eagles, by contrast, had a curiously transient quality in his recollections: it was like a tournament field, full of turbulent action, all-important while it lasted. You had to survive, to keep your feet, not as an end in itself, but because that was the price you paid—the test of your fitness.

The coal of Lindley's cigarette glowed fiercely, then arced into the night and went out.

"Good night, Jones," he said. "This time tomorrow we'll be home, with feathers in our little caps."

But the poison was already in his body. Dick had switched canteens when they were filled at midday. "This one," Clay

118

had explained, holding up the tiny bottle, "is slow but quiet. You have to allow about four hours, but it's tasteless, colorless, you can put it in anything."

In the morning, Lindley was blue in his sleeping bag. In examining the body, Dick contrived to scratch the side of the neck lightly with his ring, and let the soldiers draw their own conclusions from the tiny wound.

They buried him in the hard ground and heaped a cairn over him; and Dick went home to Eagles with lines in his face that had not been there before.

"This is the crucial point," said Melker, with sweat standing on his forehead. The air was stagnant; blue smoke hung wavering over the light. "We have to expand rapidly from a small group to a force capable of taking and holding Eagles: now I say 'rapidly,' because the longer a thing like that goes on, the more the chances add up that somebody will betray us. The safest way to do it is to do it as fast as possible: build the force, strike, and get it over. But when I say 'safest,' now that's relative: we're taking a risk, and a big one."

"Are you suggesting we pull out?" asked Colonel Rosen quietly.

"No!" Melker's forked beard quivered. "No—*that* would be sure suicide, because a lapsed conspiracy is no good, has no value to anybody except as material for betrayal, coercion and so on. I want that clearly understood: we're in, we're committed, all of us—we're going through, whatever happens."

The others looked at him watchfully: Commander Holt, Lady Maxwell, Miss Flavin with her hands primly in her lap, Dr. Belasco, Collundra, Kishor, and two big men, Cruikshank and Palmer, whom Dick had not met before. It was a select group, the inner circle of the conspiracy, and Dick felt out of place in it: why was he here?

"I also," said Melker, leaning back with a sigh, "wanted to see how many of you I could scare. Fortunately, the answer was none."

Two or three faces showed grim amusement. "We're too old at the game for that, Melker," said the Colonel.

"May be, may be, but I'm a suspicious man. Now it happens that I have some reassuring words to balance the scales. As you're aware, Dick Jones here was sent to eliminate young Lindley: now that was an experiment in more ways than one."

Rosen's interest sharpened. "Yes?"

"Lindley was in line for a key job: we are pulling the necessary strings and it appears that we'll have our man there by tomorrow. Now my feeling was that if there had been any abnormal alertness, anything even so vague as a hunch, then a man like Lindley would be bound to be on his guard. Now then, Dick, tell them how you disposed of Lindley."

Dick said, "I put the poison in my canteen, and made sure I got his when the soldier brought them back."

Melker raised his eyebrows expressively. "You see? The oldest trick in the book."

Commander Holt was shaking his head. "You took a long chance, young man."

"Not at all," said Melker. "Lindley was not abnormally alert, which was what we wanted to know, and we gained some valuable information—about Jones as well as Lindley." He glanced knowingly at Dick. "Jones, I may say that we would have warned you in advance about that aspect of the matter, if it would have helped you at all."

"I think I understand, mister," said Dick. Curiosity was overcoming his resentment. So far all this was preliminary: what was going to happen next?

"Now," said Melker, folding his hands into a steeple. "We were agreed that it was desirable to make sure of Oliver before the turnover."

"But not about the methods of doing so," put in Collundra.

"No. True." Melker drew a deep breath; his shrewd eyes twinkled. "But I am able to tell you now that we have succeeded in what we regarded as the most desirable but least likely possibility."

The others were leaning forward, excitement showing in their faces. "Have you—?" said Belasco.

"We have," Melker said, "obtained the prote of the young lady in question, and have had her duped as one of a routine requisition of servant girls. She is in this suite now. Clay has been preparing him all morning, and when he judges Oliver is ripe for the meeting— Yes?"

A dark-eyed man in Melker's livery came forward and murmured something in his ear. "Good!" said Melker. "Men and ladies, the time is at hand. If you will gather around the TV, in a few moments you'll see something interesting."

Dick found himself beside Melker as the group re-established itself on the other side of the room. The TV was on, showing a view of one of the small rooms in this same suite; but the room was empty. Judging by the camera angle, the pickup must be hidden in some piece of furniture, perhaps under a table.

Melker grinned up at him with infectious good spirits. "You may possibly find yourself a little bewildered at all this?"

"A little!" said Dick.

"It's a rare story. Perhaps we have just time for me to run

120

over the high spots. Thaddeus Crawford, the man who built Eagles, married a slave girl. It wasn't unusual in those times; the distinctions weren't as rigidly drawn. She bore him a son, sickened and died; however, Thaddeus had taken the precaution of duping her when he first got her: after all, she was a slave."

"But his *wife*?" said Dick.

"Oh, yes. Certainly. Well, mister, in his later years Thaddeus became somewhat, let us say unusual in his thinking. He grew obsessed by the fear of losing Eagles to upstarts: he wanted to ensure a succession of Thaddeuses. So he prevailed upon his son to marry the dupe of his own wife."

Dick could not repress a start of revulsion.

"Just so; however, you see, technically it wasn't incest—the dupe was a twenty-year-old girl; his mother had died at the age of twenty-five, fifteen years earlier. Well, mister, he married her and they had a son—the present Boss of Colorado. And *she* died. A congenital weakness, apparently. By this time a kind of tradition had been established, you see, and you know what tradition is in a big house; I believe there is even a widespread superstition that no man can hold Eagles who *doesn't* marry the Bosswife. At any rate, our present Boss, Thaddeus II, duped and married her when he was twenty-four. She had a son the same year—Oliver—and died in 2032. The joke is—" Melker grinned like a gargoyle, putting a skinny hand on Dick's sleeve. "The joke is, genetically the idea is all wrong. Thaddeus's son Edmond had half his mother's genes, naturally. Edmond's son, Thaddeus II, has three-quarters of his mother's genes, and Oliver seven-eighths. If this keeps up another few generations, the line will consist of nothing but genes inherited from the mother; not that that wouldn't give a good deal of variation for a while; but poor Thaddeus—*fft!*" Melker waved his hand. "He might just have well have mated his wife to his butler."

Dick felt a stiffening of the bodies around him, and Melker's glance flickered away toward the screen.

He turned. In the screen, Oliver and Clay had just walked into the room. Oliver was dressed in white and gold, gaudier than his usual costume; his hair was freshly coiffed and he looked pale. His lips moved, but whatever he said was lost in the rustle of movement.

"Sh!" said Miss Flavin, angrily. The group quieted.

"Wait here just a minute," Clay's voice said. "I'll have her brought in."

He left the room. Oliver glanced around nervously, one hand on the engraved metal stick he wore, the other fidgeting with the lace at his throat. He flung himself down on a divan, stared blankly at a picture on the wall—one side of it

121

was visible in the screen; it was Frans Hals' "Laughing Cavalier"—then got up again and began pacing back and forth.

Beside Dick, Melker was breathing stridently. He glanced that way; Melker's eyes were bright, his parted lips moist. "His mother died when he was six," he whispered. "Watch him now: watch him!"

Oliver turned at some sound not audible in the screen. After a moment, there was movement: a person advanced slowly into the room.

Like the rest, Dick strained idiotically to see around the side of the TV screen. In a moment, she moved again: the girl took another hesitant step forward, and stood looking speechlessly at Oliver.

She was dressed in the puff-skirted formal costume that had been popular in Eagles twenty years ago; there was something about the arrangement of her pale blonde hair that was even older. She was slender and awkward, and her long, green eyes gazed at Oliver with a kind of numb astonishment. Her parted lips quivered as if they had forgotten there were such things as words.

Oliver went down slowly on his knees. His arms lifted helplessly. "Oh, Mama!" he said. "Mama Elaine!"

SEVENTEEN

Dick awoke to a thunder of running footsteps in the corridor; screams, the crash of glass. He sat up, heart pounding. He blinked as lights flared on in the outer rooms. A door slammed.

"Who's that?" he called. "What is it?"

Alex came running into view, his thin face scared and paper-white. "Oh, misser, misser, they are killing people in the corridors!"

There was a distant explosion that jarred the floor. Then more screams, farther away. Dick got out of bed, thinking furiously. Turnover Day had been put off again and again, in spite of Melker's good intentions; the last Dick had heard, it was set for three days in the future.

Either they had started it prematurely, without warning him, or else there had been a slip-up and the turnover was betrayed.

The valet, shaking but still correct, was holding out his trousers. If only he knew more! "Tell me what you saw, Alex. No, not those—the dress uniform."

"Misser, it was terrible. I was in the Long Corridor, on my

122

way to the Gismo Room for the morning quota. I heard explosions, like it was gunshots. I turned around, all the people was staring, they couldn't believe their eyes. There was running a man, and then just by the little gold fountain, there was another gunshots, and he fell down. It was like a terrible, terrible dream. And the blood, you have no idea . . ."

"Who shot him?"

"I didn't see. I ran. But in our corridor, Misser Jones, it came gunshots again, and then I saw a whole lot of men running, with guns in their hands. And behind them, the red ones, shooting."

"Household Guards?"

"Yes. Shooting, shooting, shooting—I thought they would kill me. Two they did kill, they are lying there in the corridor. I saw also the black ones, Gismo Guards; but then I came in before they could shoot me. Misser Jones, what is going to happen?"

"Hell!" said Dick, jerking at the elbow-chain attached to his belt. It wouldn't give, and then it did. He pulled the chain through the sleeve, then did the same for the other side. Wherever he was going, he might need his arms free.

He knew one thing, at any rate: if the Guards were chasing conspirators, it was all up; one way or another, the attempt had failed. The only question was, how much did they know? If they had all the names, it was just a matter of time before they picked him up. The best thing he could do would be to try to get out of Eagles as fast as possible.

But if they didn't have his name, and he ran, it would be an admission of guilt; whereas if he brazened it out, he might have a chance.

In the corridor were two dead bodies, both huddled against the blood-spattered wall. Dick recognized one of them; it was Thor Swenson, with whom he had been drinking beer only the night before last. The funny thing was, he hadn't known Thor was in the conspiracy.

Up in the Long Corridor there were more bodies, both sexes, slobs as well as people.

An incongruous memory came into his mind, for no reason that he could see: the dead mongrel, back at Buckhill on his last day, with the little slob boy kneeling in tears over it.

He listened. There was no more firing, nothing to be heard except a faint, cadenced marching and a rumble of wheels that grew slowly louder. He heard a voice shouting orders. Out of a cross corridor suddenly appeared a squad of Household Guards with two field artillery pieces. Dick saw the officer in charge glance sharply in his direction, and felt a cold sweat break out on his forehead. It occurred to him for the first time that an Army uniform might be no protection

123

at all; the Army had been deeply infiltrated, and it was ten to one that some of the conspirators had been in uniform when the fighting broke out.

He didn't hesitate. He strode toward the officer, bringing his heels down hard. The guards were wrestling the two field pieces around back to back, to sweep the corridor in both directions. The officer raised his pistol. "Halt. Identify yourself."

"Lieutenant," said Dick firmly but respectfully, "there's some mistake here. General Myer is about to set up an artillery post in that same spot—he went off to see about requisitions not fifteen minutes ago. I'm his adjutant, Lieutenant Jones."

"I take my orders from Home Guard H.Q.," said the other, lowering his pistol. "Where's your sidearm?"

"We haven't been issued any yet. Look, Lieutenant, you haven't got enough men for this operation anyhow. You could be enfiladed from that cross corridor."

"We hold that, clear back to the Arcades," said the Guard officer, but his tone sounded a little less surly. "You Army puffs have got lead in your scuts, like always. Hell, it's all over—we're just here in case. You tell your General Myer—"

He was interrupted by a stentorian voice that shouted, "Your attention! Your attention! There has been an attempt on the life and property of the Boss. All of the ringleaders have been killed or captured by the alertness of the Household Guard. However, some minor members of the gang are still at large. Stay in your present locations until a room to room search can be completed." By craning his neck, Dick could see the source of the voice, a public telescreen in the plaza just ahead. Even from this angle, the picture was clear though distorted. The camera was panning over the heaped bodies of men sprawled in the Armory Courtyard; the bronze Fountain of Commemoration was visible in the background. Dick saw Melker's gnomish face, with all the meaning gone out of it. Blood was matted in his forked beard.

The camera panned up, and he saw a group of people standing near the wall, with their hands tied behind them. One of them was Clay; he glanced at the camera without expression, and looked away.

The camera moved on. Twirling slowly in the air, trussed up by the legs like a fowl from the balcony railing, was another body. With difficulty, Dick recognized the upside-down face.

It was Oliver.

The voice boomed out again: "One of the missing gang members is a woman, age about twenty, hair blonde, complexion fair, eyes gray-green. Any person found harboring this woman will be shot. Any person delivering this woman alive or furnishing information where she may be found, will be rewarded according to status, with quota advancement or high office. Any servant delivering this woman or providing such information, will be rewarded with free status."

The Guard lieutenant whistled under his breath. His loutish face was suddenly drawn and intent. Behind him, all the other guards were looking up with the same expression. They were all slaves, of course; a special kind of slave, with the privilege of bearing arms in Eagles, which made them in some ways superior to any free man; but you could see that any of them would give an arm or a leg to be a *person*. It almost never happened; it was a measure of the woman's importance to the Boss, that he should offer it.

The woman was Elaine. There was no doubt of that, from the description. It was natural for the Boss to want her accounted for—any idiot who had her might think himself qualified to lead another revolt. But if that were all, would he take the risk of manumitting slaves?

There was another possible explanation. When Melker's group had obtained a dupe of Elaine, they might have destroyed or hidden the prote at the same time. Misfiling it would have been enough: it would take forever to find one misfiled prote among the billions.

If that were so, then even if Dick's name was on the blacklist—when things settled down, if he returned with the Bosswife, that might be enough to buy his immunity. It was something: it was a chance.

Feeling the Guards' eyes on him, he glanced at his watch. "I suppose the plans have been changed again," he said. "I'd better go and check."

The Guard lieutenant nodded gloomily. Dick turned and walked away.

Which way? He had to decide quickly: but the girl might have taken any of dozens of exits from the sector of Melker's suite. There were uncountable nooks and crannies; he had less than a chance in a thousand of guessing the right one.

But when he stopped wondering where the girl might be, and thought of his own danger, he had only one instinct: *down*.

So much the better. To track a deer, you had to be a deer. Dick boarded the down escalator at the next plaza, thinking, *I'm frightened. I've got to hide—get out of sight, or they'll kill me. Down. Down deep. Make myself small and pull the covers over my head.*

Now he was on the lowest residential level. The corridors were beginning to fill up here; he passed a roving squad of Guards, and remembered just in time to straighten his back and let his footsteps fall hard. They looked at him sharply, but let him go: he was a man in uniform, moving as if he had a legitimate errand.

Looking for a way down, he saw a door he must have passed a hundred times without seeing it: two swinging panels, with the green stencilled design that meant: SLOB COUNTRY.

He pushed the door open and was in another world. Dim lights shone on the grime of the high ceilings; the walls were of unfinished cement, and the floors were bare except for catwalks of rubber mats laid end to end. A hum of voices and movement greeted him, together with a breath of stale air, freighted with sour, old smells. For an instant, it was like being back in the holy man's cave, and Dick had a curious sense of double vision—the dusty fluorescents overhead, and and flickering, oil-soaked wick below; grime and soot intermingling. Then it passed, and he was moving down the main corridor. Half-dressed slobs looked up sleepily from their bunks as he passed an open doorway. From another came the clangor of tinware and a steamy smell with soap and rotten cloth in it. An old fellow in yellow denims came by, pushing a wheeled rack full of kitchenware. Dick stopped him roughly:

"Where's the exit to the lower level?"

"Misser," said the fellow, looking frightened, "there isn't one, excuse me, except the one that has the seal on it. Nobody goes here to below, it's forbidden. It's the Boss's own seal, I will show you."

He scurried ahead, abandoning the cart, and Dick followed into the next corridor and down a half-flight of stairs. The door was grimy with disuse. It was fastened with a hasp and a padlock; the padlock had an embossed design which Dick could feel with his thumb: a "C" with a finicky shape above it, probably an eagle.

"Get me some tools," he said. "A cold chisel and a hammer. I want that door open in less than five minutes."

"Misser, we have no requisition—"

"Get 'em!" shouted Dick. The old fellow ducked away with a gesture of despair.

In a few minutes he was back, in the center of a little knot of other servants. One of them, inevitably, was Frankie. The gargoyle was carrying a toolbox. He looked unhappy. "Misser Jones, you know we not suppose to open that door without the word from the Boss heself. If you got the word—"

"There wasn't time for that," said Dick. "This is an emergency. Here—" He felt in his pockets, found a scrap of paper. "Give me a pencil, I'll sign for it."

Frankie handed over the stub of a carpenter's pencil, looking dubious. Dick scrawled, "I take responsibility for opening door in servant quarters," and signed it. The slobs looked at

126

it with varying degrees of incomprehension; probably few of them could read or write. Frankie looked unhappier than ever, but carefully folded the paper away, and took a chisel and sledge out of his toolbox. Three powerful strokes sheared through one arm of the staple that held the padlock. Frankie worked the lock free and stood back, holding it in his palm.

Dick opened the door, saw a glimmer of light at the end of a short passage. "Lock this up again behind me," he said, and stepped through.

At the end of the passage, he found himself in a wide, empty hall. The dim lights in the ceiling were not even fluorescents, but old-fashioned incandescent bulbs; they cast a sickly orange glow that left the place almost in darkness. The air was heavy and still. Silence closed in.

Dick felt alone and a little foolish. Suppose the girl hadn't come here at all? Through that door, at least, nobody had come for years. But there were hundreds of possible entrances; if he had stopped to test his hunch by checking each one, it would have taken him forever. Now, at least, he was here; if she had come this way, it ought to be an easy matter to pick up her trail on this side.

He stooped: in the thick carpet of dust there were footprints, but none looked recent. At one side of the room stood several abandoned hand trucks; there were loading bays in the far wall, closed now by metal doors. To right and left were open doorways; nothing was visible through either except darkness, picked out faintly at intervals by more dim yellowish lights.

Dick followed the left-hand corridor past still other doorways, some closed and locked, some open. Through the open doorways, in the dim light, he glimpsed piled, enigmatic masses: once he reached inside and felt the curved smoothness of a table leg. These, evidently, were disused storerooms, full of articles once prized but now forgotten. A disturbing echo of memory awakened: Ruell, saying, "He collects collections. . . . This whole mountain, in fact . . ." How deep did these subterranean storerooms go?

Guided by some obscure compulsion, he took the first stairway down.

He found himself in a clutter of objects piled helter-skelter: tables, sofas, chairs thrusting their legs at him; books sliding and squirming under foot as he moved, lamp shades shaking down clouds of dust.

In the distance, someone sneezed.

The sound echoed and re-echoed under the vaulted ceilings. Dick held his breath, listening, and after a moment heard a faraway, sliding clatter. Someone . . . someone. . . . Who else could it be?

He moved forward cautiously, trying to avoid making any

127

noise, but it was useless. A tilted chair slid out from under him, and his foot went through a fragile table-top with a crunching, rending sound.

Instantly, somewhere in the distance, there was a crash and a scurrying noise. Dick swore, wrenched the table-top loose, and clambered in pursuit. His heart was racing; he vaulted a fallen bookcase, danced precariously in a nest of chairs, climbed an up-ended divan. He stopped to listen.

Faintly, in the distance: *clatter, crash.*

For what seemed like hours, the chase went on. Dick fought his way a few yards at a time through the tangle of furniture and crates; stopped to listen; plunged forward again. Soaked with sweat, gasping like a fish in the stagnant air, he paused with one leg up over the ridge of a mountainous sideboard. There was no sound. He gulped air, held his breath for a moment: still nothing but the pounding of blood in his own ears.

He stared from side to side. In all the vast sea of tablelegs, headboards, mirrors, there was no movement under the dim lights. Impossible that she could have escaped from the vault: the nearest doors were almost invisible in the distance. She had gone to ground: she might be anywhere in that hardwood jungle—crouching under a table, or inside a buried wardrobe; lying still, trying not to let him hear her breathing, like a rabbit in a hedge.

He waited, in hopes she would lose her nerve and bolt again, until he had his breath back. Then he began to move slowly and carefully, trying to make as little noise as possible. He quartered the ground patiently, pausing frequently to listen. On the third cast, a tiny sound broke the silence—the faint creak of wood. Probably she had shifted her position. Not everybody could stand lying still on a hard surface for long.

There was an open crate full of glass-shaded lamps nearby, He took a chance: he lifted one out, a dusty dumb-bell-shaped thing, and lobbed it in the direction he thought the sound had come from. It burst with a startling crash. Shards tinkled all around.

Sharp-eyed, Dick saw a convulsive movement in the forest of chair-legs. He vaulted an Empire sofa, zigzagged precariously across stacks of nested tables, and found himself looking down into a hollow under a big desk. Curled in the hollow, looking up at him with frightened eyes, was the girl.

"All right, come out," he said.

She rose slowly, dusty and tousled in the dim light. There was something curiously pathetic about her thinness, and the smudge of dirt on one cheek. She had ripped half the skirt

128

off her antique dress, he saw: it was not the costume for scrambling around in the storage cellars.

Her frightened expression changed, doubtfully. "Oh, aren't you—"

"Dick Jones. That's right." They had met once, at the last briefing, but only for a minute.

She was trying to laugh. "Well, then, why didn't you say so? I mean, all this—" She gestured helplessly.

"Would you have believed me if I'd told you who I was?" he asked smoothly. "Come on, let's get out of here."

She put her hand in his; her palm was cool and soft. "Where are we going?" she asked as he helped her up. She brushed her long hair back from her forehead. "Can we go back up now? Golly, I must look like an awful mess."

Dick improvised lies about the turnover, which she seemed to accept without question. How young she was! His mind kept coming back to that, newly astonished by the gawky slenderness of her body, or the innocence that showed itself in every word she spoke. Had he ever been that dumb, even back at Buckhill? It seemed unlikely.

He tried to steer a course for the door he had come in by, but when they reached it, it was the wrong one. There was a short stair going down, none going up. A stronger glow of light came from the landing.

The way might be clearer one level down: heaven knew, they could waste days fighting their way through that tangle of furniture. "Come on," he said, taking her arm.

Downstairs there was another vault, illimitable, misty under the bluish ceiling lights. Crates and stacks of all sizes stood at random, but at least there was some space to move between them. Also, there were tracks in the dust that looked recent.

Dick frowned over this. He did not like the idea of meeting anyone before he could get back to the authorities with his prisoner: some officious nobody was likely to take him for the girl's accomplice instead of her captor. However, it was worth the risk to get out of here that much faster. Somewhere on this vast floor there must be an elevator or a stair going up.

Still, the aisle grew narrower and more erratic the farther they went, and the things in the crates began to get very queer, too. Here was a box taller than their heads, through whose dusty, plastic sides they could see, as if frozen in a dirty block of ice, a heap of stuffed animals—rumpled velvet pelts, button eyes staring, threadbare paws. There were teddy bears, elephants, tigers, lions, monkeys . . . all used-looking, not collector's items by any stretch of the imagination, but just junk.

Here was a long case full of books in individual plastic

129

envelopes. Some of the bindings were good, some were even elaborately tooled, but others were scuffed, cracked and torn. Dick paused to read a few of the titles: *Treasure Island; Ozma of Oz; Pepper and Salt.* Then there was a row of narrow volumes with nothing on the spines but a monogram, "TC." One was rat-gnawed; Dick took it down, pulled the envelope off, and opened it in the middle. Under an exercise in square roots, in a boyish hand, was a riddle:

"What has 22 legs and flies? Ans.: A dead football team."

Under that, a drawing of a knife, the pencil lines deeply scored. Dick shut the book and put it back.

"What *is* all this?" the girl asked. "Do you know?"

"It looks as if he never threw anything away," said Dick. He glanced at her curiously. Her face was unconcerned; she looked back at him with a tremulous smile—more aware of him than of anything so remote as the Boss's boyhood.

Curious to think that she had given birth to that boy, who was now the gray toad who ruled Eagles. In fact, if Thaddeus II had been nine or so when that journal was written, then she must have been dead for about four years. . . . It made him a little dizzy to think about it. All that, so deep now in the past, was nothing but an unrealized future to her: she was twenty again, and looked about eighteen; the best thing that could happen to her, he supposed, was to go through it all over again. A good thing for her that she didn't know.

The floor seemed endless. The sounds of their footsteps were muffled; there was a gray musty smell in the air—a smell of papers turning dusty and brittle, packed away out of the light. Everywhere stood the plastic-sided boxes and bundles, some still whole, some not. Then the character of the place began to change. They were passing a row of little buildings, standing isolated like so many crates, some faced with stone or brick on one side, bare wood and plaster on the rest. One had a sign over it, "STRIPPEL'S DRUGS"; the door had been carefully sealed, but the glass was broken out of it.

"Can't we sit down and rest for a minute?" the girl asked. "I'm so tired, I could just die."

Against the dimness inside, he could see the outlines of a table and chairs. "Careful." With a hand on her elbow, he helped her through the broken door, bits of glass snapping underfoot. The chairs were of flimsy wood, cheap twentieth century stuff, but they seemed sound, and there was not even very much dust. Probably the interior had been sealed and filled with inert gas until recently.

They sat down, surrounded on all sides by racks, display cases, pigeonholes: candy here, greeting cards, boxes of film over there, yellowing magazines and paperbacked books. The counters were crowded with cardboard displays; some had fallen to the floor. Dick idly picked one up; there were a few tiny bags of peanuts clipped to the front of it. On the back he read: "Say! Mr. Retailer! Here's a colorful counter display box that has been designed expressly to help you make MORE SALES and MORE PROFITS. . . ." A reconstruction, probably; hardly anything of this kind had survived through the Turnover years.

He was surprised to see the girl's eyes glistening with tears. "What's the matter?"

"I don't know," she said thickly. She leaned her head on one hand, rubbing the heel into her eye. The posture made her neck and shoulders look absurdly fragile; he had an impulse to put his arm around her. Her pale lashes were quite thick and long, he saw; they didn't show when she was looking up. "Don't mind me, I'm just being silly." Her lips were swollen, her cheeks softly flushed.

The chair legs skreeked on the floor. He did put his arm around her. She was soft and slender; her fine hair tickled his chin. After a few moments, she gently pushed him away. "Have you got a kleenex—I mean a tish?"

He handed her one; she blew her nose, dabbed at her eyes. She tried to smile at him. "Don't look, I must look so awful." It was true—her face was swollen and pink, her eyes swimmy, lips puffed—and yet something ached yearningly in his chest. *I'm falling in love,* he thought incredulously.

He recognized the symptoms, although it had never happened to him before. Her features, which had seemed perfectly ordinary half an hour ago, were now unique. He saw that some of them were not particularly beautiful—her ears, for instance—but this simply gave him a feeling of pleasure and pride. Anybody could appreciate her obvious points; he loved everything about her.

Part of him was dismayed by these thoughts—there was no sense nor reason in them—but the rest of him was happily conjuring up new ones, the more irrational, the better. Would he perform menial services for her?—tend her when she was sick, bathe her, feed her, dress her? Yes, gladly. Would he give his life for her? He boggled at that one, but then a fresh wave of feeling took him: maybe he would. His next reaction was one of horror: love was a horrible thing if it could make you destroy yourself. But somehow the horror only added to his pleasure.

She said apologetically, "I haven't even *thought* about drugstores for years. It was just so unexpected." She looked around, biting her lip. "Carter's Little Liver Pills. Oh, my. And there's the fountain. I don't suppose it really works."

She was looking at the dingy marble counter with the stools in front and the mirror behind. "Works?" said Dick.

"I mean, we couldn't make an ice cream soda, or anything. But maybe there would be some water? I'm awfully thirsty."

"I'll see," Dick said, and got up quickly. There were two taps over a slotted metal plate, and he tried them both, but nothing came out. "No, it's dry." Behind the counter he saw a bottle in a half-open compartment, and picked it up. "Here's some ginger ale, though."

"Oh, that would be lovely."

He opened the bottle and used part of the contents to rinse out two glasses. Then he filled them and brought them to the table.

She made a little face. "It's flat, isn't it? But nice," she added quickly, and drank some more. She set the glass down. "I'm glad you found me. I recognized you right away—and did I feel relieved!"

"You did?"

"Oh, yes. You have a very distinctive face. I always remember faces. Yours is so square and serious looking. And you have those bushy eyebrows that go up—" she twirled a forefinger—"at the corners." She was smiling at him, but her eyes were still hazy with tears. "I used to know a boy who had eyebrows like that. His name was Jimmy Bowen. You remind me of him quite a bit."

Dick felt a curious glow of pleasure, and a stab of suspicion. "Where was that?"

"Back at Dunrovin—Mr. Krasnow's estate. My father was the head of the greenhouse there. I don't suppose you ever heard of it; they say it isn't there any more." She looked melancholy again. "Jimmy and I wanted to get married, but Daddy thought he wasn't good enough for me. Then Mr. Sinescu came and saw me, and brought me back here. Of course, all this wasn't built then. There was just the one big building on top of the mountain." She shuddered delicately. "Mr. Crawford was going to marry me, they told me afterward; I think I must have guessed it, and that was what made me fall into my deep sleep."

"Sleep?" said Dick curiously. It was enough just to listen to her, but that word had jogged his attention.

"Why, didn't you know? It's the craziest thing—I slept over seventy years! I don't believe it ever happened to a human before, but they say frogs do it. I didn't wake up till just, let's see, about three weeks ago. I couldn't believe it, till they showed me all this—" She waved her hands; her eyes glittered with excitement, and her teeth gleamed white. "It was just like a dream."

"Then you mean they didn't dupe you?" Dick asked incredulously.

"Oh, *no*. They were going to, but I fell asleep first, and

132

then they couldn't, you see. That was lucky; I wouldn't want to be duped, would you?"

Dick shook his head miserably. He saw it now: she thought she was the original Elaine; she refused to believe she was a dupe, and so she had invented this deep-sleep story and managed to convince herself it was true. There was something pathetic about it; it reminded him of what he had been trying to forget.

This was the fourth Elaine. She was twenty years old, and the other three had all died at twenty-five.

This time it would be different, he told himself fiercely. The thing was, he didn't know what the others had died of: it might have been something to do with childbirth. Or it might be something she had now, without knowing it—something that could be cured, *now*, if anyone took the trouble.

At any rate, the chain was broken—she was never going to marry Oliver. He would have to improvise as he went along—get her out of here somehow without running into the Guards, smuggle her out of Eagles . . . and, he realized suddenly, probably off the continent. It wouldn't be safe to bring her home to Buckhill, except perhaps years later. . . . He had a brief formless vision of his mother and father: *But who are her people? Do you mean to say she is a dupe? A slave?*

He shrugged the thought aside irritably. He couldn't stop to worry about that now, he had too much else on his mind. If only this damned irrational thing hadn't happened to him . . . He had a mental glimpse of how it might have been—his delivering the girl to the Household officials, being congratulated for discretion, perhaps by the Boss in person; preferment, honors, steps up the ladder—planks in the wall that held Buckhill strong and safe.

Almost, he wavered. But he saw Elaine looking at him with her level green eyes; strange, strange, how there was always more meaning in her eyes than in what she said; and he put all that behind him.

There was a scuffling noise at the door. He turned, heart jumping with alarm, but it was only the gargoyle, Frankie—two of him, dressed in gray jumpers and carrying satchels.

He relaxed almost immediately. The Frankies were un-armed—of course—and no guards were coming into view behind them. They must have been sent into the vaults on some routine errand, perhaps to unearth some particular specimen for the Boss's display collections. Still, it seemed odd somehow to meet anyone in this untenanted maze. . . . It was curious, too, how slowly they seemed to be coming forward, like figures under water. Their solemn expressions did not change, but bloomed toward him with a sort of incandescent meaning. Eyes, noses, mouths were as if lit from behind;

133

Dick, forgetting who and where they were, could only stare at them in hopes of deciphering the riddle.

The last thing he heard was a sound that vaguely alarmed him, one that he had been half-noticing for some time; the faint, steady hissing of escaping air.

EIGHTEEN

He and Adam had drifted over the deepest part of the lake, and, for a dare, he had slipped over the side of the boat, down, down to the vaguely glimmering greenish bottom, weedy and dim. Now he was coming up, but it was a long way: he could see the bottom of the boat in a little circle of light, far overhead. It didn't seem to be getting any closer. He schooled himself to kick slowly and evenly. His hurting chest tried to breathe in spite of him; he tightened his jaw and pinched his nose between finger and thumb. There was a drumming in his ears. . . .

He came up with a gasp and a shudder. For a moment the illusion was still so strong that he felt the cold water streaming from his hair; then he saw that he was in a white room, and felt the cushiony hardness of a bed under his back. The light was an old fluorescent, in a bare ceiling. There was movement, a rustle of paper; a figure came toward him.

It was Frankie. "Feeling better?" the gargoyle asked.

"I guess so. My head hurts. What happened?"

Frankie grinned. "The argon knocked you out, misser. Soon as we come in the door, over you go, blam."

"The argon?" said Dick stupidly.

"In the little drugstore. All those places got a little trickle of argon coming in all the time, to take care of the leakage. We never bothered to plug it up, you know, because it don't bother you if you just go in for a minute."

A concentration must have built up, he thought fuzzily; argon wasn't poisonous, but if there was enough of it in the air, it could asphyxiate you. That had been his mistake; he had taken it for granted that the place had aired out; otherwise he never would have—

He sat up suddenly. "Where's Elaine?"

The gargoyle pointed silently. On the far side of the room was another narrow bed. She lay on it, pale, eyes closed.

Dick made a sound and tried to get up, but Frankie pressed him back down. "She all right, misser—just you lay down and rest. She come out of it any minute."

Dick lay back, feeling too dizzy to argue. Frankie clicked

his tongue sorrowfully, looking down at him. "What you doing down here anyway, misser? You look like a nice boy. What for you want to come a-sneaking down upon us thisa-way?"

Dick stared at him. "What do you mean, sneaking down on you?"

"Nev' mind. I'm asking the questions here, not you. What's your name, misser?"

Dick's puzzlement grew. "Frankie, don't you know me? I'm Dick Jones."

"Dick Jones," said the gargoyle, licking the stub of a pencil. He scrawled laboriously on a scrap of paper held on his knee. "That's righ', I guess it mus' of slip my mind. And what's her name, Misser Jones?"

Dick said nothing. Glancing down, he had seen something incredible: Frankie was wearing a revolver on his hip.

. . . sneaking down upon us . . . We never bothered to plug it up . . .

"Her name is Clarinda Jones," he said, improvising. "Uh, she's my cousin." He watched the gargoyle painfully writing. "Frankie, you haven't been upstairs lately, have you?"

"Not for a good long time," said Frankie, shaking his head. "Going to go up pretty soon, though. Now what was you and the lady doing down here anyway?"

"Running away from the turnover." He waited again. "What were you doing in that drugstore?"

"Medicine," Frankie grunted. "We had to git medicine. Which side was you on, in the turnover?"

"Neither side," said Dick, prudently. "There was a lot of shooting and, uh, Clarinda was frightened, so I took her belowstairs. Then we got lost."

"M-hm," said Frankie. He finished writing and put his paper away. "Well, we see if the Old Man believe that. Come awn."

Dick got up. "The Old Man?" He wavered for a moment, and caught himself; he was a little dizzy.

"That righ'. Come awn, don't keep him waitin'."

As they passed the other cot, Dick bent over. Elaine's head moved; her pale lids flickered open.

He was down on one knee, cradling her head in his arms. "Are you all right?"

Her eyes focused; she seemed to recognize him. "Feel so *funny*," she said. Her arms went around him weakly.

"All righ', all righ', we take her too," said Frankie behind him. "See can she wawk; git her up."

Dick shot him a glance of resentment, then turned and helped Elaine to sit up. She stood, with his arm around her. "What happened?" she asked, looking around. "Ooh, I have such a headache."

135

"You'll be all right. Com on, somebody wants to see us."

With Frankie behind them, they walked out into a bare, drafty corridor. "Turn righ'," said the gargoyle. They passed rows of stacked cartons, then an open doorway with massive machinery behind it; then a wide open space where a dozen Frankies sat at typewriters, all industriously clicking away. Then they turned again, and were stopped by a Frankie with an Army rifle.

"For the Old Man," said their Frankie, and the other one stepped aside.

They passed on into another room where two Frankies sat at desks with telephones, and were stopped again. Elaine seemed to be fully awake now, and was looking around with surprise and apprehension. While the Frankies' attention was on each other, Dick whispered in her ear. "They don't know who you are—I told them you're my cousin, Clarinda Jones. Play up."

As they moved on again, she glanced at him and nodded.

Then they were in still another room, a big room lined with what looked like enlarged floor plans. There were desks here and there, with Frankies quietly working; in the middle, at a desk with a telescreen, sat someone who was obviously the Old Man.

He looked up as they approached, and Dick's breath caught sharply. It was a Frankie, but a Frankie twenty years older—heavy-set, grizzled, with the grotesque ugliness of his features turned to something like dignity. He glanced up incuriously at them, then went on talking into the instrument in his hand.

After a moment, he looked up again. "Yes?"

"These here the two we found in the drugstore, misser."

Dick caught his breath again. Hearing one slob address another as "mister" was a shock, even when it only confirmed what he had already seen.

Down here, burrowing like moles in the subterranean parts of Eagles, the Frankies had created a world of their own. Like all the servants at Eagles, they were supposed to be "rotated" at forty or earlier: sent away to other establishments, in theory; actually, killed and disposed of. But here was a Frankie who had obviously lived at least a decade past his span; and here were others who had not been upstairs for years. Surplus Frankies, probably, duped for some special job and then, instead of being destroyed, smuggled down here. He could only guess at how long it had been going on.

The telescreen speaker clattered briefly. The Old Man studied the screen, then said into the mike in his hand: "Let me see Level Two again." The bluish light from the screen flickered. The Old Man said, "Send the heavies aroun' by the

Oval Corridor." He watched a moment longer, then looked up at Dick and Elaine.

He said, "Where else besides Eagles did Melker plan a turnover?"

Dick answered carefully. "That would be something known to the conspirators, not to me." His tone was neutral; he couldn't treat the Old Man as an equal, but there was no point in antagonizing him by unnecessary stiffness.

The Old Man said, "I let you lie to me once. Don't try it again." He turned his attention to the screen once more. "Level One." A confused roaring came from the speaker.

After a moment the Old Man looked up. "Where else besides Eagles did Melker plan a turnover?"

Dick began to sweat. Slob though he was, there was something intimidating about the fellow. Unwillingly, he said, "Melker had connections in Indian Springs and Mont Blanc and a few other places—people he was sure would take the lead in acknowledging him. But he didn't plan any real turnover anywhere but here—he didn't think it was necessary."

There was a pause. Dick stared in frustration at the TV on the desk. *What* was going on up there?

The Old Man said. "Did any of them escape besides yourself, that you know of?"

Dick shook his head numbly. "I saw Melker dead . . . and Oliver . . . a lot of others."

"Where was that?"

"On the TV—I wasn't there myself." He added, "I wasn't in the fighting at all. . . . I came away as soon as I could."

The sound of a heavy concussion came from the TV speaker. Dick braced himself instinctively, tightening his hold on Elaine's waist, but felt nothing: they were too deep here to feel the shock.

"Do you know what went wrong with the plan?"

"No," said Dick. "Somebody must have gone to the Boss. It could have been anybody, any time. We knew that could happen all along."

"It's inconvenient," said the Old Man unemotionally. "We had our plan, too—we were going to hit during the wedding." He glanced up at Elaine. "Your wedding, Miss Elaine."

Dick felt her body stiffen. He stood still and said nothing; there was nothing to say. Of course the Old Man knew who she was . . . he was old enough; he must have been in his twenties when the last Elaine was alive.

Elaine was breathing quickly, her lips half-open. A few fine tendrils of her hair tickled his cheek. Dick was watching the Old Man's intent face and speculating furiously on the meaning of what he said; he was listening to the muffled sounds that came from the TV and trying to interpret them; and all the time he was half dizzy from having her so near.

137

A Frankie came over from the wall and showed the Old Man a paper, murmuring a few words. The Old Man answered shortly, and the Frankie went away.

Another concussion came from the TV. The Old Man's face contorted briefly in an expression Dick could not read.

"As it was," he said, "we had to hit early. Communications was our most serious problem; you can understand that. Melker could count on some outside support—we could not." He was talking with a curious persuasiveness, looking from one to the other as if to make sure he was understood. "The change in timing hurt our plans very much. But at least we seem to have succeeded in Eagles . . ." He nodded toward the TV. "That was the last pocket of resistance, the arsenal over the Rose Court, and it has just been taken."

They looked at him in a stunned silence.

"You've taken *Eagles?*" said Dick. It seemed monstrous, unbelievable.

The Old Man nodded slowly, "There's over three hundred slaves to every freeman in Eagles," he said. "We only had to put out our hand."

"You'll never hold it," said Dick.

The other inclined his big head. "I am afraid you may be right. That's what I wish to tawk to you about." He turned, murmured a few words into the mike, then set it down and rose from his chair. With a courteous hand on Dick's elbow and the other on Elaine's, he urged them toward the door. Three young Frankies fell in alertly behind them. "We'll go up to the Concourse and tawk," the Old Man said.

"Who's going to take over here?"

"One of my doubles. Being duped has its advantages, you see."

They moved out along bare corridors, along routes that looked recently cleared through the jungle of storerooms, and finally reached an elevator.

Up above, the corridors were almost deserted. Slobs stood in little groups here and there, most of them wearing white armbands: many were soldiers in uniform, with their insignia ripped off. The signs of battle were everywhere—heaps of rubble and debris, torn garments, an occasional sprawled body. As they passed a cross corridor, Dick heard a single, distant shot.

The Old Man and the Frankies glanced that way, but said nothing.

In the main corridor they passed a servant with a broom and a loaded trash cart. He was a shriveled, wild-eyed fellow of fifty or more, not the type you expect to meet abovestairs at all. When he saw the Old Man, he dropped his broom and tried to hug the Old Man around the knees. One of the Frankies held him off. He was babbling something in a

138

choked voice; Dick caught the words, "see this day come." Tears were running down his cheeks.

The Old Man said, "All right. That's all right," and passed by. As they moved on, he said to Dick, "Some of them have been waiting a long time for this. That particular fellow saw his wife rotated, and his two sons—the Boss dropped them down the Tower."

They were on a short, narrow stair that led to a glassed-in balcony overlooking the Concourse. Dick had seen the place many times but had never been inside. The door had the Boss's personal seal painted on it; the door was dented, half off its hinges, and someone had drawn a ragged "X" in red chalk over the seal.

Inside, the Old Man motioned them to chairs. Through the glass wall they could look out across the wide Plaza, cool in the water-colored light that fell from overhead, with the bright worms of fluorescents marking the various levels. The great tessellated floor was empty, as it was when the Plaza was cleared for theatricals or a circus. This was the Boss's private box.

Across the Plaza, a few figures moved methodically on the stairways and balconies. They stopped at each doorway, entered, disappeared for a while and returned. It was a room-to-room search for weapons and fugitives, Dick supposed. Only when it was completed could the victors openly take power.

This was the thing that everybody had been silently afraid of for fifty years—a slave revolt—and now it had actually happened. Dick felt incredulous, staring out over the Plaza that had so recently been full of life and color. As for Buckhill—there was no use thinking about that yet, and he put the thought out of his mind.

The Old Man was saying, "I wanted to tawk to you two privately because you realize our gravest problem. There aren't many that do."

"How's that?" said Dick. He saw that the Frankies had gone away, leaving them alone. There was a TV at the Old Man's elbow, flickering silently with a succession of images, but the Old Man was not looking at it. He was staring heavily at Dick and Elaine.

"Why, how to live with the world after we've won," he said. "It isn't enough just to take Eagles, now we have to run it. We wawnted to stop being slaves: but what does that mean? What are we going to do—try to be men and ladies, while we make our misters slave for us?"

Dick felt himself flushing with anger.

"I know," said the Old Man. "And yet most of my people haven't thought any farther than that. We could make slaves out of freemen, but that wouldn't solve anything. That would

139

be the old system all over again, only worse. Becawse we'd be poor freemen, and they'd be worse slaves."

That was sensible enough. "Well, what then?" said Dick curiously. Beside him, he was aware of Elaine sitting, bent forward, listening intently. She put out her hand, and he took it in his.

"First," said the Old Man, "we must end the injustice of slavery. That comes bfeore anything else—if we can't do that, we lose."

Dick shrugged.

"What choices does that leave us?" the Old Man asked, beginning to count on his fingers. "One, we could expel all the freemen and live here by ourselves. But that would not be a stable situation, especially if it only happened here. The freemen everywhere would wawnt to recover Eagles. Furthermore, they *could* recover Eagles, or destroy it, very easily, if we were to expel our freemen—whereas, if we keep them, they might hesitate. Now, second: this is a plan that we considered very seriously—now that we have the Gismos in our hands, within a short time we could make up thousands, or hundreds of thousands, of little kits, about this size—" He held his palms about a foot and a half apart.

"In each one there would be two Gismos, and a box of protes to make the basic things that everybody would need to survive by himself. There would be weapons, and ammunition. Water, of course, and basic foods. Medicines. Tools, and electrical equipment. Each Gismo would have an arrestor of course, and an inhibitor, so that new protes could be made on it, of anything you might wawnt to dupe. Now we could take those kits and load them into planes, and drop them just everywhere, with a little parachute on each one. Many of them would be destroyed or seized by the freemen, naturally, but any slave, you see, who did get one of the kits would have in his hands the potential of being a freeman."

He sat back. "Now we believe this could be done, and once it got started, the freemen would never be able to put a stop to it. We could float those kits from balloons and just let them loose. We could even make the process automatic—set up a big Gismo, in some place in the mountains that would be hard to locate, and just put it to work automatically turning out those kits and floating them away on the wind."

He paused.

Dick could see the picture in his mind; it was vicious and clever, and he knew instinctively that the Old Man was right—once started, you could never stop it, never in the world.

"But we decided against that, too," said the Old Man. "Our reason was this. If you study your history you'll see that the whole set of injustices, and awl the bloodshed of the

140

first twenty years after Turnover, came from just such a plan as that. Somebody, we don't know who, distributed Gismos through the government mails they had then. What happened? If one man took advantage of the anarchic conditions to get himself a slave army, you couldn't defend yourself against him unless you had an army too. Now we believe that a similar process would inevitably take place if we were to follow that plan again. The slave-holding big houses we have at present would break up, and that would be desirable from our point of view, but at the same time we would create such conditions of anarchy again, that there would have to be a time of bloodshed, and then of little wars, and then big wars all over, before things would settle down into a new pattern of mister and slave.

"Now you remember I said that first of awl the injustice of slavery must be ended. That is our aim. We want to see the time come when nobody will be a slave, anywhere, to any man. So we can't drive out our freemen, and we can't disseminate Gismos at random. What does that leave?"

He held up a third finger. "It leaves just one way: for us to learn to live peacefully together, to get along and respect each other as equals—those who were freemen, and those who were slaves."

Dick tried to keep his expression impassive, but some of his revulsion and contempt must have shown in his face. The Old Man said, "You think that could never happen. Why not? Is there an intrinsic difference between a freeman and a slave?"

Dick said, "Certainly."

"Then what about the lady beside you now? Is she slave or free?"

He said thickly, "She's free. She was married to the Boss—that is—" He stopped in confusion.

Elaine's hand tightened on his arm. "Dick, that isn't right."

She thought he meant Oliver, he realized; she still didn't understand that she was not the original Elaine.

"I know, you mean she has free status. That's true. But she was bought and sold, both her parents were slaves, and moreover, she is a dupe. Now isn't it true that, according to your way of thinking, a dupe must be a slave?"

Dick shot a glance at Elaine's face; she was bewildered and uncomprehending—it hadn't soaked in yet: but it would. He turned back to the Old Man with a look of resentment. "It's a different case," he said shortly. "Things were different then—they hadn't settled down."

"But now they have?" said the Old Man. "All right: now just suppose that while you were sleeping, I had you taken to the Gismo Room and duped. That could have happened,

141

couldn't it? . . . And suppose I then had your own body destroyed—suppose I killed the original Dick Jones, and let the dupe live on. . . . Now I wawnt you to look at me and tell me: do you have any way of knowing, inside yourself, *whether I did that or not?*"

His grim face stared into Dick's. Suddenly it seemed like a very real possibility.

The sweat broke out on his forehead and he began to feel dizzy. *Was* he a dupe, without knowing it? He searched his memory, his physical sensations. He felt just the same as he always had, but that did not comfort him: he knew dupes always thought they were the originals, until told differently.

"I'll tell you the answer, sometime," the Old Man said. "Not now. I wawnt you to think about it."

"If you did—" said Dick, in a choked voice.

"If I did, what difference does it make? That's what I wawnt you to think about." The Old Man rose, and without haste left the room. Dick caught a glimpse of a Frankie on guard as the door closed.

He hunched over in furious thought, chin on his fists. "Dick?" said the girl, squeezing his arm.

He moved away. "Let me alone, just now." After a moment, he felt her withdrawing in a hurt silence. Time enough to apologize for that later: he had to think.

Down in the gulf of the Concourse, a few people were straggling out into view. At this distance he could not recognize any faces, but they were all dressed in the fashion and it might have been any normal gathering—except that there were so few, and that they moved so hesitantly.

After a while there were more of them, gathering in small groups to talk, some moving aimlessly. The Frankies and other slobs passed among them on various errands. When there was not enough room, it was the freemen who moved aside, as if trying to avoid contamination.

Suppose he *was* a dupe—a slave, then, or some horrible mixture, a quasi-slave. It was one thing to fall in love with a dupe, but it was another to imagine that you might be one.

What difference would it make? Why, all the difference. Between freedom and slobbery—between all the good, decent, proud things and all the abased, slovenly, subhuman things. If he was still Dick Jones of Buckhill, that was something in itself, no matter how bad things got: he was a man, able to look out for himself, with a name and a place to fight for.

He had to find out—but how? Suppose the Old Man should come back and say, "I lied to you," or "I told the truth." Either way, he might be lying, and Dick would be left to guess, as before.

He shivered. Down in the Concourse, the few brightly-

142

robed people were moving with maddeningly dull slowness. The world had grown dim and hateful, all the colors were flat, and time seemed to be dragging endlessly.

What could the Old Man's motive have been? He must want something, or he wouldn't bother. If he wanted some lever to use on Dick, then he might have had him duped—but what for, actually, since he could say he had done it just the same? Dick's spirits rose a trifle, then fell again. Suppose the Old Man was planning to produce some proof, later on, that the thing had been done . . .

Now what had he said, exactly? "Suppose I then had your own body destroyed—" He had emphasized that; and then, "Do you have any way of knowing, inside yourself, *whether I did that or not?*"

Well, no, of course not. A dupe couldn't tell.

And then, just before he left, the Old Man had said, "If I did, what difference does it make?" What difference—?

Suppose he *was* a dupe. He let himself frame the thought with the tense hesitancy of a man stepping close to a dangerous edge. If no one knew it, or could prove it, or even accuse him of it—in short, if he was a freeman in the eyes of the world—then effectively he *was* a freeman.

He shook his head in bewilderment. It all seemed perfectly reasonable even when it was most paradoxical. It was a side of things that had always been there, waiting to be seen, but he had never seen it before. That in itself was matter for thought.

Eagles had made a realist of him. He believed in facts, and in altering your viewpoint to fit them, no matter what they were. That was the way you survived and stayed sane; it was hard, it meant sacrifices—he had already lost many things that he valued deeply—but it was the only way.

Now, if the only *essential* difference between a freeman and a slave was an arbitrary distinction—Dick's world rocked on its foundations.

He looked down thoughtfully at the two gnome-like Frankies who happened to be on the Concourse at the moment. They were uneducated, short-sighted, vulgar and simple—typical of the lowest kind of house slob. But the Old Man himself was a Frankie—a Frankie grown to middle age, self-trained and educated into a personality of extraordinary depth and power. If you could make that out of such material, then there was no real, intrinsic difference—no reason why a Frankie should not be a freeman, or a freeman a servant.

What was happening down on the Promenade, and in the courtyards and plazas? What were people thinking, now that Eagles was in the hands of slaves? What plans and adjustments were being made; who was alive and who dead? What did it feel like—how was it shaping up? Dick felt an impa-

143

tience to be down there, moving, taking part, on any terms.

Now: The Old Man knew who Elaine was, and it was not hard to guess that he meant to make some political use of her. Furthermore, whatever it was, it was obvious that it had something to do with Dick. There would be a role for him to play; and an important one, or the Old Man would not have been at such pains to change his opinions. . . . Dick's heart began to beat faster. He thought he saw the pattern forming.

After a while the door opened again and the Old Man's heavy outline appeared. He paused to speak to the Frankies in the doorway, then the door closed behind him. He came forward and sat down.

"Have you thawt it over?" he asked.

Dick nodded. "Yes."

"And?"

"I'm willing to listen," said Dick.

The Old Man leaned back. "Awl right. You remember I said the only way is for us awl to learn to live together peacefully, as equals. I say now that is the only way out for Eagles, not only on moral grounds but as a practical matter. We can't hope to survive in any other way. But on a larger scale it is also the only way out for the human race. If we lose, here, there will be another slave uprising somewhere else, some other time, and another if necessary, and eventually one of them will win."

Dick said, "I don't know—we did all right for over a century."

"But you see how unstable it was," the Old Man said earnestly. "This is the point: the slavery system breaks down into freedom. The freedom system, if it's properly established, never will break down into slavery again. It'll be too strawng. Now in the abstract, I know you appreciate the desirability of something stable, something that will last."

Dick grinned. "Maybe, in the abstract."

"Just so. Now, coming a little nearer, do you agree with me that a mixed society could be stable, could work here in Eagles?"

Dick hesitated. "Yes."

"You understand that would mean former freemen working closely, sharing responsibilities with former slaves?"

"Yes."

"That would be repugnant to you?"

". . . Certainly."

"But you would do it, under certain circumstances?"

They looked at each other. Dick said, "Tell me plainly what you mean."

The Old Man answered, "You and Miss Elaine would be married. I think that would not be repugnant to either of you." Dick glanced at the girl; she flushed, smiling, and looked down. "Your family connections would make it very hard for any hotheads to raise a punitive force against Eagles. The fact that she is a dupe would make her acceptable to my people. It would be an ideal union for our purposes. You would serve as head of the internal governing committee, represent us in dealing with other heads of houses, and so awn."

Dick was tense with suppressed excitement. "But you'd be behind the scenes."

The Old Man inclined his head. "For a while. Later awn there are going to be elections, and if you wawnt another office than the one I give you, you can run for it. But nobody is going to have absolute power." He added, "I can honestly say that you will have more power than you were ever likely to get under the old system."

Dick nodded slowly.

"You accept?"

Dick said, "Let me talk to my father at Buckhill."

"And?"

"If he agrees, I'll accept."

The Old Man nodded. He got up and went to the door, spoke to the Frankies outside. "This will take a little time," he said. "We have to get through to Buckhill, and then of course we will wawnt to monitor. I'll have the set brought in when it's ready." He went out.

There was a silence.

Elaine said, "Dick—when he said I was a dupe: was that true?"

"It was true. This is 2149. Oliver was the grandson of the man who duped you—Crawford, the first Boss of Eagles."

She looked out the window, her face composed, hands together in her lap. "I suppose I knew it," she said. "But I wouldn't admit it to myself. I don't *feel* like a dupe—it's strange—"

"I know," he said. "It doesn't make any difference."

"Doesn't it?" She turned to look into his face. Her color was high, her eyes bright. "Not to you?"

"No," said Dick, and found that he meant it.

He moved next to her, took her in his arms. There was a pulse beating at the base of her long, pale throat. Her green eyes looked at him from behind their screens of lashes: strange, beautiful and strange.

He kissed her. She lay relaxed and warm in his embrace; after a moment she leaned back and said a little breathlessly: "And you want to marry me?"

NINETEEN

After all, what was wrong with it?

He remembered the discussions of just this possibility at the Philosophers' Club, Melker's cover group. That seemed a long time ago, and the reality was very different. Still, some of the old arguments had stayed with him. A society that used unjust methods to suppress some of its members (the catch was that you had to call slaves members of the society) was building up forces that would have to burst free sooner or later. Then, too, a society that put more emphasis on birth than ability was likely to breed ability out of its ruling class. It all came to the same thing; it was logical; and in any case, it had happened.

Run with the pack.

The corridors of Eagles were full of color and movement again: rustling, quick movement, streams of people going quickly and quietly, talking very little and that mostly in whispers. It gave a curious, tense feeling: you kept listening for the sounds that should be there.

The debris had all been cleared out of the Grand Promenade, but no repair work was being done. Nobody was riding in chairs, everyone was on foot except a few people, Frankies usually, on motor scooters. Not a uniform was in sight. Everywhere you looked there were servants walking quietly in the crowd, heads up, with an expression on their faces that you did not like to meet. Some of them were dressed in freemen's costumes: you saw the clothing, and then, with a shock, the wrong face. All weapons had supposedly been confiscated; no one was supposed to go armed except the Frankies; but Dick saw more than one ex-servant with a stick or a hand-gun, and the Frankies did not interfere.

There had been some difficulty in getting a scrambler relay to Buckhill; meanwhile they had been going ahead with talks on a tentative basis. Dick and Elaine had already had a meeting with the prospective members of the Old Man's governing committee, and now they were on their way to a run-through of the wedding ceremony which was scheduled for day after tomorrow.

Elaine, walking at his side, was pale and ethereally beautiful in a dress of green silk, duped an hour ago from a prote that had been lying unused for twenty-odd years. Her eyes were bright, and a flush burned on each cheek. He could feel the warmth of her hand, tucked under his arm: she was feverish with excitement. On either side, the armed Frankies went with eyes straight ahead, their gargoyle faces immobile, in a strange new dignity.

Things were quieting down as fast as you could reasonably expect. There had been a little disturbance earlier, when the body of the Boss had been brought down from his sanctum; some ex-slaves had thrown themselves at the corpse like wild animals, and the Frankies had had to hustle it away out of sight.

They would learn better. There had to be superiors and inferiors, even in a society without slaves.

Dick was uncomfortably aware how many slaves—ex-slaves—there were in the crowd. They seemed to be coming out of their holes, more and more, all silent and burning-eyed; the burrows under Eagles must be empty of them: he had never seen so many at once before.

Up ahead, there was a curious, swirling movement in the crowd. People seemed to be gathering at one spot near the wall, and then almost immediately it was over, and the flow moved on unbroken.

As they passed the spot, Dick caught a glimpse of a young man standing white-faced and bewildered against the wall. Blood was streaming down his cheek. Dick recognized the face; it was one of Randolph's bully-boys, a man notorious for his ingenious cruelty with slaves. No one was approaching him or speaking to him; the crowd flowed silently past.

That was a bad thing, Dick thought, with his heart beating suddenly heavy and thick. There was the only real danger: if that kind of thing got out of hand—

He had a brief, incongruous flash of memory—two garden slobs standing over a felled tree, cool shadowed in the early morning; and their axes glinted one after another: *chunk,* pause, *chunk.*

"What is it?" asked Elaine anxiously; her fingers tightened on his arm.

"Nothing. Don't worry."

He was tense, alert, but nothing else happened. The crowd flowed on smoothly. They were passing the entrance of the Little Gold Corridor now, the place where he had had his first fight in Eagles, and he glanced down it curiously, as if expecting to see Keel there. But the corridor was deserted, the stream flowing silently alone.

Crossing the Four Ways on the old black and white mosaic floor, there was a little confusion as usual; people milling in the center, dodging around each other. Echoes broke hollowly under the many-vaulted ceiling; the crowd was as thick as he had ever seen it. There was a white-hatted Lone Star man, there two Indians in turbans, there a kepi, and slaves, slaves everywhere. Deep in the center, motion slowed almost

147

to a standstill. The sound level had risen; there were voices speaking indistinguishably.

Dick saw the two Frankies exchange glances. Moving instinctively, he took Elaine's hand away and put his arm around her waist.

"Dick, what's the *matter*?"

He did not answer. Off to one side, the crowd was swaying thick. Suddenly the air was full of noise; someone had fired a gun, shockingly loud, the echoes thundering away under the ceiling. Dick saw a whiff of smoke drift up from the middle of the crowd. Then he heard a low grumbling of many voices, and the crowd seemed to contract into itself. Someone was shouting; he could not make out the words. A Frankie, not one of theirs, was trying to force his way toward the disturbance, but the bodies were too closely packed. Others were coming across the floor on the run.

The two Frankie bodyguards looked at each other wordlessly; one jerked his thumb toward the nearest cross-corridor; the other nodded. Without further discussion, they grasped Dick and Elaine by the arms and moved off rapidly in that direction. Behind them, the uproar was growing.

Running men clogged the corridor, all hurrying toward the Four Ways; most of them were slaves. Some glanced at Dick's party; a few even broke their stride. But the movement was too strong, and they passed on. In the distance, a bullhorn broke out into loud, muffled speech. It went on blaring, incomprehensibly.

They turned at the next crossing, into Jewelers' Row. They were heading, Dick realized, for the shortest route to the Old Man's temporary headquarters in the Plaza. If they could get across the Plaza itself, Elaine would be safe.

The crowd was thinning. The noise from the Ways was almost inaudible behind them. All the little hole-in-the-wall shops looked empty, and they passed one that had had its display window broken recently: crushed bits of glass were all over the pavement.

Beside him, Elaine was silent and pale. She understood what was happening now, but she was not panicking. To get her safe, he thought: that was the first thing.

There was an intermittent rumbling, trundling sound up ahead. A little farther on, they saw what it was: a little fellow in servant's gray was rolling a heavy drum down the corridor. Where it curved around the Foley Fountain, making a little plaza, the slave stopped and with great effort got his drum upright. He was still some little distance away. They saw him pry up the lid and drop it ringing on the floor. He dipped in one hand and brought it out black.

They were near enough now to make out his face. It was a seamed, gray face, vaguely familiar, with little eyes of malice. The slave held his black hand at shoulder level, palm up. When a freeman passed in orange silk and lace, the ex-slave reached out and swung his hand. It landed with a *splat*. The man recoiled, with a dark blob over half his face. It was no one Dick knew—a gray-haired man in his fifties. He stared at the slave in blank incomprehension: the slave grinned back at him, then laughed.

The man brought his hand away from his cheek and stared at it: the orange-gloved fingers were smeared with black grease. He made a choked sound and reached for the stick that was not at his belt. The slave grinned and waited.

They were near enough now to see everything: the man's flush of anger, the slave's gray cheek wrinkled in a smile. People standing around, nearly all slaves, were looking on in intent silence.

The man's hands were opening and closing. At last, pale, he turned away.

"Yahhh!" said the slave, in a raucous voice. All around him, other slave faces were bright and feverish; there was a murmur and a ripple of embarrassed laughter.

The Frankies, with grim expressions, were edging them around behind the mob. As they passed, the onlookers were moving in; a babble of voices began. Dick saw an old man-servant leap at the drum and plunge his hand in. He brought it up dripping, black to the elbow. Past him, a dignified woman in violet came forward protesting, hustled by the slaves crowding at her back. The old man turned deliberately, and planted his handful of muck squarely in her face.

The crowd closed in, and Dick saw no more.

TWENTY

For hours the crowds had been roaring through the corridors of Eagles. Once started, it went on and on, incredibly, without a pause. At first the Frankies had tried to control the mob by exhorting them over the loudspeakers; then they had thrown up barriers across the main corridors. The mob had rolled over them; some Frankies had been killed. Now the rest were staying out of harm's way, on balconies and other perches in plain view, watching. The sound of the crowd never stopped, never varied, and it was a dreadful thing to hear: a rushing, roaring, inhuman sound, beating like surf at the eardrums, with a high, almost inaudible, nerve-grating treble of hysteria in it.

From insulting and killing freemen in the corridors, the

mob had progressed to breaking down doors of private apartments, and for a while the booming of sledges had punctuated the uproar, with the crowds swarming suddenly around a door that had gone down, the corridors half-emptying, and then after ten minutes or half an hour of insensate destruction, the crowds would swarm out again until the whole thing repeated itself somewhere else.

Towards midnight, the Gismo Guards had fought a pitched battle in the Lower Mezzanine, using mortars, grenades and small arms. Someone had blasted down half the ceiling on top of them, and the concussion had been felt everywhere in Eagles. A little later, some of the slaves had begun turning up with Gismoed weapons, but by then there were no freemen left to kill.

The mob swept on. It was not satisfied by the massacre it had done all that afternoon, by the hundreds of corpses, men, women and children mangled and dismembered. It pulled down hangings, broke furniture into splinters, ripped paneling off walls, smashed lamps and ornaments, tore books. One fire after another billowed greasy, choking white smoke out into the corridors. The Frankies fought them with Gismo-fed extinguishers and hoses; the corridors streamed water and blood. The fires died, leaving a wet, acrid reek and a black mud of ash; the crowd roared on.

Every window had been smashed, and the cold air of the heights searched in through the doors hanging awry on their jambs; papers blew in gusts down the corridors between the hurrying figures, and the garments of corpses lifted in the wind. Some of the crowd had axes now, the sledges were in use again, and great strips of metal paneling came down with a clatter; masonry fell in choking clouds, marble cracked and thundered.

Transfigured faces shone in the broken light: eyes wide and aglitter, mouths grinning—masks of cruelty and triumph, all fixed and all alike. They recognized one another only by their common expression: gardener and room girl, valet, cook and craftsman, they mingled indistinguishably, running and stumbling without fatigue, staring as if drugged, croaking at each other out of their parrot-grins; grimed, shiny with sweat, bloody, blackened and staring, staring.

Dick was one of them. Dressed in rags torn from a dead slave, his face and hands filthy, he ran with the rest. The faces floating around him were like reflections of his own. He had been running and shouting for hours, but he felt no tiredness, and he did not notice that only a hoarse whisper came out of his throat now.

At the beginning, when he had robbed the corpses of clothing for Elaine and himself, he had known that only one disguise would really work: to be one of the mob, to feel

150

what they felt, to think what they thought. He had tried to tell her before they went out into the corridor; there had not been much time. They had been separated almost at once. He had not seen her since.

He had known that the only way to survive was to become one of the hunters. He had done so. He had no identity now, no anxieties for himself, no feeling of separation from the mob around him. Elaine was only a dim figure in the back of his mind. He was a drifting yell, a bright light moving, a brain full of violence and noise looking for more.

He remembered capering in the Big Plaza, holding something round and dark and shapeless that swung by its long black hair from his fist; and the shouting, joyful faces, the arms and bodies leaping to take it away from him. Then somehow he had got into the Gismo Rooms under the Guard barracks, and in the light of one unbroken fluorescent, someone was passing out bundles of dynamite sticks to the crowd, but he had seen a pickaxe and had taken it instead; and then, without any transition, he was in the Elwyn Conservatory half a mile away swinging his pick crazily through the polished glass screens that stood everywhere, hearing them scream and clatter, seeing the gashed trunks and branches full of glittering shards.

Then there was the time the man came running across the floor, hoarsely shouting, with a woman in his arms, and dashed himself against the cracked Promenade window, breaking it, and fell into the darkness outside. . . . The running footsteps, the shout, "Yahhh!" and the crash. The footsteps, "Yahhh!" crash of glass, kept going meaninglessly through his brain.

There was a heavy explosion somewhere below, and the floor bounced as if hit with a giant hammer, knocking him off his feet. He climbed erect again, a little sobered and stunned, seeing the faces around him half shocked to reason for a moment. They were in the New Gallery, and he saw the smashed picture frames hanging empty from the walls. Then the crowd was up, confused, in movement now in a new direction, down the steep ramp to the plaza behind the Sportsgarden, running hard at the bottom, and exploding out across the empty plaza, mixing with another stream of people on the far side, scattering unexpectedly in a dozen directions—some across the arcade into Jewelers' Courts, some down the tunnel toward the museum annex, some into the little rabbit-warren corridors that branched every which way from the end of the plaza. Dick found himself, breathing heavily, in a dark low corridor of empty shop window-frames, littered with bits of glass and paper. Footsteps crunched rapidly away into the distance; he was alone.

Across the corridor was a telebooth, doorless, the broken

picture tube like a blind eye. On a sudden impulse, Dick lurched over to it and pushed the buttons for a scramble call. The speakers hummed faintly; the circuits were alive, anyhow. Nothing else happened, and when he punched the combination for a relay broadcast outside Eagles, there was no response: naturally; you couldn't use these booths for outside calls unless special circuits were set up through Central Monitoring. He thought about that, aware of his own harsh breathing as he leaned with both hands over the control panel in the dark little booth. His body was beginning to feel numb with fatigue, now that he had stopped; he was sweating as he leaned there in the dark, orienting himself. Central was only two levels down; it would be easy to get there, but was the chance worth taking? He knew it was dangerous to be out of the crowd like this, out of the protective crowd feeling, but it was also a chance he might not get again.

Dick hesitated, then levered himself wearily upright and broke into a leaden run down the corridor, setting his face into a staring blankness.

Central was a huge room full of wreckage. All but a few of the picture tubes along the walls had been broken, and the control panels had been attacked apparently with axes—wiring and components chopped into, drawers opened and the contents spilled, chairs and tables overturned. Dick wedged the door shut and went feverishly from one board to another, trying to find one that was still in operating condition. It looked hopeless; the mobs must have torn through here not once, but half a dozen times.

He stood staring in frustration at the ruined panels. Then he walked slowly once more around the room.

In the corner by the door was a heap of wreckage larger than the rest, where two cabinets had been toppled over, their contents spilling out. He stirred the heap with his foot; under the sliding rubble of glass and pasteboard there was a gleam of something big and undamaged. He fished it out: it was a portable TV, of the kind used for intramural broadcasts in Eagles—six inches square by eight deep, with its own power pack and antenna, completely undamaged, not even a scratch on it.

He pried open the back, hunted up two adapter cables, and attached them to the TV's binding posts. Time was passing. He trotted back to the control panels, found two jacks marked "BCAST" and "RCVE," and plugged the TV in.

The screen lighted up. It was Channel 3, one of the usual adventure films; he caught a glimpse of a man being bowled over and shaken by a lion. He dialed quickly to Channel 9.

The screen flickered, steadied to show a gray card with
152

white lettering: "ALL CIRCUITS BUSY." The switchboard's recorded voice said, "This is Rocky Mountain Relay. All circuits are busy, please stand by."

He waited impatiently. The visual display stayed the same; the recorded message repeated itself every few seconds. At last the screen flickered and cleared again: another card, lettered, "YOUR CALL PLEASE." The voice said, "This is Rocky Mountain Relay. Please give your call clearly, naming place and location."

Dick said, "Buckhill, in the Poconos." He added, "Urgent!"

The display changed to read, "THANK YOU." The voice said, "Thank you. Your call is now being relayed. Please stand by."

A minute or more passed. The display changed to read, "SIGNALING," with a disc that lighted up and went out, lighted and went out.

After a long interval, the screen flickered and cleared again. Something dark was being withdrawn from the screen; Dick glimpsed a tall figure against the background of a familiar room. He said, "Dad—"

His voice stopped. The figure in the screen was not his father; realizing that, he saw that the tower room was in wreckage, papers spilled from the desk, windows and casements shattered. Then he saw who it was: one of the garden slobs, a big buck named Roy—standing there, dull-eyed, with a bloody butcher knife in his hand.

The mob flowed on, endlessly. Some of its members were still ferociously active; some had been overtaken by fatigue and were shuffling along, blank-faced, somnambulistic; but the human river never stopped. There was now no place where the sated ex-slaves might have paused to sit down and look at what they had won. Every chair and table had been broken, windows smashed, small objects spilled and trampled underfoot; paneling had been ripped away from walls, even the flooring pried up; Eagles had been changed, in fourteen hours, from a magnificent palace-city to a honeycomb of gray, debris-choked cells. A fire was burning unchecked now in the North Colonnades, sending up a thick dark pillar of smoke to be whipped away by the winds into the upper air. Outer walls had been battered down, portions of roofs were gone, and the cold air howled through all the corridors. Some areas were still blazing with light from high-placed fixtures; others, where the wiring had been damaged, were pitch dark or illuminated only by the weak bluish light of morning. Passing continually from light to darkness, to half-light, the people looked at each other out of stunned wooden faces, jaws slack, eyes filmed. They went on moving because there was nothing else left for them to do; and because they felt that if they should stop, it would somehow be terrible.

The explosions continued at long intervals. The roof of the Rose Court came down, burying hundreds; the Long Corridor was blasted into rubble. There was a puff of smoke against one flank of the Tower; scales of gold glittered briefly, each a hand-worked panel nine feet square, but so small in the distance that they looked like pollen, drifting and gleaming, then gone.

Dick was watching from a balcony overlooking Marson Court, now open to the sky. An explosion had torn off the whole roof, exposing the rubble-strewn court with its balconies, stairways and descending levels, all silent and mysterious, like something just dug up by archaeologists. The cold wind whipped by overhead with a shriek, fingering the balcony as it went; Dick stood gripping the rail, buffeted and numb. He had been wandering without thought or feeling for hours, ever since the call to Buckhill. Now, from this height, he could see the roofs of Eagles spread out around him. Many other rooms were gaping open to the sky, like rotten teeth, and in them he could see other figures standing, staring up as the dawn brightened.

Down below, the roofs fell away in dizzy leaps. The mountain swooped down below them, blue-shadowed, with the broken line of the funicular like a hasty chalkline in the darkness. The shadow pooled deep at the bottom, but Dick could just begin to make out the blocky shapes of the airport buildings, and the wrecked planes on the field.

Another puff of white caught his eye, and as he turned to look, the sound came muffled after it, a swallowed roar in the wind. More scales of gold drifted away from the side of the Tower, and the whole tall structure appeared to lurch. Faintly, on the wind, came a grinding protest. In the dawn, against the silken blue of the sky, the Tower was more beautiful than he had ever seen it. It rose now like a golden tree, limbless and eaten hollow, shining in the naked beauty of its wounds, with its mighty buttresses, like roots, gripping the mountain.

Another white puff bulged out from the side of the Tower. It trembled visibly, like a tree at the axe stroke; then he saw it lean.

The enormous shaft of the Tower leaned, very slowly, and went on leaning, with incredible nightmare slowness, forever and ever, growing larger against the bright sky and yet still leaning, while distant seismic ripping and crackling sounds came on the wind; and still it was leaning nearer, so that he could see the scaly pattern of gold panels in its framework, and the dull light glinting off the pinnacle as it went over, now faster and faster, while panic held him in a tingling, breathless waiting, too shocked to shout, and still faster, resistlessly, like all heaven falling to smash the earth, larger and larger like a moon descending, and then it flashed down, with fountains of gray rubble flying at its torn-up roots, and somehow failed to destroy him; and looking down he saw it dissolve into golden chaos while the lazy fragments of roofs came spiraling up into the air around it: then the mountain shook under him, once, twice and again.

In the long, unreal silence, the orange-gray cloud of dust slowly spread and trailed away in long, diminishing streamers into the air. The open places among Eagles' roofs began to blacken with figures crowding up, standing to stare. There were no more explosions. Underfoot, Eagles seemed to breathe more slowly; the sense of frantic movement was gone. People were coming up wearily, singly, to stand in the open and look around them in wonder.

Over the back of the world the sunrise was spreading its wings of majesty, gold billowing into scarlet, pierced and purpled. Flecks of yellowish cirrus rode infinitely high in the pure dome of air; the pale light was slowly spreading, bringing depth and roundness to the flat earth.

TWENTY-ONE

Going down from the courtyard into the mass of corridors, he saw the Frankies moving again purposefully through the apathetic crowds, and realized that all through the night and morning he had not once recognized the familiar face. It was as if the Frankies had been submerged in the mob mind, just as he had been himself; and only now, when individual faces were being worn again, could they be told from anyone else.

At the corner where the smaller corridor entered North Passage, two Frankies were setting down heavy bundles of rifles. Each had a .375 Winchester slung over his shoulder, the same make and caliber as the rifles they were now unwrapping, aclatter on the floor. As Dick paused to watch, they began stopping passersby, shoving a rifle at each, saying something, pushing him away. Moving nearer, Dick found himself clutched, given a rifle, pushed off; the Frankie saying hoarsely meanwhile, in a mechanical monotone, "Get to a roof or a window. Make it quick." There were distant shouts in other corridors; some of those with rifles were drifting off, others following more slowly. The Frankies handed out the last of their weapons, pushed a laggard or two again and repeated the order, then went away. Slowly, trying to shake some alertness into himself, Dick went back the way he had come.

The Frankies were organizing a defense: then Eagles must be under attack, and from the air. Eagles had always been considered impregnable from the air, but he realized now, with senses sharpening a little, that with the citadel in ruins, the defenses at the bottom of the mountain shattered and unmanned, it was a different thing.

The giant on the mountain had been crippled and mutilated; now the harpies would come.

Climbing again into the open courtyard, he saw them: slender, tilt-winged shapes, bobbing and swooping in the violent up-currents. Each one was trailing a fierce tail of fire; he could make out the tiny bubble, and the pilot's head. They were two-man aircraft of a type he had never seen, modified copters with a makeshift rocket assembly at the tail. The rockets gave them enough power to maneuver in the winds at the mountaintop; even so, they were swinging wildly in the treacherous updrafts, and Dick saw one pinwheel against the side of the mountain, exploding into a bright flare that drifted downward, a spark, diminishing. Each one must have a Gismo in it, he realized dazedly, to make it possible for a plane of that size to use sustained rocket power: in ordinary times, no one would have dared to try such a thing, not even the Boss; it must have been done on the spur of the moment. . . .

He was dimly aware of a popping of gunfire somewhere to his left. Turning to look, he saw a cluster of dark figures with rifles on an exposed platform, just before a sudden blossom of masonry expanded around them. One of the swift, bobbing planes passed erratically over and rose in the updraft; he saw its rocket flaming distantly as it turned to dive again. Others were crisscrossing over the broken field of Eagles' roofs, a landscape as skeletal as the Moon's, with topless towers gaping like the shattered mouths of cannon. Here and there, other white puffs spouted briefly where the planes passed. Dick saw no bombs falling, and realized that the tiny flyers must be firing explosive shells. More roofs winked into ruin as he watched. Under the candid sky, the gray corruption seemed to stir itself, like something half-alive, writhing in pain.

There was a clatter of feet and three men came straining up the staircase below him, breathing in hoarse gasps, with a mounted machine gun between them. Ignoring Dick, they set the gun up near the parapet. A plane swooped overhead, quick as a hummingbird; they trained the gun futilely after it, then turned it toward a more distant plane and began firing. Deafened, Dick saw the ejected shells spring out glittering in the pure air. Across the roofs, other guns were

156

flashing. A plane burst in midair, first a fireball, then a greasy drifting smoke; wreckage whined and rattled around them, and Dick crouched instinctively under the parapet.

The useless rifle was still in his hands; he looked at it and swore, in a monotone, without knowing what he was saying. The machine gun was still firing a few yards away; others were coming into action, and he could see the heavier flare of mortars in several places. One fired just as a plane went over it; there was a heavy burst of gray smoke where the gun had been, and fragments went spinning. Then out of nowhere there was a tilt-winged plane diving as Dick looked up. It was growing with impossible speed, and he could see flickers of light at its wingtips; and as he ducked, straining close to the parapet, he saw bullet-puffs march irregularly across the balcony beside the machine gunners. Then there was one bright flash at the nose of the plane, and simultaneously parapet and gunners lifted to a heavy blow.

Rubble pattered down around him. When he could see again, half the balcony was gone; there was no sign of the gun or gunners. His head smarted; he put his hand to it and drew it away, smeared with blood and masonry dust. He could not tell whether he was badly hurt or not.

He staggered to his feet, still gripping the rifle. One last explosion fountained up, over where the Promenade should have been; then the broken huddle of buildings lay silent and dark. There was no more gunfire, and the swift planes were circling or hovering.

Numbly, he saw that the stairway he had come up was gone. He was marooned on the balcony.

Out beyond the lower slopes of Eagles, one of the planes was beginning a series of curious maneuvers: dipping close to the roofs, pulling up in an abrupt climb, hovering, then beginning again. Straining his eyes, he saw a flicker of motion between roofs and plane at the bottom of its dip. It was a hairline, a cord or cable with a dot of something at the end of it, whipping violently in the wind. Then something happened, it was cast off or reeled in, he couldn't tell which. As the plane dipped once more, there was another flicker—he saw the line shoot out, and this time stand taut in the air between the roofs and the plane.

The plane hovered, pitching violently in the up-currents, but holding its place. Other planes were beginning to go through the same maneuvers; one or two of them struck and held almost immediately.

Then he saw dark shapes sliding down the cords—men in heavy flying suits, helmeted, with gear slung around them. Like kites, the planes hung everywhere over the gray waste; and men were swarming over the ruined roofs.

Dick saw a man with a rifle appear suddenly on the rim of

a tower; he could not hear the shot, but one of the invaders threw up his hands and fell. The others nearby took cover, and faintly Dick heard the chatter of automatic rifles. The man on the tower spun outward, his weapon floating away, and fell twisting out of sight.

Planes which had successfully dropped their men were cutting the cords and moving off; new ones, an apparently endless supply, were taking their places.

The planes were working nearer. In the full daylight, the invaders' leather jackets gleamed, their goggles shot glints of white. Some were going down into Eagles, disappearing; others, with climbing gear, were working their way systematically over the roofs.

The balcony under Dick's feet shuddered to an abrupt subterranean roar. Black smoke swirled up, carrying a confused echo of screams and shouts. A few hundred yards distant, another black plume shot out of an open roof.

Dark scrambling figures began to appear on the balconies again—slaves, waving their arms to show they were weaponless. The invaders closed in around them. More spurts of black smoke came up; more slaves appeared. If the invaders had already discovered that all the freemen in Eagles had been slaughtered . . .

A few hundred feet away, on an exposed balcony smaller than his, Dick saw two figures come into view, a male and a female. The buck was a familiar stocky shape, with immense, heavy shoulders and a grizzled head. As he turned to look up at the sky, Dick recognized the Old Man. It was only then that he looked again at the girl, and saw that it was Elaine.

Dick stood up slowly. She was in slave's rags, her hair disordered and her face blackened, but he could not mistake those green eyes, or the characteristic gesture with which she put up one wrist to wipe her forehead. She had not seen him yet.

The Old Man turned sharply, recognized him, and seemed to gather himself. He took Elaine by the arm as if to point her out. Staring intently across the gap, he called, "Dick—!"

The appeal was unmistakable. Mercy for mercy; a favor for a favor. If Dick could save his own neck and Elaine's, then he ought to be able to save the Old Man's, too.

Now he saw recognition in the girl's face, and she held her arms out, calling, "Dick! Oh, Dick!"

Too soon, an invader plane was dipping towards them. The grapnel shot out, caught the peak of a nearby roof, and held. A second plane put down its line a few hundred yards away. Dick saw the goggled faces staring down at them, and he saw the uniformed figures emerge from under the planes' bellies, beginning to slide down the taut lines.

His mind was working feverishly fast. Everything came

together, the slave turnover, Elaine, the Old Man, all his life at Eagles, Buckhill . . . and without any conscious intention, his arm came up with the rifle. The stock fitted itself into his shoulder. Over the bead sight he saw the Old Man's startled face.

He squeezed the trigger, and saw the blocky figure fall.

Elaine stood in an attitude of frozen horror for a moment, then turned and ran for the stairway. In a moment, she was gone.

The Old Man, with a spreading bloodstain on the front of his smock, rolled half over on his side, then dropped back and lay still.

The invaders, disengaging themselves from their droplines, were staring across at him. "Who's that?" called one of them.

"Dick Jones of Buckhill."

They were climbing across to him, cautiously, holding their guns ready. "That's right, I know him," said one. He was a lean youngster, with Puget Sound colors in his shoulder patch; the other one, older, was wearing the Boss of Salt Lake's insignia. "Good thing you shot that slob when you did," he said, climbing over the parapet. He showed Dick his sub-machine gun, grinning tightly with excitement. "I had my finger on the trigger."

A furious gush of white suddenly sprang up in the middle of the field of roofs, tall as a geyser, carrying whirling clouds of fragments with it. The balcony staggered with the shock. "My God, did you see that?" cried the younger officer, as if unaware of what he was saying.

"Something big must have blown."

"My God, my God," the younger one went on saying, his eyes bright and feverish. Suddenly he swung up his rifle and began firing at some figures that had appeared on a nearby open roof. A few dropped, the rest went out of sight. "There's never been anything like it," said the young man, staring around him with a fascinated and happy expression.

Dick glanced across at the body of the Old Man, lying motionless and somehow smaller than it had been before. He saw the empty stairwell down which Elaine had vanished, and looked out across the smoking field of roofs, almost unrecognizable now: the places where he had followed Keel by moonlight, fought Ruell, made love to Vivian. . . .

"I don't know if you've heard what happed at Buckhill," the older officer was saying at his ear. He hardly heard the words. "Bad luck—your family all massacred. Slobs hiding in the woods, but they'll get 'em sooner or later."

"I'll do that myself," said Dick, without turning. He wanted to fix this last sight of Eagles in his memory, just as it was. There was his youth, deep down there, buried in ash and locked under the fallen rooftops. All right, let it lie.

He looked to the east, toward Buckhill. There was no feeling left in him now: but he knew he was a Man at last, and had his work ahead of him.